Evil Never Dies

(a sequel)

by

Maria Savva

The Spider - Book 2

Published by:
Rose and Freedom Books
P.O. Box 55285
London N22 9EU
England, U.K.

Cover design by Evening Sky Publishing Services

A catalogue record of this book is available from the British Library

ISBN: 978-0-9928345-4-8

Also by Maria Savva

Novels:
Coincidences
A Time to Tell
Second Chances
The Dream
Haunted
The Spider

Short story collections:
Pieces of a Rainbow
Love and Loyalty (and Other Tales)
Fusion
Delusion and Dreams
3
Far Away in Time
Lost and Found

Other short stories by Maria Savva appear in the *BestsellerBound* anthologies and *The Mind's Eye Series*, and have been featured on *The Write Launch* online literary magazine

Acknowledgements:

Thank you to the following people, without whom this book would never have been finished:

Fabulous editor: Bob Helle
Amazing beta readers: Darcia, Shahnaz, Kim, Julie
Awesome cover designer: Kat McCarthy, *Evening Sky Publishing Services*

Chapter One

Rex Weaver hovered over the remains of the spider.

I will seek my revenge for this, my friend. One of the most beautiful spiders, crushed to death by an imbecile. Has he no respect for the life of the most magnificent creatures on Earth?

Rex fumed inwardly as he surveyed the empty room. Roisin, Hugh, and Robbie were somewhere not too far away, perhaps in the kitchen. Rex could hear muffled speech, and there was laughter, too.

How can they kill a supreme and innocent being and then carry on with their lives as if nothing had happened? This is what I have had to put up with all my life. Humans have no respect. Despicable life forms. They think they've killed me, but I can't be stopped. I will achieve my goal, I will become a spider again and rise to power. I will find a way to put my plan into action; I will not rest until I do.

George went into the bathroom as soon as he got home, and splashed his face with cold water. He could see the anxiety in his own eyes reflected back at him from the bathroom mirror.

On the drive home, a maelstrom of emotions thrashed through his mind, but overwhelmingly guilt: his conscience screamed at him, urging him to return to the house and retrieve the spider.

What if someone walks in and the spider kills them? It would be my fault. Rex said... What am I thinking? There is no Rex. He's dead. I put a poisonous spider in a house where people will be living. What if it kills them? It will be my fault...

What if Robbie and Roisin go to the house? He shrugged away the thought.

The incessant worrying ate at his brain on the way home, causing him to narrowly miss driving through red lights and hitting innocent pedestrians; he was a quivering wreck by the end of the journey. George had been under the illusion that delivering the spider was all he had to do to get his life back. But it wasn't Rex hounding him now, it was his own mind: he had done a terrible thing.

'Looks good in here. Hopefully, this new purchaser will exchange and complete quickly and we can forget about this place once and for all,' said Hugh.

'Hang on, what's that on the floor?' said Roisin as they stood by the living room door.

'Don't worry, it's only the spider I killed. I should've thrown it away.'

Roisin huffed. 'Typical! Quick, get me a tissue so I can get rid of it before the solicitor gets here. There's some in my handbag; I left it in the kitchen.'

Hugh went to the kitchen and returned shortly with Roisin's handbag. 'I'm okay with trampling on them, but not really brave enough to pick them up,' he said apologetically.

Roisin giggled as she took the bag from him and fished out a travel-pack of tissues. She carefully placed a tissue under the remains of the spider. 'Whoa, I don't think I've seen a spider this big before.'

'Yeah, looks even bigger squashed like that.'

'Ow!' squealed Roisin. 'It... It bit me... But how? It's dead, how could it...?'

A hollow, yet potent laugh echoed through the passageway. George placed his hands over his ears. *I'm imagining it. It's the trauma of dealing with that spider. Rex is gone... The deal was done... He's gone.*

The laugh sounded for a second time, audible despite George covering his ears. He slowly lowered his hands and looked around him, fearful.

'Yes, George, it's me,' said a booming voice, one he recognised.

'I gave you your spider. Go away. Leave me alone.'

'It's dead.'

'It was alive when I left it there—'

'Trampled underfoot by a man not worth a hair on that precious spider's leg. However, I am pleased to report that karma has seen fit to repay him. The spider bit her. Poetic justice. His child will die, and possibly his wife too... Well, strictly she's your wife. I can't keep up with all the shenanigans.'

'Roisin? What's happened to her?'

'Hugh killed the spider.'

'What have you done to Roisin?' George demanded. 'You said you'd leave us alone.'

'I made no promises. You only heard what you wanted to hear.'

The raucous laughter buzzed through George's ears as he ran to the front door and back to his car.

'Ambulance... Please hurry... Eight Goldfern Road... A spider bite... Not sure. She's... She's in pain... Sweating... S-she's pregnant...' Hugh gasped for breath after spluttering out the details to the operator over the phone.

George stalled the car a couple of times, struggling to concentrate.

He could hear the sound of an ambulance before he reached Goldfern Road, and as he pulled the car around the corner the vehicle came into view. It was pulling up outside number 8.

He parked at the end of the road and watched the scene with bated breath.

'You're going to be fine, Roisin.' Hugh sat beside her as they waited for the ambulance, holding her hand tightly.

'Mummy!' Robbie's screams were piercing.

Hugh picked up the boy. 'Shhh... Robbie, Mummy's going to be okay.'

'But she looks scary. Why is she doing that, kicking her leg?'

'She's not feeling well because the baby's coming, that's all. She'll be fine.'

George looked on from a distance as the ambulance parked outside 8 Goldfern Road.

Theo was standing outside his front door watching the scene. George prayed the old man wouldn't notice him. Thankfully, he appeared too engrossed in the goings on at number 8.

A familiar face approached Theo's house: Lisa. She stood at his gate and the old man walked towards her. Both wore concerned frowns. Another neighbour joined them.

George glanced around and saw that a few of the residents of properties across the road had come out of their houses. Many others peered from windows. Net curtains twitched with the morbid curiosity that surfaces at such times.

Unnerved by the growing crowd of onlookers, George hunched lower in his car. He watched a stretcher being carried from the house. Hugh and Robbie followed it into the ambulance. Robbie was shouting, 'Mummy! Mummy!' George desperately wanted to go and comfort the child, but how could he explain what he was doing there?

The paramedics closed the doors of the ambulance and the vehicle pulled away. George wondered whether the spider was still in the house. Rex had said Hugh killed it. So what happened to Roisin? If the spider bit her maybe that's why Hugh killed it.

After the ambulance departed, Theo and Lisa remained outside for a short while with the other neighbour, having an animated discussion about what had happened, it seemed.

Shortly, they dispersed back to their houses and the net curtains in surrounding properties stopped twitching. The street became as silent as it had been when George delivered the spider earlier that morning.

The key to the house was in his pocket. He'd taken it with him when delivering the spider in case he needed to go inside. He drove the car further along the street and stared at the house, darkness emanating from its core as if some unseen presence were staring at him, daring him to enter. The unsettling memories, like wisps of grey cloud, wound their way into his mind, refusing to give him peace. He took a deep breath as he parked the car.

Chapter Two

Glen woke up and turned around to see Petula asleep in bed beside him. It brought a smile to his face. He rolled over and took his mobile phone from the bedside cabinet, couldn't wait to tell George what had happened.

'Hi, George.'

'Glen.'

'Don't sound so pleased to hear from me.' Glen chuckled. 'I've got great news and wanted you to be the first to know.'

'Go on.'

'Me and Petula are back together. Amazing, ain't it? Listen, do ya wanna meet up in the pub? I'm sure she'd love to see you again.'

'Um... I'm tied up right now.'

'How about lunchtime? About one?'

'Okay.'

'Why d'you sound so gloomy?'

'I'm at Number Eight.'

'What the— Why?'

'Long story.'

'You can tell me more at lunchtime. Gotta go.'

Petula had awoken and was looking at Glen.

'Morning, beautiful.'

'Huh, I very much doubt I look beautiful first thing in the morning.'

'You always look beautiful to me, Pet.'

She smiled. 'Who was that on the phone?'

'George. I've arranged for us all to meet at lunchtime.' He kissed Petula on the forehead and got out of bed.

George placed the key in the lock with some trepidation, unsure what he'd find on entering the house.

He walked in and gasped: the walls were covered in the same wallpaper he'd seen when he and Glen found themselves trapped in the basement. Webs, spiders, everywhere. The dim lighting, almost yellow, cast a sepia tinge. George gasped when he noticed Rex seated on the staircase ahead of him, dressed in the hideous spider costume. 'But...

you're dead.'

'That's the thing about the undead, George, we can do whatever we want.'

'I don't understand. Roisin and Hugh were selling this place. Why does it look like this? I'm dreaming, aren't I? You're not real.'

'I need to make a deal with you.'

George began to tremble and perspiration formed on his brow. The haziness of the lighting and seeing Rex again was making him queasy. 'None of this is real,' he said loudly, in the hope it would all disappear.

'What have I told you about reality? It's an illusion. Do you understand that now?'

The front doorbell sounded and instantaneously the house reverted back to the modern design that Glen's builder friends had achieved; gone was the spiderweb wallpaper and the yellow lighting. Rex had also disappeared.

George looked around in confusion. There was the inevitable questioning of his sanity, which had become second nature ever since he and Glen were captured by Rex. He answered the door and saw two smartly-dressed men standing outside, one carrying a briefcase; both wore grey suits.

'Hello. We have an appointment with Hugh and Roisin. I'm their solicitor. This is the estate agent,' said the taller of the two men.

'They're not here. They've had to rush to hospital. Roisin is unwell.'

'Ah, nothing serious I hope?' said the estate agent.

'I'm not sure what happened.'

'Could you ask one of them to get in touch with us when they're back, please?' said the solicitor. 'And send our best wishes to Roisin.'

'I will,' said George.

The two men walked away.

George was left stunned at how quickly his perception of the house had changed. Once again he wondered whether he should seek help through therapy.

He closed the front door and turned around. The house had not reverted back to the creepy spider lair, but Rex was seated on the stairs.

George exhaled loudly. 'Look, Rex, or whoever... *what*ever you are; I kept to my side of the bargain and now Roisin has been taken to hospital.'

'She'll live. Now, where were we before those men rudely interrupted us? Ah, yes, our deal.'

'No more deals.'

'You don't get to choose. This might feel slightly uncomfortable.'

'What?'

'The deal didn't work out. Do you expect me to simply forget and let you off? That isn't going to happen. You started this. You killed me, remember? I'm the one who gets to tell you what to do. That's how it works, you see. You murder someone, they decide your fate.' His laughter boomed through the house, coming from somewhere external it seemed, even as Rex's mouth opened and closed.

George stood still. 'What do you want from me?'

'Your body. I need to use your body for my mission. I would have preferred a spider, but there isn't much time. If I don't find a body to possess soon, I will fade away. I can feel my energy flagging.'

'No way.' George turned to escape through the front door but felt a heavy weight on top of him.

Chapter Three

Roisin opened her eyes and squinted against the bright lights. Sitting to her left she saw Hugh.

'Roisin? You're awake!'

'I...' She coughed to clear her throat. 'Wh... Where am I?'

'You're in hospital. But don't worry, you're all right.'

'What happened? Is it the baby? Is the baby all right?' She eyed her stomach, a sense of fear creeping up on her.

'Try to rest. The doctor said you had a reaction to the spider bite.'

'That damn house.'

'We missed the appointment with the solicitor, but I phoned him a few minutes ago. He said we could meet up when you're better, or in the circumstances he might send us the paperwork to sign instead. The buyer still wants to go ahead, as far as I know.'

'Good. I'm never going into that house again, even if we never sell it. It's cursed.'

'The solicitor said a man was at the house and opened the door for him. That's how he found out we were at the hospital.'

'Who was at the house?'

'All I know is it was a man. The description sounded like your ex, but—'

'George? What would he have been doing there?'

'Do you think I left the door open? I was so panicked.'

'But what would George have been doing there?'

'Maybe it was someone else, a neighbour maybe. It's not important now. You should rest.'

'Where's Robbie?'

'I took him back to your mum's; he was a bit shook up and I didn't like him seeing you like this.'

'Like what? What do I look like?'

'You look fine, but you were sweating a lot and convulsing. Robbie freaked out. Don't worry about him, though; your stepdad was at home when I got to your mum's house. Robbie's with him.'

'Thanks. Hugh, it was so painful. It stung so much. But I can't remember much else.' She instinctively lifted her hand, which shook with an involuntary spasm, as if it didn't belong to her. 'What happened to me? Is the baby all right? It doesn't feel right. I feel different.'

Hugh looked down at his hands.

'Hugh?'

The door opened and a nurse walked in. 'Good, Mrs Barnaby,

you're awake. The doctor will come and see you soon. How are you feeling?' She approached the bed and checked the monitor at the bedside. 'Would you like anything to drink? Can I get you some water?'

'Yes, please. Nurse, is my baby going to be all right?'

'I'll get the doctor.' She gave a terse smile and left the room.

'Why won't anyone answer me? Hugh?'

He closed his eyes briefly, then touched her hand. 'Darling, I can't lie to you. The baby... The spider bite brought on the labour. You had the baby. You probably don't remember; you were pretty drugged up. They had to give you drugs for the pain.'

'Drugs? But what about the baby, where is she? Wouldn't the drugs have harmed her? How could I have the baby without knowing?'

'They had to go ahead with the birth. The baby was... I can't say it.'

'What?'

Hugh smiled but it appeared to take enormous effort. His eyes were red and she noticed him wipe away a tear.

'Hugh, talk to me.'

'There were complications.'

'What sort of complications?'

'I'm sorry, Roisin.'

'What are you sorry for?' Her mind felt groggy. 'Where is she?'

Hugh hung his head. 'The poison was too strong, and—'

'What are you saying?'

'She... The doctor should explain. I'm still in shock.'

'Are you saying what I think you're saying?'

Before he could reply, the nurse returned to the room with a doctor.

After helping Roisin to sit up in bed so she could drink some water, the nurse left the room. The doctor then told Roisin what Hugh had been unable to. Roisin wasn't interested in the details and sat in stunned silence throughout, unresponsive to his words. Words could not bring her daughter back.

When the doctor left the room, Roisin turned to Hugh. His face reflected her sorrow. 'I want to be alone.'

Hugh took her hand. 'I can't leave you like this. We'll get through it together.'

She pulled her hand away. 'Please, I need time to myself.'

'I'll be outside if you need me,' he said, touching her cheek where a tear had fallen.

Roisin watched as he left the room, and then sat staring ahead, listening to the bleeping sounds coming from the machine at her bedside. An overwhelming sense of grief and loss took over. Incomprehension.

Everything had changed so quickly. She prayed this was a hallucination brought on by a drug she'd been given, but she could not shift the hollowness within. Tears fell. She wanted to hold her child, the child she'd carried for so many months with wishes, hopes, and dreams for her future.

This is because I cheated on George.

Beneath the surface of the happiness she'd found with Hugh there existed a critical voice, and it had become louder in recent weeks—a voice telling her she didn't deserve to be happy. *I'm being punished. I deserve it. My baby's dead because of me.*

The plans made for the little girl that she'd been looking forward to welcoming to the world were obsolete. So many preparations in anticipation transmuted into reminders of what could have been. The pretty, pink clothes that she'd stored in the chest of drawers would never be worn; the large white teddy bear that she'd named Harold, after her favourite teddy from her childhood, sat in the cot waiting for the child who would never come home.

Diana. She'd already chosen that name for her daughter. Diana had been the name of her first best friend at school; a pretty girl with rosy cheeks, and curly brown hair that fell in ringlets. Her cheeks were always red and rosy, but the blush on those cheeks turned out to be the sign of a degenerative condition, and at the age of nine Diana was taken away from school to be cared for at a local hospice. Roisin never saw her again. As a nine-year-old it hadn't taken her long to replace her best friend. She'd almost forgotten Diana, but at the age of fifteen a mutual friend told her Diana had died at the hospice soon after her tenth birthday. From that day onward, her past friendship with Diana became much more significant to Roisin, colouring her thoughts as a teenager, as she navigated a world that seemed to hold less magic since she'd learned of her death. So much of her world view had been influenced by those innocent childhood conversations, and she'd been carrying memories, many of which had helped her to make sense of the world throughout her formative years.

Hearing of the loss of her friend was akin to some part of her being snatched away, and it made her realise that perhaps a small part of her may have been holding out hope that one day they'd meet again.

The loss of Diana remained with her. There were many times, over the years, when events as trivial as a children's birthday party, for example, or perhaps the sight of young girls playing in a park, would remind her of her friend and often bring her to tears. In her mind the nine-year-old remained eternally young, untouched by the passing of time, so full of life and brimming with curiosity and wonder.

She had intended to name her daughter after the friend she would never forget—as a tribute. In a cruel twist of fate, this baby had been snatched away too, and now instead of a name in common, the connection between the two would be loss, grief, and unfulfilled dreams.

Chapter Four

Glen glanced at his watch. 'I'm sure I told George to meet us at one. It's nearly quarter past. D'ya think I should phone him?'

'Is he usually on time?' asked Petula.

'Like clockwork.' He took out his phone and called George's number.

'Hello.'

'Hi, George.'

'Who's speaking?'

'What, you didn't check the caller ID? Not the paranoid George I know.'

'Glen? Hello.'

'Your voice sounds different. Have you got a cold?'

'No.'

'What's up? You coming?'

'Excuse me?'

'You're supposed to be meeting me and Petula, remember?'

'Er... it completely slipped my mind. Where should I meet you?'

'The Red Lion, of course.'

'The Red Lion.'

'You sound different.'

'Perhaps I do have a cold coming on.'

'You *are* still coming though, right?'

'The Red Lion, you say? Is that a public house?'

'A what?'

'Where is it?'

'What?'

'The Red Lion?'

Glen laughed. 'Just get here as soon as you can, you moron.'

There was silence on the line.

'George, are you there?'

'The Red Lion. Is that the one on the high street?'

'No, the one in Timbuktu. What's happened to you?'

'Never mind, I'll look it up.'

'Look it up? Bloody hell, we've been coming here for years.'

'I'll be there shortly.'

'It's like you're on a different planet. George?' Glen shrugged. 'He's hung up.'

'Is he coming?' asked Petula, frowning. 'That sounded like a weird conversation.'

'It was bloody weird. He sounded strange. Stranger than usual. I swear sometimes I'm convinced he's got early onset Alzheimer's.'

Petula wound a lock of hair around her finger and appeared glum for a moment.

'You okay, Pet?'

'Um, yeah. D'you think he doesn't want to meet up because I'm here?'

'Why would you think that?'

'Y'know, because of the way our relationship ended in uni.'

'Don't be daft, that was a hundred years ago.'

She picked up a drink coaster from the table and focussed on that as she spoke. 'I know how close you two are. Maybe he thinks I'm no good for you.'

'I'll be the judge of that.' Glen kissed her cheek and put an arm around her. 'Stop worrying, will ya? I'll get us some drinks while we wait for George. What d'ya want?'

'Gin and tonic.'

'Coming up.'

Rex arrived at The Red Lion at 1.35 p.m., a flustered glow on his cheeks. Spotting Glen at once, he made his way to the table where he was seated next to a dark-haired woman.

'You found the place then?' Glen chuckled. 'You okay? You look like you could do with a drink.'

'I'll get myself one.' Rex turned away and headed towards the bar, wishing he'd never come. He wasn't confident he could get away with pretending to be George. This man, Glen, was his best friend, he knew everything about him. Rex took a deep breath and reminded himself that he was inside George's skin, he just had to try to stay calm.

'Good to see you, George,' said the barman. 'What can I get you?'

Rex ordered a brandy and immediately regretted it, wishing he'd said 'the usual'; if the barman knew George on first-name terms, he would surely know what he usually ordered.

The barman raised his eyebrows. It was clear he was surprised by the order. It was obviously not George's "usual".

'Do you still have the number for that plumber you recommended last year?' asked the barman. 'I might need him again.'

'I'll have a look at home,' said Rex hoping that would suffice. He paid for his drink and walked away before the barman could engage him in further conversation.

'Not having your usual then?' said Glen, raising an eyebrow as Rex sat opposite with his glass of brandy. 'Have you had a rough morning?'

Rex coughed. 'I wanted to try something different.'

'The George I know would never drink that stuff.'

Rex reddened. 'I've changed recently, after everything...'

'Ain't we all. Oh, my God, how rude am I? I haven't introduced you two. Well, you know each other from uni, but George meet Petula; Pet, meet George.'

'Hi,' they both said.

Rex stiffened, unsure how well acquainted George had been with Petula.

'It's good to see you again,' she said, in an apparent attempt to break the ice, then turning to Glen: 'It's amazing that you and George are still friends after all these years.'

'Amazing?' blurted Glen, 'A bloody miracle, more like. It's only because I'm so good natured, or I would've told him to piss off years ago.'

Rex remained silent, eyes fixed on the table.

'Are you sure you're okay, George?'

'Yes,' snapped Rex.

'You don't seem yourself, y'know.'

'I'm fine. Perhaps I shouldn't have come today. I have a lot on my mind.'

'Like what?'

'I'd rather not talk about it.'

'Is it because Petula's here? We could meet up later at mine, if you'd feel more comfortable. I hate seeing you like this. What's happened? Is it that spider-man again?'

'Spider?' Rex stared into Glen's eyes, wondering if George had spoken to Glen after seeing him at 8 Goldfern Road in the morning; but then he relaxed a little, certain that couldn't have happened.

'You've got that look in your eyes, like you're a zombie.'

Rex shook his head and glanced at Petula and then back at Glen.

Glen gasped.

'Wh-what is it?' Rex downed his brandy in one, avoiding eye contact with Glen, concerned about what he would say next.

'For a moment there I thought your eyes were— Bloody hell, are we ever gonna get over that man? Your eyes... they were completely black —y'know, like The Spider's eyes—but they're back to normal now. Must've been a trick of the light.'

'What spider?' asked Petula, wrinkling her brow.

14

'Remember I told you about that weirdo who dressed as a spider.'

'Oh, yeah.'

'Pet, did you see his eyes just now?'

'No. I hate spiders. I feel itchy even talking about them,' she added.

'I should be going,' said Rex. There was always a sense of anticlimax whenever he heard that his eyes had turned black. He always hoped it meant that he would somehow miraculously transform into a spider, but despite his hopes, it never happened.

'George, when I called you earlier, you said you were at Number Eight. What were you doing there?'

'Nothing. I really have to go,' said Rex.

'We'll talk about this tonight at mine. You free at about eight?' asked Glen. 'You're freaking me out.'

'Your house. Please remind me where it is.'

'Oh, my God, you're kidding me, right?'

In a moment of inspiration, Rex leaned in and said, 'Glen, this is quite embarrassing, but I seem to have temporary amnesia. I hope it's temporary. I was, as you are aware, unable to recall where this public house was situated—' He waited, unsure whether it sounded believable.

'This amnesia, did it involve swallowing a dictionary by any chance? Why are you talking like that?'

'It must be an effect of the amnesia.'

'Maybe you've been abducted by aliens and replaced with a more eloquent version of yourself.' Glen chuckled.

Rex looked at his hands, which were not his hands at all, and for a moment the sensation of being in a different body caused him to feel discombobulated. 'I can't even remember where *I* live,' he managed to splutter. 'I know it's number twelve, but I'm not sure of the name of the road or how to get there from here.'

'Bloody hell. Right, you live at twelve, Doncaster Lane, off the high road. Turn right out of the pub. Wait, are you being serious?'

'Yes.'

Glen shook his head. 'I live across the road. Nineteen-A, Hilborne Crescent. Come and see me tonight at eight—we should talk about this. Chances are you're gonna need therapy.'

'Hmm... I'll see you later. Nice to see you again, Patricia.'

'Petula.'

'Er... yes. Petula. Like the singer. Did you know that there was a moth named after her? I like moths. They're tasty.'

'Tasty?' Glen baulked. 'OMG. What's wrong with you?'

'I hate moths as much as I hate spiders,' said Petula.

'Um. I was joking.' Rex faked a laugh.

Glen and Petula joined in the laughter.

'Right, well, I'm glad you ain't lost your sense of humour,' snorted Glen.

Rex stepped out of the pub. *I really could go for a succulent moth right now,* he thought. This was getting confusing. His taste buds belonged to the spider whose body he'd possessed before George's. That brandy had tasted disgusting. It had been his favourite drink when he was in his own body.

He recapped the addresses: *Twelve, Doncaster Lane, nineteen-A, Hilborne Gardens... no, Crescent. And, that girl—Patricia... No, Petula, like the moth. There it goes again, a hunger pang for moths.*

He tapped his pocket; there were a couple of sets of house keys. As George had visited 8 Goldfern Road this morning, with any luck one of the sets of keys would allow him access to the house.

He'd wanted to stay at the house earlier, when he possessed George's body; it was the only place that felt like home. Unfortunately for him, one of the neighbours saw him. Rex had stepped outside the front door after possessing George because the act made him feel claustrophobic, as though he were trapped inside a dark, constricting object; almost as if he'd ended up inside a sealed box. It took him a couple of minutes to adjust and left him breathless.

Theo had greeted him with, 'George! What are you doing here? I had no idea you were in the house. I heard you sold it. Are you thinking of buying it again? What happened in there? Why was the ambulance here?'

The barrage of questions left Rex even more nauseated.

Rex hated Theo. He'd been the one who'd complained to the council when Rex was renovating 8 Goldfern Road. The last thing Rex needed was to draw attention to himself. It would seem suspicious that George was at the house after Roisin was bitten by the spider. Theo wasn't the kind of man to keep anything secret; Rex decided he would have to leave as soon as possible. He'd lied to the old man: 'Oh, hello, Theo. I was just checking on the house. The door was left open after the ambulance left.'

'Really? I was outside and I'm sure the door was closed.'

'It was on the latch.'

'Right, I see. But why was the ambulance here? What happened to the girl?'

'I don't know. I should go; I have an appointment in town.'

'I won't keep you. You must come and visit though, you and your friend Glen. It would be good to catch up.'

Rex had nodded and forced a smile at Theo while fantasising about killing him.

He'd walked away from the house pondering how easy it had been to possess George's body. The initial claustrophobia hadn't lasted long, and although far from comfortable inside an alien body, he found he was at least able to function without too much difficulty.

He wondered about George. He didn't have any memories of George's life. His soul seemed to have vanished, or perhaps it was being suppressed by his own. Rex caught himself and realised he shouldn't think about it. He had to concentrate on his mission. Now that he had a body, he would try again to put his plan into action.

Chapter Five

As far as George could tell, his eyes were open but he couldn't see. For a moment panic took hold. *I'm blind. Oh my God.* He recalled the unexpected meeting with Rex. But Rex was dead. What had really happened?

A blue light fizzed at one side of his sightline. It grew larger and he floated towards it. *Where am I? Am I dead?* Had Rex killed him, in revenge?

'No, you're not dead,' a high-pitched voice sounded in response.

Hearing this unexpected reply caused further disorientation. Had Rex captured him again and put him in the basement, plied him with sleeping-spider gas? But that wasn't Rex's voice. It sounded feminine, almost angelic.

'Your body has been possessed. Your soul is in limbo. You must return to your body or you will lose all energy. When a soul loses its energy, it enters the void.'

Possessed? H-how do I return to my body?

'This will happen naturally if the spirit that is possessing the body decides to leave, but otherwise there must be a battle with the possessor to reclaim your body.'

I can't see a thing. Where am I? Who are you? How can you hear me? I can't feel my mouth. I'm thinking, not speaking. What's happening to me?

'As far as we know you were forced out of your body by a malevolent spirit. You have arrived at the centre for lost souls. You were found by one of our angels. We have ascertained that, most likely, the force of the possession caused you to lose consciousness. We can try to help you back into your body.'

Why can't I see you?

'Our identity must be kept secret. We cannot reveal ourselves.'

Where am I?

'I already answered that question.'

The centre for lost souls?

'That's correct.'

Yes, but where is that?

'It's not important for you to know. Now, I gather the last person you saw was Rex, someone who is undead. You believed you saw him?'

Y-yes... How did you know?

'We know your life history; it's written in your soul. Tell me more about Rex.'

He was planning to kill a group of people, and he captured me and my friend Glen. We managed to get away, but I killed him.

'This spirit may be seeking revenge for his death.'

We had a deal. I found a spider for him, so he could possess the spider's body. But the spider was killed.

'I will find out more about Rex and locate him.'

Uh... thank you.

The blue light fizzled out, leaving silence. *Hello?* George repeated the word in his thoughts. No response came. He was alone in the abyss once again. It reminded him of the time when he and Glen were held captive at 8 Goldfern Road. This time, however, as far as he could tell, he had no physical body—arms, legs, etc. There was an uncomfortable sensation of floating in the ether, lost in space. He attempted to reach out an arm, but there was no arm to flex, he wanted to kick out a leg, touch something, but it left him numb. He was George Barnaby, that much he knew, but he only existed as thoughts, it seemed; thoughts without a body.

The last thing he remembered was the meeting with Rex. He'd told him that Roisin's baby would die. Could Rex be living and breathing inside his body? He recalled the times Rex's disembodied voice had threatened him. Inexplicably, Rex had found a way to possess his body. How did Rex make the transition?

Rex returned to 8 Goldfern Road in the evening, preferring the cover of darkness so as to avoid snoopy neighbours.

He walked around the house shaking his head at what he saw. The magnificent wooden web had gone.

A key turned in the front door. He looked around the living room but there was nowhere to hide. Sighing, he turned to face the door as footsteps approached.

'George? I thought I recognised your car outside. What are you doing here? How did you get in?'

Rex wrinkled his brow. It took him a moment to remember he was in George's body. Hugh stood at the door. Rex resisted the urge to attack the man in revenge for what he had done to the spider. Instead he forced a smile. 'I own this house,' he said.

'I have no idea what you're doing here or what you mean. Roisin and I own the house.'

'This house was left to me in the former owner's will.'

'We... We bought the house from the executors. They didn't mention you.'

'You're trespassing.' Rex reached out, 'Give me the keys and get out.'

'Understandably you're upset because Roisin left you. I played my part, but life doesn't always turn out the way we plan it. Roisin and I have had very bad news today. We lost our baby.'

'My heart bleeds for you. Now, give me my keys.'

'This house belongs to me and Roisin. If you think otherwise, take it up with your solicitor. *You* are the one who's trespassing, and if you don't leave I'll call the police.'

Rex realised there was no point arguing, the executors had sold the house. He'd been sure Glen and George bargained with the executors and asked to keep the house rather than the sale proceeds. He had seen them in here with the builders. They must have only been renovating it to sell it on. He let out a frustrated sigh. 'I'm going, but this is not the end of the matter. I'll make sure you pay for killing that spider.'

'How do you know about the spider? Did you leave that poisonous spider here?'

'No.'

Rex left the house, concerned he may have said too much.

He fumbled in George's jacket pocket and found a car key fob. Hugh had said George's car was parked outside, so Rex pressed the remote button in the direction of the front gate. Lights flashed on a small red car. He mused that it was not as nice as the car he'd owned in his lifetime, and wondered briefly who'd taken the car after his death.

The blue light fizzed to his left-hand side and George was instinctively drawn towards it. As unsettling as all of this was, it comforted him to know he wasn't alone.

'George, we now have more information about Rex. He is indeed a malevolent spirit. He cannot die. He is one of those who roam eternally without a body.'

Um... I think you've forgotten that he has my body.

'Don't worry, we haven't forgotten. He is able to possess bodies, yes, but none will ever be his own. His sinful nature is far too great, therefore his soul cannot be reborn.'

How did he possess my body so easily?

'Malevolent spirits are able to do this relatively easily. Having no conscience, they are ironically more adept at using their instinct and can more naturally move from one state to another. Someone like you, with a purer soul, will suffer more because your conscience is constantly creating blocks, so you must work much harder to break through these.'

I don't understand.

'It's not necessary for you to understand. I will help you reenter your body.'

But how do I know I can trust you? I can't see, and I have no idea where I am.

'I will take you to where Rex is, and I will teach you how to see as a spiritual being. You can then reclaim your body.'

But... how long will it take?

'It's hard to estimate, but we know Rex plans to kill. If he does kill while he is in your body, well... I don't need to explain what the consequences would be.'

I'd be arrested for murder?

'Yes.'

Does that happen? Do evil spirits possess bodies and kill?

'Of course. It's very common.'

What happens to the innocent souls?

'There isn't time to explain. We must find a way to get you back into your body. As time goes on, there is more of a risk Rex will kill while possessing your body, and every day your soul loses energy by being apart from its rightful body. After a while you will lose all energy.'

Lose all energy? Die, you mean?

'Come on, we must go.'

Chapter Six

Rex sat on the sofa in Glen's flat while Glen went to make coffee.

'Don't worry, I boiled the kettle this time,' said Glen, chuckling as he entered the room and handed a mug to Rex.

Rex took the mug and nodded.

'So,' started Glen, 'what's up with you, George?'

'I told you, it's temporary amnesia.'

'You need to get help. You ain't been the same since spider-man got us.'

Rex peered at him.

'Stop doing the zombie stare and tell me what I can do to help.'

'The house on Goldfern Road; I was there just now, before coming here. Hugh arrived there shortly after I did.'

'Hugh? Roisin's fella?'

'It's so unfortunate that the house has been sold. There must be a way of getting it back.'

'We told the executors we didn't want the sale proceeds, remember? It was your idea; you said the money was cursed because of Rex.'

'I've changed my mind.'

'What?'

'We can tell the executors we want the house.'

'No... No, it's been sold. It's too late, mate. Forget about that house. What possessed you to go near the place?'

Rex glanced at him. 'You asked if you could help me.'

'Yes.'

'I want a wooden web.'

'Why on earth—'

'My therapist advised me to recreate the scene of the capture so I can go in there without feeling threatened. That's why I wanted the house, you see. But if we can't use Number Eight, I suppose any house will do. I will need a web, though.'

'Wait, rewind. I didn't know you were seeing a therapist.'

'I am. Things were getting on top of me.'

'But why would this therapist tell you to get a web? That's ridiculous. Are you sure they know what they're doing?'

'Apparently that would be the best way for me to overcome. You do want to help me, don't you?'

'Uh... yeah... But the wooden web was freaking weird; how are we gonna get one of those? Didn't Rex say he built it himself?'

'I know how to make one.'

Glen's eyes widened in question.

'I looked it up on the Internet.'

'How would—'

'I also know how to make sleeping-spider gas.'

'Now you're starting to freak me out. How would you know how—'

'Trust me, I did some research.'

'You don't have to make sleeping-spider gas.'

'Yes, I do. Everything has to be exactly the same. I want one of those costumes too.'

'The spider costume?'

'Yes.'

'Now I know you're joking.' Glen burst out laughing but his reaction was met with a stare and a frown that caused him to freeze momentarily. 'You're doing it again.'

'What?'

'Staring.'

Rex looked at his hands.

Glen stood up. 'So let me get this straight, you want to copy what The Spider did, but won't it trigger the bad memories?'

'My therapist says it might help me.'

'How do you remember everything in so much detail about the house and The Spider? That's odd, ain't it?'

'Uh... yes, I suppose so.'

'I don't know what to say.'

'Please say you'll help me.'

Glen shrugged. 'It sounds crazy, but okay, I'll help. Let me know what you want me to do.'

George was hovering somewhere in space, in complete darkness. He soon realised that the voices he could hear were his own and Glen's, but the conversation was taking place without him being present.

He concentrated on the blue light flickering beside him. *What's going on?* he asked.

'Rex has possessed your body and now everyone believes he's you.'

So, Glen is talking to Rex, but he thinks he's talking to me?

'Precisely.'

George listened to the conversation in disbelief. Rex was planning to build another web, perhaps attempt his "master plan" again, and Glen would probably help because he believed he'd be helping him recover from the trauma of what happened at 8 Goldfern Road.

I have to get back into my body. How can I do that? he asked urgently after Rex and Glen's conversation had ended.

'First you must learn to see. Without being able to see yourself, you cannot reenter your body.'

How can I do that?

'Humans are spiritual beings inside a body; when you leave your body, you can still see. The seeing comes from within. Think about people who have spoken of out-of-body experiences.'

What if someone's blind as a human?

'That's their human journey. Everyone has a different journey. As a spirit they will be able to see.'

But it's science. You need the different parts of the eye: the retina, optic nerve, cornea, etc. Without those you can't translate the light into shapes.

'I will prove to you that you can see as a spiritual being; it is one of the lessons you will learn on this journey.'

Why is there a blue light whenever you're around?

'It's part of what I'm teaching you. If you stop trying to use senses to work things out, nature provides the answers you seek. It's easy when you know how. I know everything about you because I am relying on what you humans call a sixth sense. Intuition.'

It doesn't make any sense to me.

'That's because you've been trained to look for explanations. If there is no explanation for something you simply don't believe it. However, can you explain how you're able to hear me, and hear the conversation you just heard, without ears? How are we communicating if you have no mouth, no voice?'

George was silent for a moment.

'Lost for words, are we?'

Well...

'Are you starting to understand?'

Well, I...

'Come with me, we have work to do.'

Chapter Seven

Hugh and Roisin were sitting on the sofa in her parents' living room. Close together but both lost in their own insular worlds, it seemed.

Hugh had driven them home from the hospital in silence. He'd been mostly silent this past week, only speaking when necessary. Roisin appreciated the silence; there was so much noise in her head that she could not contemplate having to deal with any external communication. Perhaps Hugh felt the same.

Roisin found it difficult to comprehend that she'd given birth whilst unconscious. Not only had she lost the child, but there was no special memory of its birth. Part of her was grateful; maybe this way she could live in constant denial, pretend she'd imagined it all. But even now there were reminders. She was producing milk for the baby that would never learn to suckle.

It came as a shock when they were told the baby would have to be registered and that they'd have to discuss funeral arrangements.

The funeral loomed like an unwanted visitor. Roisin didn't want to attend. Her mother said she understood, but urged her to reconsider, 'You'll regret it if you don't go.'

Regret. The word had been used a lot.

When the nurse said she could hold the baby and she'd hesitated, she was told, 'You might regret not holding her.'

When the nurse suggested they might want to have a photo of the baby, Roisin looked at her in horror.

'I will take a couple of photos and keep them with the records, in case you regret the decision not to take one,' the nurse said, solemnly.

Naming the child. Again she was told it might be best, and she might regret it if she didn't.

When the registrar asked if they'd chosen a name, Roisin almost said 'Diana'. But she couldn't do it, didn't want the name to take on connotations of death. They had settled for Baby Thompson—using Roisin's maiden name. A child without a name.

Regret. The word featured highly in her thoughts, and an overwhelming numbness prevailed.

Hugh had visited her at the hospital every day. George hadn't collected Robbie from school on Monday. His teacher had phoned Hugh and he ended up having to collect him as no one was able to get hold of George. George usually looked after Robbie during the week. He knew the baby had died. Roisin wondered if it could be a twisted revenge message, perhaps, to let her know he didn't care about her baby conceived with another man. Hugh told her that George simply said, 'My heart bleeds for you', without emotion, when he'd heard of the baby's death. It didn't sound like George.

Hugh and her parents took it in turns to take Robbie to school and collect him. When Roisin asked Hugh why George couldn't look after him, he'd said he hadn't been able to ask him as he wasn't answering his phone. Roisin wondered whether they'd had an argument. Did Hugh stop George taking Robbie? Maybe he needed to be with Robbie after the loss of their child.

'I think George put the poisonous spider in the house,' said Hugh—the first words he'd spoken since they returned from the hospital.

Roisin coughed to clear her throat. 'Why would you say that?'

'He was there last week, on Saturday. After I left the hospital, I went to check on things and he was there.'

'At Goldfern Road?'

'Yes.'

'What was he doing there?'

'He demanded the keys, said it was his house.'

'That doesn't make any sense.'

'I know.'

'So... So what did you do?'

'I basically told him to piss off. He left, but he threatened me.'

'Threatened you?'

'He said I'd pay for killing the spider, seemed pretty upset about it. How did he even know I'd killed the spider? Did you talk to him?'

'No. He must've spoken to someone at the hospital. That's an odd thing to threaten you about, though. Why would he care about the spider?'

'I told you, I think he put it there.'

'It doesn't sound like George. None of it sounds like George. I still don't know why he didn't take Robbie this week when he knew we had so much going on at the hospital. I'll have to go and see him.'

'You're in no fit state to go anywhere. You need to rest.'

'I'm fine. I rested at the hospital. I was going stir crazy in there.'

'I'm going to speak to the solicitor on Monday, see if we can rush this sale through. The sooner we're rid of that house, the better. I think you're right about it being cursed.'

'Why didn't you tell me any of this before? You never said you saw George at the house.'

'I'm sure I did. Remember I told you that he said "My heart bleeds for you", when I told him we lost the baby?'

'Yes, but—'

'That was the last I saw of him. I don't know why he was there or how he got in. He had this deranged look in his eyes. I was glad when he left.'

'I should speak to him. It would be better for him to air any grievances with me. Maybe the divorce has got to him. He's on his own, remember. It must be tough going through the divorce on his own with no one to talk to.'

'He's a grown man.'

'It's out of character. He's usually so keen to take Robbie to stay with him. What if something's happened to him?'

'You can't start worrying about George. You need to worry about yourself. Get some rest.'

Chapter Eight

Roisin stood outside the house frowning. The walk had worn her out. It was against doctors' orders; she'd been told to rest for at least a couple of weeks, but she couldn't rest without finding out why George was behaving so out of character. It had been going around and around in her head since Saturday when Hugh told her about his meeting with George at the house.

She still hadn't shaken the haunting belief that the baby died because of her selfish actions, betraying George. She held a strong conviction that adultery was wrong. It had plagued her parents' marriage. Her father's affairs caused her mother stress and anxiety, and Roisin witnessed her mother's endless tears at a vulnerable age.

Unable to forgive her father, she always told people he'd died, when in reality he left the family home after his umpteenth affair when Roisin was eleven years old. He attempted to contact her a couple of years later, but his letters and phone calls went unanswered.

Despite knowing how much enduring pain her father's deception had caused, she'd done the same to George. Her stress level throughout the pregnancy was high, and she'd worried it would harm the unborn child. Now the self-fulfilling prophecy had shaken the foundations of her life. An inner critical voice would forever remind her that there was an element of karma at play in what had occurred.

Roisin's head throbbed. The lack of energy made her light-headed. She thought about turning around and going back home. But she'd come this far and couldn't contemplate walking home without resting first. There was a sofa just beyond the living room door, a few metres away, and she wished for nothing more than to sit down and rest.

She owned a set of keys for the house, but rang the doorbell instead.

George answered the door and she couldn't help noticing how tired he looked. Guilt rose to the surface of her mind again, so she avoided looking at him as she entered the house without an invitation. 'I won't be long, but we have to talk,' she said, walking into the living room and sitting on the sofa immediately. She took a moment to appreciate how comforting it was to be seated, as though she'd run a marathon.

'Um... I was on my way out,' she heard him say.

'I won't be long,' she repeated, her frown etching thick wrinkles around her eyes. The front door was open. She could hear the traffic clearly and feel the breeze. 'You should close the front door.'

'I must insist you tell me why you're here so we can resolve this quickly. I'll be late for an appointment.'

Roisin folded her arms and winced slightly at the pain in her stomach. 'I'll get straight to the point. Did you put that poisonous spider in the house?'

'No.'

Her shoulders relaxed and she closed her eyes briefly, only then realising how tense her jaw had been. 'Do you have any idea who did?'

'Why would I?'

'Hugh said you knew about the spider, and that you told him you own the house.' She took a couple of deep breaths to ease her pain.

'Hugh is mistaken,' came the response.

'You didn't threaten him, then?'

'Threaten him? No, of course not. Why would I?'

'What were you even doing there, and how did you get in?'

'The door was open. I went there because I mistakenly believed I lived there. I must have remembered it as a place I'd been to before. I'm suffering from amnesia and sometimes my mind plays tricks on me, invents illogical things. The things I say... I seem to have no control over what my mind believes to be true. At the time I spoke to Hugh, I couldn't even remember where I lived. Glen had to tell me.'

Roisin's eyes widened, and through a haze of dizziness she was able to mumble, 'Amnesia? Is that why you didn't collect Robbie from school?'

'I didn't know I had to collect him.'

'You forgot?'

'It's the amnesia.'

'But if you're suffering from amnesia, how do you know who I am?'

He observed her coyly. 'Certain bonds are hard to break. I'd know you anywhere. In a thousand lifetimes.'

She fought against the redness rising in her cheeks. 'Hmm... The amnesia seems to have affected your character. You were never very romantic, George.'

'In all honesty, there are things I remember easily. I remember faces, people. Other things I've completely forgotten. It was probably the trauma of being captured by that man.'

'Captured? What do you mean?'

'In the house. You know, the spider-man.'

'What?' Feeling sleepy and listless, she found herself unable to concentrate on what George was saying.

'I don't know how much George told you.'

How much George told me? Roisin wondered if she'd misheard, but didn't have the energy to question what he'd said.

'I'm on my way to see the doctor,' he continued. 'I must be going, or I'll be late.'

She used a hand to steady herself as she rose from the sofa. 'We'll talk about this another time. I'm not sure it would be wise for you to see Robbie when you're in this state. Let me know when you're better and we'll sort out the arrangements then.'

'I'll be in touch when I'm better. Yes.'

Roisin left the house, confused. She couldn't put her finger on it, but George had changed. His mannerisms were unusual, and his voice sounded different.

She was certain she must have looked pale and sick when she was speaking to him, yet he'd never asked if she was all right, didn't offer her a glass of water. He was usually observant of her moods. Today he'd seemed so keen to get rid of her. She reminded herself that they were no longer a couple and she'd betrayed him, which meant he probably didn't care about her anymore.

Unanswered questions wreaked confusion in her mind; why had he said he was captured in the house? She remembered what the neighbour had told her: the man who used to live at 8 Goldfern Road had been obsessed with spiders. But George didn't have anything to do with him... Or did he?

Chapter Nine

'What's that red mark on your arm, Rex?' asked his mother as they sat at the table for dinner.

'Nothing.'

'Let me see. Were you stung by a bee?' Her brow was knitted tightly as she inspected the wound.

He pulled away from her grip. 'It was just a stupid spider.'

His father chuckled. 'A spider bite? Hey, Rex, with any luck you'll get superpowers like Spider-Man.'

Rex had been thinking the same thing.

When the spider crawled along his arm in the playground earlier that day, he'd winced at first, but didn't want to anyone to know he was scared, so he slowly edged a finger up to the spider intending to flick it away as quickly as possible. At that moment, he'd felt a sharp pinprick and the spider pounced, landing in a nearby bush and disappearing.

A drop of blood fell from where he'd been bitten. He held in a scream.

'Wow! I didn't know spiders could jump,' Bob had said.

'What's that?' asked Jeff, his other friend. He pulled Rex's arm towards him and inspected the wound. 'You should see the school nurse. It might get infected.'

'It won't,' said Rex. 'It's nothing.'

Terence stared at him.

Terence had been picking on him for years. Rex knew that if he started crying over the bite, Terence would call him a baby and start mocking him again. He bit his lip and held back the tears.

Terence was the oldest child in the class, and the tallest. He towered over most of the other children. He'd managed to recruit a few intimidating boys into a gang and they picked on the younger children. They spent their days collecting small change from the children's lunch money and issuing threats. Terence had apparently decided he quite enjoyed making fun of Rex. The gang were forever picking on him. The reason Terence had chosen Rex as a victim was not clear, but he'd been a small, skinny boy at the time and perhaps easy prey.

Rex knew he had to pretend it hadn't hurt him, so he said, 'Maybe I'll get superpowers, like Spider-Man, now the spider has bitten me.' He looked Terence in the eye while saying it.

Terence laughed and walked away, turning back towards Rex briefly to say, 'Make sure you bring me a sandwich for lunch tomorrow. And none of that tuna crap. Ham or egg would be good. If you don't, I'll flush your head down the loo again.'

Rex sighed in response, enduring the pain as best he could.

That night, the pain became unbearable and Rex could no longer hold back from *screaming.*

When his mother arrived at his bedside she found him with a swollen arm, and lips that were turning blue; large spots were appearing on his face and body.

'Oh, my God! Jeremy! Quick! Call an ambulance!'

Rex spent a week in hospital. He'd suffered an allergic reaction to the spider bite. He was happy to be away from school. Terence and the gang had relentlessly bullied him for three years and he'd been forced to endure all kinds of humiliation. He never knew why they picked on him more than the other children. It made him paranoid.

When Rex came out of hospital, Terence's first words to him were, 'So, Spidey, have you found your superpowers yet?' Rex's nickname became "Spidey". The gang would collect spiders and throw them at him, put spiders in his packed lunch, and even made him eat one. That was the worst thing they could have done, because Rex had become fond of spiders since he'd been bitten, seeing it as a possible way out of the situation: if he got powers like Spider-Man, he'd easily defeat the bullies. He'd cried as he swallowed the spider—the bullies thought it was because he was scared, but his tears were for the innocent creature that had died because of them, and vowed he would make them pay.

Each time Terence's gang picked on him, Rex wished he could find within himself the special powers to make them fear him. He'd been convinced the spider bite would leave him with superpowers. He never did manage to access them though, and with every failed attempt he became increasingly bitter and jaded about it.

Over time, his school friends kept their distance, not wanting to be seen with him and leave themselves open to being picked on. Rex didn't understand why they'd abandoned him, hadn't stood up for him. This exacerbated his sense of exclusion. No one liked him. Slowly, he turned inwards, sliding deeper into a reclusive existence.

Chapter Ten

One of Rex's enduring regrets was that he had never been able to take revenge on Terence and his cronies. It was one of the things that was now a top priority. He had the perfect cover being inside someone else's body, didn't have to worry so much about being arrested because George would be charged with the murders after he left his body. It made planning the murders so much simpler.

Initially, he'd thought of rebuilding the wooden web and finding the ingredients for sleeping-spider gas, and he'd almost recruited Glen to assist with this, however, he realised it was something he had to do alone. Besides, he didn't like Glen and had avoided him all week. As much of a buffoon as Glen appeared to be, there was something telling Rex that the man might somehow guess that George wasn't really George. He had to be careful.

It had come to him in the middle of the night after he'd tossed and turned for hours—the perfect way to kill Terence and the gang.

The following day, Rex sat at the desk in George's house and began searching the Internet. He found Terence Black on Facebook without much effort, and as luck would have it the man had remained friends with the former gang members.

The photos on the men's Facebook pages showed them happy and smiling. They appeared to have settled down, married, had children. There was no evidence of any regret over the way they'd treated him at school. This made Rex angrier. With every smiling image, his blood boiled until he was sure there would soon be steam escaping from his ears and nose. These treacherous men had gone on to lead charmed lives after the years of hell they'd put him through.

George's Facebook page was already logged in, so Rex requested each of the men as friends. He spent the next half an hour pacing the living room cogitating about what had happened to him at school, whilst the smiling Facebook profile photos of Terence and the others flashed through his mind's eye.

When he returned to the computer he saw that two of the men had accepted the friend requests. One of them was Terence. He proceeded to send him a message:

Dear Mr Black,
You don't know me, but I am a solicitor. I've been
trying to contact you about the death of your
former school friend, Rex Rodenbury. Forgive

me for contacting you on Facebook, it's not very professional, but Rex's will did not include your address. He was a rich man, and left you a substantial amount of money in his will. I am holding the will at my office. Please contact me so that we can arrange a suitable appointment.

Yours sincerely,
George Barnaby, Solicitor.

Rex waited.

A reply arrived after ten minutes.

Dear Mr Barnaby,
This must be a mistake. I'm sorry to hear that Rex died but he was never a friend and I couldn't accept any money from his estate.
I treated him badly at school. Perhaps you could give the money to charity.
Thank you,
Terence Black

Rex stared at the reply. *You're not getting away so easily, Terence!*

Dear Mr Black,
This is not a mistake. Rex did make it clear in his will that he forgave you for the way you treated him at school, and he believed you would be living under the weight of unbearable guilt. He went on to have a blessed life. His estate is worth millions. He would like you to take the money as a parting gesture of forgiveness.
Yours sincerely,
George Barnaby, Solicitor.

After clicking "send", Rex re-read the message and gasped. *He would like you to take the money? It should have been past tense.*

He kept his fingers crossed, hoping that Terence wouldn't notice.

Thank you for clarifying that, Mr Barnaby. I still

34

**don't understand why he's left me this money
but if it's a dying man's wish… Would
you mind sending me a formal letter from your
firm, please? There are so many scammers on
Facebook, I want to make sure this isn't a
wind-up.**

**Dear Mr Black,
I will of course write to you and the other
beneficiaries when I have an available
appointment.**

**Are you perhaps willing to let me have an e-mail
address for you and the other beneficiaries:
Jake Brother, Frank Tesla, and Nick Gunther?**

**I will send a letter with details of my office and
the appointment via e-mail as it's more secure
than Facebook.**

**Yours sincerely,
George Barnaby, Solicitor.**

Rex waited, wondering if Terence would fall for this, whether it sounded legitimate.

Terence sent Rex a list of the men's e-mail addresses within the next ten minutes.

I've got you in my web, thought Rex, with a toothy smile on his face.

Chapter Eleven

'I'm worried about George.' Roisin sat opposite Hugh at the kitchen table and took a sip of her coffee.

Hugh raised his eyebrows. 'Why?'

'I've had a call from his boss. Apparently he hasn't shown up for work for over a week.'

'So what?'

'Hugh!'

'What? How do you think it makes me feel? He's been given fair access to Robbie but just goes AWOL, and I can't see my son.'

'I understand why you'd feel like that, but I think there's something wrong with him.'

'All the more reason why you shouldn't let him near Robbie.'

Roisin put down the slice of toast she had been about to bite into. 'You're such a hypocrite.'

'How?'

She shook her head. 'You go on and on about how unfair it is not to be able to see your son, yet you're saying I shouldn't let George see Robbie.'

'That's different. Abi doesn't have a good reason to stop me seeing Liam.'

'Maybe she does!'

Hugh finished his coffee and stood up. 'Why has this conversation suddenly turned into an argument? See how toxic George is? He isn't even here and he's coming between us.'

'No! It's your attitude that's causing the problem. I'm worried about George.' She held her head in her hands.

Hugh sat down again and took a deep breath. 'He's a grown man. He can look after himself. You need to worry about Robbie.'

Roisin looked at Hugh. 'His boss can't get hold of him on the phone. I tried calling him yesterday a couple of times and left a message about Robbie's school play, but he never replied. Don't you think that's strange?'

'No comment.'

'Hugh—'

'Whatever I say, you'll twist it into something negative.'

Roisin stood up and walked towards the kitchen window. 'Maybe he really does have amnesia. I thought he was making it up so he could get rid of me.'

'As long as he doesn't forget to transfer the money for the house

36

purchase to us, I don't care.' Hugh stood up. 'I'm going to work. Maybe you should go and see him again. Remind him the sale is this Friday; we can't afford for him to forget. It's bad enough we had to push the sale back a week because you were in hospital. George could be using amnesia as an excuse to stop the sale and prevent us being able to buy our place. Have you considered that?'

Roisin sighed and turned to face him. 'He wouldn't do that. He can't, my name's on the title too.'

'I know, but he has to sign everything, and he has to authorise the money from his share of the proceeds being sent to our solicitor.'

'I'm sure that's already been agreed, hasn't it?'

'You should check, we don't want anything going wrong. Chances are he hasn't responded to the solicitor if he's not returning your calls. They need his consent to proceed to exchange and complete on the day.'

'What if he's ill? I can't help blaming myself.'

'How could it be your fault?'

'You know... cheating on him.'

'I doubt that's what's caused his madness.'

'He's not mad.'

'We'll have to agree to disagree about that.'

Roisin folded her arms. 'You can be worse than a child sometimes.'

'Thank you, Abi.'

'What?'

'That's the sort of thing she used to say to me.'

Roisin approached him and closed her eyes briefly. 'Hugh, we're going to have to try to put the past behind us if we're ever going to find a way forward.'

Hugh nodded and turned around to leave.

'Wait, there's something else. Remember what I told you about the Goldfern Road house—the man who used to own it being obsessed with spiders?'

Hugh turned towards her and shrugged. 'The serial killer? I thought he died.'

'Well, yes. George said... It sounded as though George had been in the house.'

'He *was* in the house. I told you. He was claiming it was left to him in a will.'

'Yes, but before that. He said he'd been captured. What if he knew the spider-man and that's why he thought the house was left to him in his will? I was so tired I can't remember exactly what he said.'

'He's probably pretending he's got amnesia, so he can cover up. It's not beyond the realms of probability that George was a friend of this man and may have been planning to murder people too.'

'That's ridiculous.'

'That spider could've killed someone.'

'George didn't put the spider in the house.'

'You believe him?'

'Of course I believe him. He wouldn't do something like that.'

Hugh held up his hands, 'I'm just saying; we never really know people—a lesson I learned from living with Abi all those years. People are good at hiding who they are.'

'I'm not having this conversation. I have to let George know his boss is looking for him. If he gets fired he'll have no money coming in, and there'll be no maintenance for Robbie.'

'But are you well enough to go and see him?'

'I'm not ill, I've just had a baby.' Her face fell as she instantly regretted her words, and she noticed the gloom that spread over Hugh's face reflecting her feelings.

'Please be careful, Roisin. He's been acting bizarrely—all this talk of being captured and being left a house in a will. What was he even doing at the house? He could have been planning to kill us by putting the spider in there.'

'Ridiculous! Whatever he thinks of us, he loves Robbie and he would never put his life at risk.'

'Maybe he's going through some kind of breakdown, might not be aware of what he's doing. You hear this sort of thing on the news all the time—men going crazy and killing their ex-wives and kids.'

'He's not like that.'

'Be careful, that's all I'm saying.'

Rex walked around the house and became curious about the large boxes in the hallway and in the kitchen. Up until today he'd ignored them, having other things on his mind. He distantly recalled George saying he was selling the house.

There was a knock on the front door.

He rolled his eyes. He didn't know the people that George knew; it would undoubtedly be a person he didn't recognise. He went to the door, and peered through the spyhole first. His spirits lifted when he saw Roisin. He'd always found her attractive, and ever since her last visit he'd been wondering whether he could try to rekindle the relationship George had once had with her.

He opened the door and smiled. 'Nice to see you again, Roisin.'

'Is it? Why haven't you been answering my calls? I was worried about you.'

'Sorry, my mind is all over the place... It's the amnesia.'

Roisin walked into the house without waiting to be invited. 'I see you haven't made much of an effort to pack. You do realise you have to complete the sale by Friday so you can transfer the funds to my solicitor, don't you?'

'Friday? What day is it today?'

'Tuesday.'

'I didn't know about the sale... Amnesia...'

'Do you even know who your solicitors are?'

He shook his head.

'Bloody hell, George. I'll help you. Good thing I know some of your passwords, hey?'

She breezed over to the computer and sat down. 'Right, I'm going to check through your e-mails and make sure everything's been organised for the sale. Have you found a place to rent yet?'

He looked at her with a blank expression.

'Never mind, it doesn't matter. How have you been managing if you've forgotten everything? How have you been shopping without your PIN number, for example?'

'Um... Contactless mainly. And George had quite a lot of cash in his wallet.'

Roisin raised her eyebrows at him, and he realised what he'd just said. 'When I say *George*, I mean me, of course.' He followed with a laugh and hoped she would say nothing more about it.

She shook her head and turned her attention to the computer screen.

Rex stood watching as she typed. She appeared so masterful. He'd never had a girlfriend. Relationships with the opposite sex had eluded him. There was Felicia, who'd stolen his heart when he was nineteen, at university, but he'd taken so long to muster up the courage to ask her on a date that a fellow student beat him to it; he'd had to witness their blossoming affair, filled with envy, for the next two years. He took a moment to remember Felicia and wondered whether her relationship with Dennis had lasted. His attention was diverted to the present when Roisin spoke.

'By the way, George, I had a call from your boss. He said he couldn't get hold of you. He didn't sound happy that you haven't been to work.'

'I have no idea what work George does.'

39

Roisin spun in the chair to face him, eyes wide. 'Why do you keep referring to yourself in the third person?'

'Um... the amnesia. I mean, it sometimes makes me feel like I don't really know who I am anymore.'

Roisin's brow furrowed. 'What did the doctor say?'

'It's a reaction to a traumatic event.'

'Short-term amnesia, yes? You will get your memory back?'

'It's too early to tell.'

'Robbie misses you.'

'I miss you.'

'We're getting divorced. I'm with Hugh now.'

Rex touched her shoulder. 'Remember what we had. Perhaps it's the reason I'm suffering this trauma. Maybe our break-up has done it.'

'*Remember what we had?* That's an odd statement from someone who claims to have amnesia.'

'Some things are unforgettable.'

'I'm helping you because we have a child together and he needs both of us. I need to check these e-mails.'

Rex surmised that the way Roisin had looked at him meant she still loved George, whether she would admit it or not. He decided to bide his time and work out a way to seduce her. The idea of having sex with her caused all kinds of effects on his body. His heart beat faster and he was perspiring. The sensation of an erection was the worst thing. This past week or so, of all the things he'd had to get used to living in another man's body, by far the most nauseating was having to go to the toilet and handle someone else's penis. That part of possessing a body he could do without.

An hour was spent organising the completion of the sale of the house where George and Roisin had once lived as a happily married couple.

George had received e-mails from the solicitor dealing with the matrimonial home sale with last-minute queries and asking for details of where the funds should be transferred on completion of the sale. Roisin discovered that George had arranged to rent a small one-bedroom flat close to Robbie's school. The tenancy agreement awaited a signature, and Roisin arranged for him to return it with the deposit to the letting agent.

Finally, he made a call to his boss and explained he was suffering from amnesia and would have to take leave from work. His boss sounded sympathetic, but requested he send a doctor's certificate as soon as possible.

'Right, so you need to get on with packing your stuff as soon as you can, and remember to ask your doctor for a certificate.' Roisin stood up and stretched, glancing at her watch. 'That didn't take as long as I thought it would.'

'I can't get a doctor's certificate because I can't remember who my GP is.'

'But... But you said you went to the doctor.'

'I lied. I was embarrassed. I haven't been to see anyone.' He pouted for effect.

'Listen, I'll go with you to the GP. I have to leave now, but let's meet tomorrow and we'll go together. I'll be here about nine, after I've taken Robbie to school.' She touched his cheek.

Rex put a hand over Roisin's. It felt good. He leaned in and kissed her on the mouth.

She pulled away and then looked up at him briefly from under her eyelashes.

He noticed she hadn't resisted the kiss, and dared to believe this would be the start of a beautiful evening. The illusion was shattered, however, when she slapped him across the cheek.

'Don't you dare do that again! I'm with Hugh.'

He watched her leave and heard the front door slam shut. A smile spread across Rex's face. It was a sign of passion, wasn't it, to slap a love interest across the cheek?

Chapter Twelve

Roisin knocked on the front door at 9.15 a.m., waking Rex from a dream. The dream had been quite vivid. In it he had relived his possession of the spider's body, which had brought about a sense of calm, but that came crashing down when Hugh stomped on the spider. Now Roisin had woken him from the dream and once again put an end to his happiness. Waking hours were a nightmare, sleep was the only time he got any peace. He hated living in George's body.

By the time he pulled on a dressing gown and went downstairs, Roisin had already let herself into the house and was sitting in the living room waiting for him.

'There you are,' she said, glancing at her watch. 'I told you I'd be here at nine, didn't I? We'll have to hurry if we want to see a doctor. It's impossible to get an appointment at short notice these days. Why aren't you dressed yet?'

Rex's head throbbed. He sighed and said, 'I know you want to help, but I would prefer to do this on my own. It's bad enough forgetting my whole life, but having to feel like a child who needs his mother with him at the doctor's is, well, humiliating.'

Roisin stood up. 'But I was doing you a favour, you said you didn't know who your GP was.'

'I'd prefer it if you just give me the address. Really, I'd rather go alone.'

'I could drop you off there. I have the car with me.'

'No, thanks for the offer but I'll be fine on my own.' He held in his frustration.

Roisin frowned, scribbling the address onto a piece of paper she found on his desk. 'You've always been so stubborn. At least you haven't lost your personality.'

'Thank you,' he said, taking the slip of paper.

'I've also written my number there, in case it isn't on your phone.'

'It's on my phone.' Rex had been toying with the idea of phoning her after her last visit and had seen the number on George's mobile.

'I thought you might have deleted it because of the divorce.'

'I wouldn't do that. You're the mother of my child.' He walked towards her.

'Yes, but you haven't been answering your phone.'

'It's the amnesia. I don't remember who people are, and it's embarrassing if I answer the phone and they expect me to know them.'

'It must be hard. Look, please call me if you need any help.'

He felt her hand on his arm and looked into her eyes.

'It's not a problem if you need help, okay? I want you to get better so you can see Robbie. We might be divorced, but it doesn't mean I don't care about you.'

Rex smiled and became more alert. He remembered the evening before, when she'd flirted with him; it was happening again—offering help, giving him her number. He leaned in, risking another slap on the cheek, but she walked away.

'We're divorced. I'm with Hugh.'

She's warming to me... regretting leaving George. He followed her out of the door and called her name.

Roisin turned around at the front gate, squinting against the sun.

He held up the slip of paper. 'Thank you. I appreciate this. You were always so good to me.'

With a tense smile and a wave, she walked away.

As much as he hated being in George's body, he knew he would have to try to remain in it as long as possible so that he could take advantage of this situation.

He noticed Roisin stop to look at him briefly before getting into her car. 'I'll get her back for you, George,' he muttered under his breath, 'but I will have my fun with her first. It's the least you can do for me.'

He took the piece of paper she'd written on and proceeded to tear it into tiny pieces. He couldn't risk seeing a doctor.

Chapter Thirteen

Derek's garage struck Rex as the ideal place for a murder. It would be the perfect way to take revenge.

He'd never liked *Uncle* Derek. He wasn't actually related to him but someone Rex's mother had started seeing behind his father's back when Rex was a child. His mother lied and told Rex and his father that Derek was her cousin. He used to visit the house whenever Rex's father went away on business. Derek was well-connected to the criminal underworld. A nasty man, he'd threatened Rex that if he told anyone he dabbled in crime, he'd make sure he paid for it.

When Rex's parents died, Derek pretended to care and even helped Rex to get up and running with taking over the family business. One day, quite unexpectedly, he departed without saying goodbye. Soon after Derek's disappearance, Rex discovered that a substantial amount of gold was missing from the safe. With no trace of a break-in, Derek was undoubtedly the culprit. Being afraid of the man, Rex didn't report it.

Derek breezed into Rex's life briefly a few years later. He'd attempted to steal more gold and jewellery; Rex caught him. By then he'd developed deadly concoctions, including the sleeping-spider gas. He'd scared Derek enough to warn him off.

When there was a burglary at the jewellery shop a couple of months later he knew it was more than likely Derek's handiwork, but had no evidence. He'd always harboured a yearning to take revenge, knowing that Derek would believe he'd had the last laugh. Their paths hadn't crossed much in the years since.

Derek used to be a mechanic, although it was mainly as a cover for other more shady dealings; there was a garage at the rear of his property. He lived alone. It would be easy enough to get rid of him without anyone finding out.

The last time Rex saw the man was three years ago; he'd had a problem with his car and needed it fixed quickly. Being a Sunday, he couldn't find a mechanic to assist on short notice, so even though he hated him he'd gone to see Derek. He remembered Derek saying, as he was leaving the garage, 'You should visit more often.'

I'll be visiting you now, Uncle, thought Rex with a grimace, *It'll be the last time we see each other. The last time you see anyone ever again.*

It had been easy enough to get hold of a gun. Ironically, it was because of the criminals he'd met through Derek that he knew where to get one. None of them recognised him in his new body, of course, but he told them Rex sent him.

He'd also purchased some chemicals, and used his scientific knowledge to create a liquid, similar to the liquid he'd used in his guns at 8 Goldfern Road, that would sedate his victims almost immediately. He'd tested it on a neighbour's cat and it had worked perfectly. The only missing ingredient was venom from a spider; that irked him, but he knew there was little he could do about it.

It was dark when he arrived at Brimstown Avenue. An alley on the side of Derek's house led to the back garden, and the shed that had been converted into a working garage. As Rex walked along the alley, he decided it would perhaps be better to fake Derek's suicide. It would be far easier to get away with than a shooting in this residential street, and besides, he couldn't risk getting caught at this stage.

Rex approached the garage and listened out for any noise from within. Once he'd established that Derek wasn't inside, he broke the lock and entered the garage. There was a car in there. He planned to find Derek, knock him out, bring him here and set up the scene.

A couple of hours later, Rex left Brimstown Avenue. It had worked out exactly as planned. On breaking into Derek's house, he'd found him snoozing on the sofa. He recalled seeing an old trolley-like workbench at the back of the garage, and it occurred to him that he would need something with wheels to lift and move Derek.

He returned to the garage and wheeled the wooden bench back to the house. As luck would have it, Derek's sofa was about the same height as the bench, so that made it easier to lift Derek onto it. He covered Derek from head to toe with the throw from the sofa, just in case there were any nosy neighbours looking out of their windows. He wheeled Derek to the garage marvelling at how easy it had been to do this and how the man was, surprisingly, still asleep.

Once his victim was safely in the driver's seat of the car, Rex turned on the ignition. Derek woke up when the car engine sounded, and protested in his half-asleep state, but Rex used the barrel of his gun to knock the man out before exiting the garage pulling the door closed behind him. He cursed his luck at having to use the gun. The scar on Derek's head would make it obvious his death hadn't been suicide. Rex put it to the back of his mind; the idea was that he would set the garage alight when all the victims were in there, so hopefully forensics wouldn't be able to discern the scarring from the gun when Derek's body was ravaged by the flames. This positive thought brought a smile to his face. He congratulated himself on one small victory, he was now in possession of the keys to Derek's house, which would make carrying out the other murders so much easier.

On his way back to George's flat, Rex wondered whether he should have waited and made sure Derek was dead. What if he came to and managed to get out of the garage? Surely the fumes from the car would suffocate him. *Derek saw my face...* But then Rex remembered that he didn't look like himself. Derek wouldn't know who had left him in the garage.

Rex parked his car by the side of the road. Thoughts were bombarding him; something was unfinished. He couldn't afford to leave any clues. The neighbours would surely hear the car engine running in the night. If someone found Derek, they'd notice he had been hit on the head. There was also the possibility that someone had seen him earlier in the back garden. His thoughts giving him no peace, he headed back to Derek's house.

When he reached the exterior doors of the garage, he heard the purr of the car engine. He knew, from a cursory glance online about the effects of car fumes, that Derek would surely be dead by now. However, his concern was for his own safety. The fumes would have reached dangerous levels, so entering the garage would be a risk. He decided to pull open the garage doors and wait for a while for the fumes to disperse. He found a dust-mask in a drawer in Derek's house, but doubted it would be enough to prevent him inhaling deadly gases. He used the mask, and also wrapped an old shirt around his nose and mouth before entering the garage. He ran in and out at lightning speed, just stopping long enough to turn off the car's ignition. Once out of the garage he caught his breath after removing the shirt and mask. Derek was dead; there was no doubt.

He closed the garage door and left the house.

One down, four to go, thought Rex. He felt pressured to get the murders over with before anyone started looking for Derek. He was a lonely man as far as Rex knew, unlikely to receive many guests, but he couldn't be sure as he hadn't had much to do with him in recent years. What if someone visited him and noticed something awry?

A couple of days later, Rex sat on the sofa in 7 Brimstown Avenue, in the exact spot where Derek had been snoozing.

After arriving at the house, he'd gone to the garage. Derek's head was visible in the driver's seat, unmoving. Perfect.

Rex had sent identical letters to the four bullies via e-mail, inviting them to meet him at the house. Only the appointment times were different.

He'd invited Jake at 1 p.m., Frank at 2 p.m., and Nick at 3 p.m.

Terence was due at 4 p.m. He planned to save him till last, and show him what he'd done to the others before killing him. Having accepted that the fantasy of killing them as a spider was unattainable, he regretted not being in his own body for this. Watching them die through the eyes of the boy they'd tortured would have been the ultimate revenge. George's eyes were far too placid; anger did not exude from them as easily.

At 12.58 p.m. the doorbell rang. Rex planned to kill the first three quickly. He'd had a silencer fitted to his gun to reduce the noise, so he'd shoot them and then store the bodies in the garage. He planned to use one of the petrol canisters he'd seen in there to set the place on fire and get rid of the evidence.

Jake Brother stood outside the front door holding hands with a small boy, who appeared to be about six years old. The boy smiled at Rex when he saw him, as did Jake.

'Hello, I'm Jake.' The man held out his hand.

'Rex,' said Rex, then caught himself, 'Um... Rex Weav—Rex Rodenbury's will, yes? I'm George.' Flummoxed, Rex took a deep breath and shook Jake's hand. He hadn't expected to see a child.

'If you don't mind me asking, I'm curious as to why everyone has different appointment times,' said Jake. 'I called Nick yesterday and he told me he's coming later, and he'd spoken to Frank and Terence; they said they had different appointment times too.' Jake walked past Rex into the house as he spoke.

'There is a reason for that,' said Rex, thinking on his feet. 'Your gifts from Rex are quite different, and he specifically requested in the will that you should be told of them separately. Please take a seat.' He hoped that would satisfy Jake's curious mind, but began to lose confidence in his plan, kicking himself for not anticipating that the four friends would obviously discuss this unexpected turn of events.

Rex sat next to Jake on the sofa. 'Would you like a drink?' He'd planned to put his specially formulated liquid sedative in the drink and then shoot him as soon as it kicked in. He looked at the little boy with the messy brown curls and big blue eyes, and gulped, unsure he could go through with killing him as well.

'A cup of tea would be nice, thanks.'

Rex shook his head and closed his eyes letting out a sigh.

'Is something wrong?' asked Jake.

Rex quickly composed himself. 'No. I'm fine.'

'Stop playing with the plant, Damon, you'll kill it,' scolded Jake, as the young boy pulled at the leaves of a rubber plant.

Rex stood up. 'I'll make the tea.'

He went to the kitchen. Once inside, he pulled the door closed, perhaps a bit too forcefully, then regretted it. The last thing he needed was to draw attention to himself. Jake might warn the others about him. There was no alternative, he'd have to send Jake away and rearrange the meeting. He clenched his jaw wishing away the swarms of frustrated emotions threatening to erupt into anger.

He exited the kitchen. 'Mr Brother, I've had a call from my office and must leave to see a client urgently. I'll rearrange your appointment.' He lowered his voice and moved closer to Jake, 'Next time, it would be best if you leave the child at home; the matters we will be discussing are not suitable for young ears.'

'Oh... Um... yes. Oh well, let me know when you want me to come again. Ideally next week, as the boy will be in school. I don't have anyone else who can look after him this week; my wife's working abroad.'

Rex nodded.

'Are you able to at least tell me how much money he left me?'

'Sorry, I have to go straight away. It's very urgent.'

Jake stood up and reached out a hand to shake Rex's. 'Come on, Damon, we're leaving.'

Rex followed him to the door.

Jake appeared so normal and happy. His life had turned out well. He recalled the time Jake had held him against a wall, aided by Terence, when Nick kicked him in the groin. Echoes of their laughter filled his mind as the memory surfaced.

Damon looked like Jake. Vexation brewed as Rex watched Jake wave at him whilst strapping Damon into his car seat. *Perhaps I should have killed him and the boy*, he thought, going back inside and slamming the door behind him.

The clock above the mantelpiece ticked loudly; Rex noticed the time: 1.13 p.m. If he only killed Nick, Frank, and Terence, it would be obvious to Jake that he'd killed them. Identity wasn't a concern; he couldn't care less if George was locked away for the murders, but three of them wouldn't do. The whole gang had to pay for what they'd done to him. They all had to die.

Rex took George's smartphone out of his pocket and sent e-mails to the men, cancelling the appointments—rearranging them for the following week—then stomped out of the house in frustration.

Chapter Fourteen

Roisin walked into the living room and noticed Hugh hide something behind his back. She raised an eyebrow. 'What's that?'

'How was your day?' he replied.

'What are you hiding? Let me see.' She approached him and he stood up and sidled past her, out of the room.

'It's a bottle! Is that alcohol? Hugh?'

He turned to face her and held up a half-empty bottle of whisky in a shaky hand. 'So what? I'm a grown man. If you caught Robbie with this, that would be a problem—'

'Stop making light of it! You're an alcoholic! You swore to me you wouldn't drink again.'

He sat on the stairs and hung his head, placing the whisky bottle on the floor next to him.

Roisin leaned down and took the bottle. 'Did you drink all of this?'

'I've been trying to forget stuff, but I can't.' He stood up. 'How do you stay so calm? How, Roisin? We've just buried our child.' He was swaying slightly from side to side.

Roisin held her forehead. 'It hasn't been easy for me either.' She felt selfish, knowing she'd pushed Hugh away whenever he'd attempted to talk about losing the baby.

She looked at him and remembered how dejected he had been at the funeral. Roisin and Hugh kept it as close to them as possible; there was no need for anyone else to know they were burying their child. They'd discussed it and decided it was best to face it alone. They invited Roisin's parents and sister, but only because they were already aware that the funeral was being arranged.

Roisin had worried that Hugh would drink after the funeral, but he hadn't. She'd been proud of him.

'I called to talk to Liam yesterday,' he said through sniffles. 'Abi won't let me. She said she'll take me to court if I go anywhere near her or Liam; says she can get a court order to stop me seeing him. She says Liam's scared of me and doesn't want to see me.' Tears began to leak from the corners of his eyes.

Roisin moved closer to him and put a hand on his arm. 'She can't stop you seeing him forever. Let's forget this, forget today. You have to stay off the booze and I'll help you try to get through to her. She must know that Liam needs you in his life.'

'She hates me, and he's going to grow up to hate me because she'll be telling him I'm a loser. And it's true, isn't it? Why are you with me?

49

Why haven't you thrown me out?'

'That's the whisky talking. I'll make you a cup of coffee.'

Hugh followed her into the kitchen.

'My whole life's in such a mess,' he said, sniffing as he sat on a wooden chair by the kitchen table.

Roisin busied herself filling the kettle with water, her mind drifting to what George had said the last time she saw him. Her heart had been pining for George in the past week, which struck her as absurd considering she'd just moved into the new house with Hugh. It felt wrong, having these feelings for George while living with Hugh, and yet they existed. George had appeared so vulnerable the last time she saw him; he was so much more like the man she'd originally fallen in love with. He'd apparently forgiven her betrayal. She told herself to be sensible. Going back to George would be exactly that, "going backwards".

She tried to focus her mind on the future with Hugh. They should be happy. But everything had changed. The obvious change was the big hole where their hopes and wishes for the new baby had once resided. Roisin knew she would never come to terms with the tragedy so instead made every effort to accept it, move forward regardless. She often caught herself wondering if she was merely putting off the grieving. Would it come flooding forward at a future date, like a tsunami, washing away everything she held dear? But that had already happened, and here she was, dealing with the destruction in the best way she could.

Hugh had changed. Sometimes she felt bad when she resented his behaviour, his tendency to use alcohol as an escape. He was grieving too, she knew that, yet selfishly she was not allowing him to do it his way. But she reminded herself there was a child caught in the middle, and her reaction to Hugh's drinking was a protective instinct. She wouldn't allow him around Robbie if he started drinking again.

They'd moved into their new house; the money from the sale of the home she'd lived in with George had come through, and Hugh and Roisin borrowed money from their parents to top up the extra they needed until the Goldfern Road property was sold. In a way, Roisin welcomed this, because it forced her to stay, not make any rash decisions to pack up and leave, as tempted as she was to run away.

The money from the sale of 8 Goldfern Road would come through in the next week, which would enable them to repay her parents and Hugh's parents. That would at least get rid of one of their immediate problems.

'Things will sort themselves out in time,' she said, speaking her mind.

'I can't handle much more of this. You're stronger than me,

Roisin.'

'You were there for me when I had problems with George; without you I wouldn't have got through.'

'Without me you wouldn't have a broken marriage and you wouldn't be mourning a dead baby.'

'Hugh!'

'That was insensitive, sorry, but I lost the child too. I might not have been carrying her, but—'

'I know.' Roisin sat opposite him as she waited for the kettle to boil. 'Stop blaming yourself for my broken marriage. I did that myself. Well, with some help from George. I would've divorced him whether or not you came along; I think I was looking for a reason to leave him.'

'What am I going to do about seeing Liam?'

'Do you want me to phone Abigail?'

'No. She hates you. The last thing she said to me was "go back to your bitch and leave us alone".'

'Hmm... She's bound to resent me. I don't expect to be her best friend, but I could speak to her; she's a mother.'

'She's not like you.'

'You managed to agree about what to do with your house when you divorced, right? So surely you can agree about Liam.'

'The house was easy enough, we sold it and she took the bulk of the proceeds, claiming she'd put most of the money into the purchase. That may have been true, but I was the one paying the mortgage. I didn't argue with her, though. She said she needed to set up home with Liam, and the house had to be suitable for him. I agreed because I wanted what's best for him. Now she doesn't let me see him.'

'You're his dad. You have every right to see him. Try talking to her again.'

'It's not worth it.'

'Liam's nine, right? He's getting older; he'll be making his own decisions soon.'

'She says he doesn't want to see me.'

'You should take her to court. Have you threatened that? Maybe if you tell her you'll go to court if she doesn't let you see him—'

'I wouldn't know where to start.'

'I'll help you.'

The kettle boiled and Roisin stood up to make the coffee. She couldn't help thinking back to how much simpler her life had been with George. She blinked in an attempt to forget.

Chapter Fifteen

'What colour do you see?'

Black.

'Concentrate.'

George could only make out the blue fizz that was always there when the angel was around, and he was filled with frustration, being unable to see whatever he was supposed to be seeing.

'You need to think beyond what is right in front of you. Your senses give you a good idea of your environment. You can pick up images by what you feel, and become aware of your environment by concentrating.'

It's not working. There's only black, and a blue light when you're around.

'You see the blue because you've made a connection in your mind between that and me. I am not a colour. I am a spirit. You can't see me.'

So what's the blue fizz then?

'You've created that in your consciousness to represent me.'

I don't understand.

'Because you're caught up with what you've been taught about seeing.'

I'm trying, but I can't see anything.

'I'm going to tell you what is in the room. It might help. This room will be your home for now. You'll remain here until you're ready to repossess your body. This is your living room; the living room in the new flat you rented after you sold your home. Rex inhabits this flat, and he spends the majority of his time in this room. It will be better for you to remain here until you're ready to reenter your body.'

Is he in the room now?

'No. There is a window to your left. The curtains are half open, so there is daylight leaking through. Concentrate and tell me whether you're able to distinguish that light.'

George was once again overwhelmed at finding himself alone in the blackness with the solitary company of a voice in what had once been his head. Even stranger than hearing the voice, was that he had a sense of space but not much else; he had no sensation of body parts at all. He concentrated on being in a room with a window to the left. An orange light flashed and then all was black again. He concentrated on being in the room and the orange light began to build and then remained to his left, out of sight of his non-existent eyes.

'What can you see?' came the voice.

There's an orange light to the left. Is that the window?

'The curtains are orange and the light filtering through has an orange glow. Well done.'

Do you know when Rex is coming back?

'No, but you'll know when he returns.'

I'll hear him?

'Yes, and with any luck you will see him. Keep concentrating. I'm going to leave you alone.'

But I don't know how to possess a body.

'I'll be back to show you how when the time comes.'

Rex returned to 7 Brimstown Avenue and waited for his prey, five days later than originally planned.

The first to arrive was Jake. Without the child. Rex didn't waste any time. He was frustrated at having had to change the date of the killing and this stirred impatience within him. By the time Jake arrived, he had no patience left. He served him a glass of water with a dose of his liquid sedative and went on to shoot him in the head as soon as the man became dozy. After using the workbench to wheel the body into the garage, he spent the next twenty minutes cleaning up the blood from the immediate area around the sofa. Regretting his haste, he realised he'd have to be more prepared next time to avoid getting blood on the furniture.

He covered the sofa with a clean throw found in one of the bedrooms, to hide the hideous spattering of blood, and had only just finished tidying up when the doorbell sounded. Frank had arrived.

By 5 p.m. the four men had joined "Uncle" Derek in the garage, and Rex doused the bodies with petrol and tied a rope to the car inside the garage. He unravelled the rope so that it reached almost to the back door of the house and then lit it with a match. He watched as the rope slowly caught alight and burned along its length, weaving its way towards the garage. Soon the entire place would go up in flames. Rex ran out of the house and into his car before that happened. He deleted the e-mails he'd sent the victims using George's smartphone, and didn't think of them again. They were mere flies, unfortunate flies caught in his web and obliterated.

When Rex got back to George's flat, he found Glen waiting for him outside.

Wretched man, what is he doing here?

'Hi George, how come you never invited me to a housewarming? We have to get a party set up.'

'A party?'

'Yeah, why not?'

'I'm not in the mood for a party.'

'Okay, maybe not a full-blown party, but a nice housewarming do. Something to celebrate your move.'

'George would hardly be celebrating having to move out of his house so that he could give money to his ex who's moved in with her lover.'

'Oh, right, yeah, sorry mate. But why did you say it like that?'

'Like what?'

'You said "George wouldn't be celebrating", as if you were talking about someone else.'

'It's the amnesia.'

'Right. Probably the amnesia stopped you inviting me round too.'

'I only moved in on Friday. I'm still settling in.'

'I could've helped you move in.'

'I can't talk now. I'm busy.'

'I'm worried about you, and I'm not the only one. Roisin was on the phone to me this morning. She said your boss phoned her again. He was asking about that certificate from your doctor.'

'Maybe there was a delay. You know what doctors are like. He said he would send it.'

'Did you even go to the doctor? Roisin thinks you didn't.'

'I'm fine. I don't need a doctor.'

'Yeah, if you don't mind losing your job. You ain't even been to a therapist, have you? The last time we spoke, you said your therapist was advising you to do some crazy shit. It didn't sound right, y'know, building the wooden web and—'

'I don't have to do that anymore,' said Rex, curtly.

'Good, 'cos it sounded like a stupid thing to do.' Glen shuddered exaggeratedly. 'I wouldn't wanna be reminded of any of that creepy stuff.'

'I don't mean to be rude, but I'm busy, so—'

'Busy with what? Can you even remember what your plans are for today?'

'Amnesia only makes you forget the past. I'm perfectly capable of running my life, thank you.'

'Ruining your life?'

'I said *running*.'

'This is serious. I'll come with you to the doctor. I can explain what's happened, and they'll give you a certificate you can take to work. If you lose your job, how will you afford the rent on this place?'

'My memory is coming back.'

'Right, so you remember where you work?'

'Yes, I'll go tomorrow.'

'Why don't I go with you? I can explain things to your boss.'

'I'm perfectly capable of explaining everything to my boss. Was there anything else?' huffed Rex.

'Yeah, you look a bit rough, mate. What've you been doing? Is that blood on your coat? Did you have an accident?'

Rex took a deep breath, remembering his coat had been lying on the sofa when the first victim met his gruesome end. There was a large brown mark on it; unmistakably dried blood.

'Mate, if you've been out on a killing spree and you're caught, the best reply you could give the police is you can't remember. What better proof is there for that than a certificate from your GP saying you've got amnesia?' Glen doubled over with laughter. When he stood up a frown formed on his face as he surveyed the stains on the coat. 'Seriously, mate, do you need to talk? Were you in a fight?'

It occurred to Rex that he couldn't be sure how easy it would be to leave George's body, and if caught by the police for the murders he would need a defence. 'I think getting a certificate from a doctor would be a good idea.'

'I'll come with you,' said Glen. 'We'll go first thing in the morning.'

Chapter Seventeen

The charred remains of five men have been discovered in a garage on Brimstown Avenue. Firefighters were called to the scene yesterday evening when residents of neighbouring properties reported what sounded like fireworks exploding, and noticed smoke rising from the back of number seven Brimstown Avenue. At present the identities of the dead are unknown, although the owner of the property is believed to be amongst them. A neighbour stated that the house was occupied by a man who lived alone. He said the man kept himself to himself and rarely received any visitors. Police are appealing to anyone who saw people go into the house to come forward. The only CCTV camera in the vicinity appears to have been vandalised. A local resident has reported seeing a man in his twenties or thirties with dark brown hair enter the house early yesterday morning, and said that the man had a set of keys. The name of the property owner has not yet been disclosed by police investigating the incident...

Ben Gibbons gaped as he watched the news. The day before, he'd been outside Derek Cole's house and had seen a man leave, running to his car, before the garage at the back went up in smoke. He'd been intending to go into the house to confront Derek, or "Del", as he knew him. If he'd gone into that house he may have become a victim. Five men. Even *he* had never killed so many in one day.

Part of him was in awe, but a bigger part of him reeled with frustration and anger. How dare this man take away his link to what could have been the biggest haul of his life? Del knew where the gold was hidden. He'd taken the knowledge with him to the grave. Ben had spent years using numerous contacts and resources to track Del down.

They'd been good friends years ago. They'd carried out a burglary together and stolen gold worth a six-figure sum at the time. Del had promised Ben half of the gold. Ben specialised in burglary; he knew how to disarm alarm systems and could break in even where there were the most secure locks. Del wouldn't have succeeded in stealing the gold without him.

After the burglary, Del told Ben that they had to be cautious in case the police were looking for the gold. He said he'd hidden it somewhere secure and would get in touch and let him know when he could have his share. The gold had been stolen from a jeweller's owned by a family Del knew well, so he said he would watch them and see what they were going to do about the stolen gold before deciding on the next move.

Ben waited for months. He'd become frustrated so had tried to contact Del, only to find he was in prison. At first he believed he was in prison because of the burglary. He'd visited him and found out he was in there for an unrelated offence. Del told Ben he would be released soon and would be in touch.

Ben waited. Months turned into years.

He went to Del's house and was told by a woman who'd answered the door that Del had moved away. The woman explained Del was her ex, that she hated him, and would have him killed if she found out where he was. She'd even asked Ben to let her know if he caught up with him.

He'd failed to locate the man for many years. Now he'd come full circle, back to the house where Del had always lived—he'd never left. He'd been avoiding sharing the gold, Ben presumed.

Precisely when he'd been on the brink of discovering what had happened to the gold, Ben's dreams slipped further away. This serial killer was to blame, this man who'd killed Del and those four other men. Who was he?

Ben was no stranger to crime, and he himself regularly killed people time and time again with little or no remorse. It was a way of life. It began when he started taking drugs at a young age; then it escalated when he became part of a gang. There were disagreements and there were killings; an unescapable element of the world he moved in. But he'd never killed that many people in the space of a few hours. The young man, who appeared harmless, dressed like a banker in a smart suit, had apparently taken these murders in his stride, and in broad daylight. He was either suffering from a mental illness, or was even more of a hardened criminal than Ben or anyone Ben had ever known.

Ben remembered how he'd followed the man's car from Del's house, curious to see where he was going, not even suspecting at the time that anyone had died in the house. He reflected on how the man had appeared so casual; not like someone who'd just committed a string of murders.

When the man parked his car and approached a residential building, another man was waiting there; the murderer and this man entered into a heated conversation. The other man also wore a smart suit. Ben imagined they might be some kind of mafia gang he hadn't come across.

He'd driven back towards Del's house afterwards, but the road had been cordoned off by the time he got back there. He'd still had no idea what had happened.

Watching the news now, he realised there was obviously more to the innocuous-looking murderer. Had he known about the gold? Ben resolved to find out more about him.

Rex watched the early-morning news with a mixture of intrigue and delight. One of the things he'd learned from Derek, as a teenager, was that before committing any crime it was prudent to make sure any CCTV cameras were out of operation; he felt a sense of accomplishment—he'd made the police's job much harder. He was slightly annoyed at the neighbour who had reported seeing him enter the property. He wasn't ready to leave George's body yet. How much time would it take them to identify the bodies of the victims? He had been counting on the remains being so burned as to be impossible to identify. The men would of course be reported as missing, and investigations into their comings and goings would be carried out. Any police checks on social media would link back to George's Facebook page and the messages he'd sent to Terence. It wouldn't be difficult to connect that evidence to the deaths at Derek's house. Ideally Rex needed enough time in George's body to get rid of Hugh and Glen, seduce Roisin, and then to find a deadly spider to possess.

Chapter Eighteen

There were no seats available at the GP surgery when they arrived. Glen approached the front desk.

'Hi, I need an emergency appointment for my friend.'

'You'll have to wait, sir. The doctors are fully booked today.'

'We don't mind waiting.'

Rex stepped forward.

'Can I take your name, please?'

'Rex Weaver.'

Glen coughed. 'Um... his name is George.'

'George. I said that, didn't I? George Barnaby.'

'You said Rex Weaver.'

Rex felt his (or George's) cheeks redden. *I have to be more careful.* 'I have amnesia.'

'He has amnesia,' repeated Glen to the woman behind the counter.

'Right. George Barnaby. Date of birth?'

Rex shrugged.

'It's May. Eleventh of May, 1980,' said Glen.

'Thank you. Please take a seat and a doctor will call you when they're free.'

'There aren't any seats,' said Rex to Glen as they turned away from the receptionist.

'There are now, that couple have just got up.'

They walked over to the uncomfortable-looking plastic chairs near the exit and sat down. For a few moments neither man made a sound.

Rex thought about his slip—saying his name—would Glen be suspicious? He doubted it. This man was a buffoon, forever joking and making fun of life. He didn't possess any perceivable intelligence.

Rex fantasised about getting rid of him. This was the man who'd hit him with a brick and sprayed him with the gun containing the tranquilising liquid at 8 Goldfern Road. The garage had gone up in flames, so he would have to find somewhere else to take Glen and make sure he never made it out alive.

'George, that was weird,' said Glen eventually, disturbing Rex's musings.

'What was?'

'You said your name was Rex Weaver. How did you even know what his surname was? Even *I* didn't, and I was the one who was mainly dealing with the executors.'

'It was on his will. Didn't you see it?'

'Oh. No, I don't remember. Maybe I did. But how come you said your name was Rex? Are you still having those nightmares? If you are, you should tell the doctor.'

'I'm fine. I don't even know why I'm here.'

'To get the certificate. Stop being stubborn. At least Roisin will be off your back if your boss stops phoning her.'

'Roisin.'

'Your ex.'

'I know who she is.' Rex looked Glen in the eye.

Glen averted his gaze 'Stop staring at me, you freak. You've got that zombie look in your eyes again.'

'Do you think Roisin still loves me?'

'What? Am I a marriage counsellor now?'

'She came to see me last week, to make sure I was all right. She wanted to accompany me to the doctor. If she's that concerned about me being ill, she must have feelings for me.'

'You're not telling me you wanna get back together with Roisin, are you?'

'We had a good marriage until Hugh came along.'

'She cheated on you, who's to say she wouldn't do it again? And besides, she lives with him, doesn't she? And you're divorced. I hate to break it to you, but it's over.'

Rex thought about getting rid of Hugh; if he was out of the picture there'd be no one to stop him having his way with the beautiful Roisin. He could comfort her, and one thing would lead to another. 'I think she still has feelings for me, that's all.'

'Remember to add "delusional" to your symptoms when you see the doctor,' said Glen.

George's name sounded over the loud-speaker system. The two men made their way into the doctor's room.

Rex sat alone in George's flat after Glen had left. He hated Glen. He once again fantasised about killing him, but realised he'd have to slow down on the murders.

Rex's ultimate goal was to find a spider; a poisonous one. He'd walked in a spider's skin, but it wasn't enough; he needed to inhabit a spider's world. As a spider, his life would be endlessly more fascinating. He loved to imagine catching prey in a web, an authentic woven spiderweb, poisoning them, and then finally eating them. It had been a lifelong dream, a dream ended by Hugh and his cowboy boots. He hated Hugh, as much as he hated Glen... Maybe more. He couldn't be sure how much of that was George's feelings from within his body. George probably hated the man too; after all, he'd stolen Roisin.

He remembered that George had found the Brazilian spider quite quickly. The supplier's details might be on his computer or phone. Rex pulled George's iPhone from his jacket pocket. There were three missed calls from "work". Rex's thoughts strayed to the certificate he'd obtained from George's GP signing him off work pending further investigation into the "patient's loss of memory/amnesia?" The question mark the GP had added to the certificate seemed to signify he didn't believe him. He was informed he would be receiving a referral to a specialist clinic soon—an appointment he'd already decided he would miss.

Rex flicked through the messages on George's phone and found an intriguing one from someone called Tom sent at about the right time to be linked to the poisonous spider.

Jess found out where to get what you asked for. They'll deliver to your house in a couple of days.

Jess... Who could this Jess be? Perhaps Roisin knew. He would ask her.

Just then, the front doorbell rang.

Rex wondered whether Roisin had come to check on him. A smile perked up the corners of his lips. He walked out of the flat and opened the communal door.

A man stood outside. A tall man, over six feet in height.

'George Barnaby?' Boomed the enormous visitor's voice.

'Who's asking?'

'I've come for payment.'

'Payment? Um... I thought I paid online.'

'Are you trying to be funny? I should warn you I lost my sense of humour after killing a few people.'

Rex gulped. 'I'm... This is concerning the rent, yes?' He recalled Roisin setting up the direct debit for him. His brain felt muddled.

'This ain't about any rent. The delivery man told you the boss would be dealing with collection of the payment. And the boss wasn't happy to find you'd moved away so soon after the delivery. You weren't trying to avoid paying, were you?'

'Oh... um... Is it about the gun?' whispered Rex, leaning as close as he could to the towering man.

'I'm losing my patience. How many more illegal rackets have you got going on, man?'

Rex exhaled. 'The gun. Um... '

'No! This is about the spider. Y'know? The killer spider you ordered. Where's the money?'

Rex smiled instinctively. 'The spider. How wonderful! I was going to get in touch with you. I need another one.'

'I don't deliver, I collect. And if I can't collect, I break things. Comprende?'

'Break things... right. Um... I'm sure we can find a way—'

'Your time has run out. I don't get paid to chat. I'm going to count from ten backwards. When I get to one, I want the five hundred pounds or you lose a limb.'

'Let's be sensible.'

'If I was sensible, I wouldn't be in this game.'

'I need to make a phone call.'

'You've got ten minutes,' growled the man, walking away towards a black estate with tinted windows.

Rex still had the gun; he yearned to take this ogre somewhere he could put a bullet in his head. He felt nostalgic for the house at 8 Goldfern Road; it had been so easy to catch his prey there. This man wouldn't have stood a chance. He yearned to recreate that setting, take back control. George's weak human body was useless to him.

The man outside meant business; he'd killed several people before. Then, Rex reminded himself that he was dead already. He was the one who had the upper hand. Even if this blood-thirsty debt collector killed George, *he* would still exist. He wouldn't have a body—a minor setback. Now that he knew how to possess a body he could easily find another victim. But then he remembered Roisin: he'd never win her over if he didn't look like George. He couldn't allow this man to kill him.

He pulled out George's mobile phone and called Roisin.

'Hi George, I'm glad you phoned. Your boss—'

'Sorry, I don't have time to chat. You wouldn't happen to know my pin number for my Visa card, would you? I need to get some cash out.'

'No, sorry, I don't. Can't you go into your bank and explain what's happened? I'm sure they'd let you get cash over the counter.'

'You couldn't lend me five hundred pounds, could you?'

'You sound anxious. Are you in trouble?'

'No. Don't worry, I'll sort it out.'

'I would help if I could, really, but I don't have that kind of money to hand. How are you, George? Robbie keeps asking about you. He's not sleeping and he's not eating properly. He misses you so much. And your boss keeps phoning. Haven't you been to the doctor yet?'

'I've been to the doctor. I'll take the certificate as soon as I can.'

'Make sure you do.'

His brow creased into a frown. 'I have to go.'

Rex noticed the large man pacing outside the house; he approached him, less intimidated now. 'I have to go to the bank,' he explained.

'I ain't got time for this. I have to be somewhere else in ten minutes. We'll make a deal. Listen carefully, because it's important, and you don't want to get it wrong, because if you do, you die.'

'Death is an illusion,' said Rex, confidence growing.

'What did you say?'

'I might be dead already. *You* might be.'

'Are you threatening me?' The man leaned down closer to him and stared into his eyes.

Rex met his stare.

The man backed away, as if startled. 'How did you do that, man?'

'Do what?'

'Your eyes, they went completely black, like completely, even the whites.'

Rex was sure he could see fear in his eyes. 'Perhaps you should be careful who you threaten,' he said, feeling even bolder. 'Some people possess certain powers.'

The debt collector blinked a couple of times and then said, 'I'll be back in two hours. Be ready with the cash, or I'll... I'll make sure you pay in kind.'

'But if I'm already dead what can you do to me?' Rex let out a belly laugh.

The man backed away looking fearful but as though he were covering up his unease. 'Have the money ready for me, you creep. I don't scare easily.'

'Don't you ever wonder what happens to the people you kill?' asked Rex walking towards him at a steady pace, head held high. 'What if I'm one of them, back from the dead?'

'Make sure you have the money when I return,' he replied, screwing up his face in confusion or vexation.

'I'll be waiting for you to return, don't you worry,' said Rex, arms folded. He couldn't help marvelling at how easy it had been to unsettle this hardman. His eyes changing colour to black may have helped. As the same thing had happened at the pub when he was with Glen, Rex dared to dream that he might be becoming a spider; what if the transformation

64

took effect naturally, as he'd hoped it would ever since being bitten by a spider? He walked back into the flat. Instead of going to the bank, he decided to devise a way to kill the debt collector when he returned. He had a gun; he only had to work out the best way to lure him into a trap.

Chapter Nineteen

George had been listening to sounds in the room for what seemed like days but must have been a few hours. It still didn't make sense to him that he could hear without ears, and this made him more inclined to believe the mysterious voice. Perhaps, if it were all true, he would also be able to see without eyes.

It seemed so fantastical; he wondered whether he'd become trapped in a delusional box for eternity. The more he thought about it, the more he began to doubt his own mind, while at the same time painfully aware he had no "mind" but still survived—a concept which confused him. How could he think if he didn't have a body with a brain? Everything he'd learned about life and death was turned inside out. He was inexplicably alive, without the essentials required to sustain life. He'd existed in this state for days, maybe longer, and hadn't eaten, or drunk any water.

The single most plausible explanation, even though he had always been sceptical about such phenomena, was that Rex had possessed his body.

He remembered what the voice told him: if he didn't get back into his body soon, he would cease to exist. He wasn't even sure whether the voice was real or imagined.

Being stranded alone brought home to him how much of his former life was valuable and positive; how much he'd overlooked by concentrating on the negatives. All the negative aspects of his former existence paled in comparison to living this non-life. A *something* without a body.

There was a flurry of wind. *Rex?* The voice said he would know when Rex entered the room.

George concentrated, with nothing to show for the concentration; no furrowed brow, no squinting eyes. He listened without ears for any sound, and strained to see without eyes. He heard a voice and a noise. The voice had been a deep voice, but muffled... *Rex?* The noise sounded like a metallic object falling onto a hard surface. *Concentrate, concentrate...*

Then it happened, like a miracle; a small area of circular light became wider and wider before him. A man came into view: the man he'd once been. It reminded him of stories he'd heard about out-of-body experiences, seeing himself from afar. He appeared to be further away than he actually was, like looking through a telescope. He held a shiny object: a gun. *Oh my God, he's going to kill someone... maybe already has killed.*

George might have turned pale if he still had a face. The

realisation hit him that if this man had shot someone, CCTV would have caught his image, or they'd have his fingerprints. This was the ideal cover for a serial killer like Rex: to live in another person's body and commit heinous crimes.

The mad thoughts continued to run through George's non-existent brain, perplexing him even further. There was no way out. Perhaps he could try to get back into his body now, if he made a concerted effort. But what if a crime had already been committed? Did he really want to go back only to be sentenced to life imprisonment?

'You can see him, can't you?'

The blue light fizzed at the edge of George's line of vision. He made an effort to look at it, but the light remained far enough away that he could not see it.

I can, replied George.

'So, all you have to do is imagine yourself falling forward. Go on. Now is your chance. Your energy is fading, you may not have much time left.'

But he's killed someone. He's got a gun. That's why he wanted my body, isn't it? To carry out a killing spree.

'He's planning to kill a man. He hasn't killed him yet. However, I must warn you before you claim your body back, he has already killed five men while he has been in your body.'

Five men? How on earth...?

'There were no witnesses, but he contacted one of the victims using your Facebook account, and also sent e-mails to the victims, in your name.'

But criminals hack Facebook accounts all the time, and they can get the e-mail addresses of people on a "Friend" list if they do that. That would be a defence, surely.

'There are no guarantees.'

So you're saying I might be sent to prison for multiple murders? Is it even worth going back into my body? Will I go to prison?

'I cannot predict the future. The future changes frequently; it cannot be seen with any certainty.'

But what about fortune tellers? They predict the future.

'They use the power of suggestion. They tell people things in such a way, suggestively, so they behave in a certain way. If you can make a person believe in an eventuality, then it will happen.'

But there are things beyond our control.

'It's always cause and effect.'

Yes, Rex caused these men to die and the effect will be I'll end up in prison.

'There is a way around even the hardest things.'

I'm not sure I want to go back and face up to all of that.

'You cannot stay in your current state. If you lose your energy, which is waning, you will go into the recycle path and your soul will be prepared for the next life. You will no longer retain the memories of the life you led as George Barnaby. Don't be afraid; we have the power to help you if the need arises.'

The blue light disappeared before George could question further.

Who is this freak? wondered George. *He's killed five men and wants to kill more?* Rex's favourite number was eight; could that be how many people he planned to murder?

George decided not to think about it. He would get back into his body, so preventing any more murders, and then work out what he could do to cover his tracks for the past few days, or weeks, or however long it had been. Concentrating on the image that he saw before him, he fell forward into the scene.

It took him a second to realise what had happened. He walked over to the mirror and stared in awe. He'd overcome Rex's efforts to destroy him. There was a hollow scream and a voice—Rex's voice—shouting, 'Noooooooooooo!' The sound drifted further and further away until nothing but a distant echo.

George turned around and saw the gun on the floor. He'd never used a gun before, had never even seen a real one. Was there a correct way to pick it up to avoid accidentally pulling the trigger? He decided to wear gloves, to avoid fingerprints.

He went into the kitchen and put on a pair of washing-up gloves. He fished a plastic carrier bag out of one of the drawers.

Trembling, he returned to the living room and picked up the gun, holding it at a distance with the barrel facing away from him. Paranoia took hold, as if this inanimate object might decide to attack. He carefully placed the gun inside the plastic bag.

Not knowing where he could dispose of it, he decided to put it under the bed for now and maybe ask Glen what to do. He remembered a conversation he'd once had with Glen when he'd mentioned he knew where to get a gun. George thought back to that conversation and recalled that it had taken place when they were in the pub with Tom and Jess—the first time he'd mentioned 8 Goldfern Road. Before everything had changed.

Chapter Twenty

'Maybe it was losing the baby.' Hugh sat on the sofa with his head in his hands.

Roisin had been peering down at him, her hands on her hips. She dropped her hands to her sides and flopped down onto the sofa beside him. 'I lost the baby too, you know.' The words sounded empty, as if read from a meaningless script. Numbness was the overriding feeling—perhaps a coping mechanism. She'd shed no tears over losing the baby, not since first finding out the news at the hospital. On more than one occasion, whenever she'd caught Hugh wiping away tears, she'd worried that she'd become hardened and cold. Would nothing ever bother her again? Those thoughts were always quickly discarded as life went on, whether taking Robbie to school, or cooking, or one of the hundreds of other endless household tasks calling out for her attention.

Hugh reached over to the side table and took a tissue. 'I hate to say it, but you're becoming like Abi.'

Roisin knew he was a bit drunk, upset about not seeing his son, upset about the baby dying, but being compared to that woman caused deep scorn to rise inside her. 'I'm nothing like Abigail. How dare you even—'

'You're cold, Roisin. Like ice.'

His words echoed the thoughts that were constantly haunting her. She stood up.

He stood to face her.

She lowered her eyes. 'Have you considered that maybe I care too much?' The words were mumbled, her head full of doubt.

'We lost our baby, and now Abi is refusing to let me see Liam. What do you expect me to do? I can't sleep and I've lost my appetite. Booze is the only answer.'

She raised her eyes to meet his. 'You're deluded, Hugh! The alcohol makes things ten times worse. Do you want me to leave you? You're pushing me away. I need you to be there to talk to, but you're always out of your head on booze. When you started drinking again, I warned you, but you continued. Look at you, you can hardly see straight.'

'It's George, isn't it?' he slurred.

'What is?' A blush covered her cheeks as she recalled their recent kiss. The confusion made her dizzy. She'd left him, and had been about to have a child with another man. George had been so angry before. They'd tried to get past it, but it hadn't worked then; it wouldn't work now. Yet there remained a small part of her that yearned to return to an

69

uncomplicated existence with George and Robbie. The desire gained momentum every time Hugh presented with a bottle, can, or glass in his hands. Hugh's drinking had spiralled out of control in the past couple of days. It was how Hugh dealt with problems. He used drink as medication, comfort when he needed help.

'You're an alcoholic.' A sharpness pervaded her tone. 'If you don't get professional help—'

'Like I said, it's George. You want to get back with him, don't you?'

'Why are you bringing him into this?'

'You've been spending time with him.'

Had Hugh somehow got the impression that she was going to leave him, could that have started him drinking again? A wave of guilt descended; she would feel awful leaving him if it caused him to seek solace in his addiction. 'Let's get one thing clear, I am not going back to George.' She paused, allowing herself time to reflect on what she'd said. The words sounded like a lie. These feelings for George were unexpected. It was natural, though, wasn't it? Her conscience battled to find a reason. *He's the father of my son, that's why I love him. Love?* The word surprised her.

'You keep phoning him.'

Hugh's words brought her mind back to the present. 'We discussed this already,' she said, brushing his accusation away. 'The drink is clouding your thoughts, Hugh. George is having problems at the moment. You know that. He has amnesia. I had to help get him back on track with the house move—you even suggested I go and see him, remember? And you know his boss kept phoning me. Stop accusing me of stuff. It's over between me and George. Forget any doubts you have.' She sat down again.

Hugh sat on the armchair beside the sofa. 'I'm not coping. Do you think I want to keep drinking? Booze takes away the thoughts, helps me forget.'

'I'm getting rid of all the alcohol in the house.' Her gaze was fixed straight ahead, avoiding his eyes. 'Then we're going to get in touch with a solicitor and see whether you can arrange regular contact with Liam. You're his dad, you've got rights. We've got to sort things out. We've made a commitment, setting up this new home together. You have to clean yourself up. I don't want Robbie seeing you like this. Life isn't easy, but we can get through it together. Don't be selfish and act like you're the only one with problems, or it's over.'

'Maybe you're stronger than me. I need a drink.'

'One more drink and you're out! I'll make you some coffee and then we'll decide what we're going to do. If you can't stop drinking, you'll have to be referred somewhere by your GP. There are clinics—'

Hugh stood up. 'I don't want to lose you. If I lose you I'll have nothing left.'

She stood to face him. 'Then you need to try. All I'm asking is for you to stop drinking. If you care enough about me, you'll stop. It's your decision.'

Chapter Twenty-One

Rex's soul dwindled into the darkness; he'd slipped from George's body as a heavy presence took over. His screams went unheard.

Blackness surrounded him. Scorching heat was his only companion. The sensation of falling through a tunnel was overwhelming. He didn't have a body anymore, that much he knew; he felt weightless.

Falling and falling, further and further, nausea plagued him. Then a light filtered in his direction. He wondered whether this was what people who had near-death experiences often talked about. Shortly, the dark became complete.

Rex heard a low buzzing, which had been going on for a while. He was in complete darkness. He'd been here before, except this time he couldn't move, wasn't in control. When he'd been killed by George, he'd found it easy to navigate his way around, to possess the body of the spider, to possess George's body. This was markedly different. He was able to think, but that was all. Nothingness consumed his surroundings. Darkness. The low buzzing was becoming annoying. He wanted to shout out for it to stop, but found he was unable to express himself in sound.

'You who were Rex Rodenbury,' a voice boomed.

I haven't gone by that name for years.

The person, or thing, behind the voice was able to hear his thoughts.

'It's your name.'

I changed it.

'Regardless, you were Rex Rodenbury.'

Weaver.

'Ah, yes, your obsession with spiders caused you to change your surname. As far as we are concerned, you are still Rodenbury.'

Who are you? Where am I? How are we even communicating?

'You're in the waiting room. We can read your thoughts.'

Waiting? Waiting to go where?

'Where would you like to go?'

I'd like to go back to Earth, but this time as a poisonous spider.

'Ah, yes, you have always wanted to be a spider.' The voice followed the statement with a loud laugh.

Why is that so funny?

'In your next life, your existence will be as a spider's prey: a fly.'

The buzzing became louder and Rex sensed frustration at not being able to speak to challenge the voice. *A fly? Huh. I won't be a fly!*

'You will be a fly. But only for a short time. Flies have a life-cycle of... oh... perhaps fifteen days, a month sometimes, but we will make sure yours is brief. You're a cold-blooded killer, and you will live as a fly to be killed by the one you possessed.

The one I possessed? The spider? But it died.

'George. George will have the pleasure of killing you.'

But George is the killer, he murdered me.

'He who lights the fire shall pay the consequences. You struck the first match.'

I refuse to be a fly.

'You will have no say in the matter.'

Chapter Twenty-Two

George wandered around the flat. The removal boxes he'd packed when he was living at the house he'd shared with Roisin were dumped in the hallway, making moving around quite difficult. A handful of the boxes were open, and essential items like the kettle and toiletries had been taken out. George didn't like the idea of Rex rifling through his personal items. Thankfully, the majority of his belongings remained untouched.

He picked up a box labelled "kitchen", aware he needed a distraction from his negative thoughts, and made his way into the kitchen. It was tiny compared to the kitchen in his former home, and he doubted the appliances would fit as neatly on the worktops. As he placed the box onto the table, he a buzzing sound coming from somewhere in the room. He'd had a fear of wasps and bees ever since one of his friends was stung and ended up in hospital with a severe allergic reaction. From the corner of his eye he spotted a small black housefly. Relieved, he pulled out a piece of newspaper from the box he'd been carrying, rolled it up, and swatted the fly until it fell and landed in the sink. He turned on the tap, and was reminded of the spider that had appeared in the kitchen sink in his old house. He blinked away the unpleasant memory as the fly spiralled down the drain.

The next twenty minutes or so were spent unpacking items from the boxes and tidying the kitchen. As he was about to look for another storage box to unpack, the front doorbell rang.

George went to the buzzer: 'Hello?'

'Open up or I'll break the door down,' came a gruff voice.

'Who are you?'

'Buzz me in you clown, before I smash your windows.'

'I think you might have the wrong person. I've only recently moved in. Perhaps you were looking for the people who lived here before?'

'I'm losing my patience. Open up or die.'

'I'll call the police.'

'Believe me, the police will be very interested in your criminal activities,' came the reply.

George feared this could be connected to the murders Rex had committed.

He walked into the hallway trepidatiously. He couldn't be sure whether Rex had arranged for someone to come over.

He approached the communal door, intending to try to get rid of the man, not wanting to let him into his flat. On opening the door, he saw a tall man outside. The man was intimidating, due to his size and the stern frown he wore. 'H-hello.'

'This ain't a meet and greet. Have you got the money, or do I rearrange your face now?' growled the man.

'Um... money? I'm not sure I know what you mean.'

'I've already warned you.' The large man pushed past George and slammed the door behind him, almost knocking George over. 'I've doubled the debt to a thousand. Pay up, or pay the consequences.' He drew a gun from his inside coat pocket.

George backed away and found himself up against a wall in the narrow hallway.

'How do you expect me to give you that much money—'

'You said you were going to the bank, remember? I've run out of patience.'

'Please, please, don't shoot. Let's talk about this sensibly.' George held up his hands.

'I'm not a loan company. I collect. That's my job. The boss's instructions are that I should kill you if you don't pay up.'

'Can I at least know what I'm paying for?'

'Are you for real? How many times? The fucking spider!'

Spider. The word echoed in George's head. Unwanted thoughts of Rex, the house, and the poisonous spider swam around in his mind making him queasy. 'Oh... yes. Of course, the spider.'

'At last!' said the man. 'Wow, the lights are on but there's no one home. A goldfish has a longer concentration span than you, man.'

George struggled to recall if there was any money in the boxes he'd packed. He did keep an old biscuit tin with savings, but couldn't remember whether Roisin had taken it when she'd moved out.

'I'll be one minute,' he said, walking into his flat, closely followed by the debt collector.

Once inside he turned to face the ogre. 'Um... could you move out of the way, I have to get that box.' He pointed to a box labelled "kitchen". He'd already unpacked the other kitchen boxes, so this was his only hope.

George noticed that the man's hand was shaking as he held the gun towards him, and he wondered if he was on drugs.

Nervously, George fiddled with the sticky-tape that sealed the box. He sighed when he managed to pull it open and breathed with relief when he saw the old tin inside the box. He lifted it out and opened it. There was at least two thousand pounds inside, as he'd been saving for over a year.

The collector grabbed the box from him and said, 'This'll cover it.' Once again he pointed the gun towards George. This time he had a grin on his face. 'Huh, you're not as confident when you have a gun pointed at you, are you?' In a flash he had gone, leaving George stunned.

Chapter Twenty-Three

Ben Gibbons had been tagging the man he'd seen talking to the murderer. He hadn't built up the courage to approach him yet, but today he decided he would face his fears and have a chat with him, see what he could find out. He now knew his name was Glen. He hadn't seen him with the killer since the day of Del's murder, but had a hunch that this man knew a lot about him. Ben's gut instinct had never let him down in the past.

He watched from his car as Glen exited his flat talking on a mobile phone. He saw him cross the road and enter The Red Lion.

Ben waited outside for a few minutes.

When he entered the pub, Glen was seated at a table at the far end of the bar next to a scrawny looking black-haired woman. They were smiling at each other, and intimate—seated close together and touching each other often as they spoke.

Ben was about to approach them, when he saw the murderer greet the couple and take a seat next to them. The murderer then went to the bar and bought drinks before returning to the table. Ben decided to find a seat close by, to try to listen in to their conversation.

'How you doing, mate?' asked Glen as George returned to the table with the drinks. 'Have you got your memory back yet?'

'My memory? Why would you ask that?'

'It's worse than I thought. It kind of makes sense, though, that as you have amnesia you'd forget you have amnesia.' He laughed.

'Amnesia?'

'Blimey. This is getting annoying, having to recap stuff every time I see you. I might start recording our meetings. Do you remember getting the certificate from your GP? You did take that to your boss, didn't you?'

'My boss. Oh no, I forgot to call in sick. My head's been all over the place...What day is it today?'

'Um... Friday.'

'Shit. My boss will be wondering where I am. I'm surprised he hasn't been phoning me.'

'Er... He *was* phoning you. Blimey, this amnesia is worse than we thought.'

'He must've told you I had amnesia.'

'Your boss didn't tell me you had amnesia.'

'I wasn't talking about my boss.'

'*You* told me you had amnesia. That's why we went to get the certificate.'

'What certificate?'

Glen shook his head. 'I'll come to yours with you after so we can try and find it.'

'Glen, I need to talk to you.' He looked at Petula, apologetically. 'Alone.'

'Right, but Pet's my girlfriend; whatever you wanna tell me you can say in front of her. She won't tell anyone.'

'This is Petula?' George narrowed his eyes at her.

Petula blushed. 'Glen, maybe I should leave you two alone. I can see you tonight.'

'No, stay and finish your drink,' encouraged Glen. 'I'm worried about you, George. I already introduced you to Pet, remember?'

'You didn't,' murmured George.

'You had amnesia, so you probably don't remember.'

'No, I mean what I said: it wasn't me, it was Rex.'

'Rex?' Glen glanced sideways at Petula. He leaned in and whispered to her: 'Rex is the man who captured us, the one who used to dress as a spider.'

'The serial killer?' she said, a bit too loudly.

'Shhh...' said Glen.

'Sorry.'

'You told me you were seeing a therapist.'

'I'm not. Rex said that. That's what I want to talk to you about. I don't wanna talk about it in public. We should go to yours.'

'There's no one here.' Glen glanced around the pub. 'Only a couple of people: that lonely looking bloke, and the old woman over there. They're not gonna be interested in our conversation.'

George turned around. The "lonely looking bloke" caught his eye and then quickly turned away. 'The lonely bloke looks like he can hear what we're saying,' whispered George.

'We'll go back to mine after we finish our drinks,' said Glen. 'I know I've said it a thousand times, but I have to keep saying it if you don't listen, don't I? You badly need to see a therapist.'

'Probably,' said George. 'You probably will too, when you've heard what I'm going to tell you.'

Chapter Twenty-Four

'Remember how you studied spiders and learned how they kill their prey?'

The voice was starting to irritate Rex. He was once again floating without a body in the stifling heat and darkness, with no sound other than the voice. *Leave me alone.*

'Don't worry, you will be alone in the next life. You'll become a fly again. How *was* that, by the way?'

Rex recalled the sensation he'd had of flying and the loudest buzzing sound he had ever heard. He'd been aware of light and of different shapes moving slowly. He remembered the excruciating pain he'd felt when everything turned black, and the sensation of his whole body being trapped under a heavy object.

'Yes, yes,' said the voice, inexplicably picking up on his thoughts, 'the death you suffered was painful, but not lengthy. This time will be different. This time you will be caught by a spider, and you will know what it feels like to be trapped in a web.'

When will this end?

'End? You're in eternal Hell.'

Ben watched as the group left the pub. The conversation they'd been having was strange to say the least. They kept referring to a man called Rex. He'd heard them mention a serial killer. They'd talked about amnesia; it sounded as though the man was using it as a cover story. If his friend believed he had amnesia, he'd get away with it; he was brazen. Ben waited a couple of minutes before following the group out of the pub. He stood across the road and saw them enter Glen's flat.

'The last time we were in this room together—well, you would have thought we were together. You thought you were talking to me, but you weren't,' said George.

'Right. How much have you had to drink?'

'I'm being serious. Somehow—and I don't know how he did it— Rex possessed my body. I don't know if it was days or weeks. I was in complete darkness waiting to get back into my body.'

'Rex, the spider-man?' asked Petula.

George looked at her, as if only now realising she was in the room.

'Yes, the one I told you about, sweetheart,' said Glen. 'The man who captured us. Rex was haunting George. He was a ghost. He did some fucked-up things like making me turn into a spider. I didn't believe that, but then he turned George's ex-wife and her new man into spiders, and we thought we'd killed them but it wasn't real. After seeing it with my own two eyes, I had to believe George. But possession?' He turned to George. 'How can you prove it?'

'Didn't I seem weird to you? Wasn't there anything different about me?'

'You always seem weird to me.'

'Be serious, Glen.'

'You did say something strange when me and Pet met you in the pub; you said you liked eating moths.'

'Oh, yeah, I remember that,' said Petula.

'I couldn't get it out of my head,' continued Glen.

'And, you'd forgotten where you lived,' added Petula.

'We thought that was the amnesia,' said Glen.

'There wasn't any amnesia. Rex didn't know enough about me and my life, so he was saying he had amnesia.'

'Now you come to mention it, I remember you saying that you knew how to build a wooden web and how to make sleeping-spider gas. I thought that was odd because you were supposed to have amnesia, so it didn't make sense that you remembered those things.'

'See? That's proof. He made up the amnesia. And that's not the worst thing. He killed people when he was in my body.'

'What?'

'I was told he murdered five men and was planning to kill more.'

'George, I need you to answer a question for me. Don't take it the wrong way, but... did you kill those men?'

'Y-you think I—'

Glen put up a hand to stop him speaking, 'Mate, I'm only asking because you killed those criminals in the house as well as Rex when we were trying to get away from—'

'So now you think I'm some kind of serial killer? You know as well as I do that it was self-defence.'

'By that stage we had managed to escape from the house, so technically it wasn't self-defence.'

George held his head in his hands and then blurted out, 'Whose side are you on here?'

'It's just—'

'You have a convenient memory because if I remember rightly, you were the one who shot those men with that fluid gun; that might have been the thing that killed them. They collapsed.'

'Whoa!'

'Guys,' interjected Petula, 'please stop arguing. We should be trying to work out what to do next.'

George let out a breath and stood up. 'It's obvious you think I'm some kind of deranged murderer.'

'That's not what Glen said.'

'Mate, sorry,' said Glen. 'It's just, I'm not sure what to believe, but I'm gonna go along with you. Who knows, maybe we're both traumatised after being captured. I did see what Rex did to Roisin and Hugh so I know he's capable of unbelievable shit.'

George closed his eyes and sat down. 'I can't believe you would think I—'

'You know what I'm like, I always speak before I think,' Glen said.

'You're my oldest friend, if you think I'm capable of murder I don't stand a chance with the police.'

'It won't get that far.'

'Five men were murdered and my body was used to murder them.'

'They need evidence. And besides, you've got a certificate from your GP saying you had amnesia,' assured Glen.

'But I haven't got amnesia.'

'You'll need the certificate. Your boss was annoyed with you for not letting him know what was going on. I don't think he's seen the certificate yet.' Glen put a hand to his mouth.

'What?' said George.

'I've just remembered, when we were at the GP surgery, they asked for your name and you said Rex Weaver.'

'See? That's proof.'

'Also, when I met you—or Rex—on Wednesday, outside your flat, there was definitely blood on your coat. You could get done for murder. Who did he kill?'

'I don't know the details.'

Glen stood up. 'We have to try and find this certificate. You can use it if the police question you. In the meantime, we have to think of watertight alibis. No one's gonna believe you were possessed.'

Chapter Twenty-Five

'Do you remember Isabel, my friend who was babysitting Robbie when we went out a couple of weeks ago?'

Hugh looked up from the kitchen table, a glum expression on his face. 'The girl with the pink hair?'

'Well, yes, it was pink then—she likes dying her hair,' Roisin continued as she prepared Robbie's packed lunch for school. 'I was talking to her about how Robbie hasn't seen George for ages and how worried I was about it. Then we got into a conversation about her cousin whose husband left her and then applied for access to their children. She went to court and used this free service to help her with the court hearings; they gave her advice too. I took their number. You could call them.'

'Why were you telling her about my private life?' growled Hugh.

'I wasn't. Haven't you been listening to me? We were discussing Robbie and George. Isabel is a good friend of mine.'

'What's happening about that?' asked Hugh, taking a sip of coffee.

'What?'

'Robbie and George.'

'I'm not sure. I want to go and see George again and see whether his amnesia has improved. Robbie was up for hours last night, asking where he was. I keep telling him "Daddy's gone away for work", but it's getting harder to keep up the pretence.'

'I know he was up for hours, why do you think I'm in such a bad mood this morning? I didn't get any sleep.'

'That's what it's like when you have kids. You should understand that.'

He hung his head. 'I'm not dealing with any of this very well. I keep wanting to go and see Abi, to try to reason with her, but I can just picture her glaring at me. She's a bitch.'

'Do you want me to speak to her?'

'We've had that conversation. No.'

'Fine, look.' Roisin found her handbag and took out a piece of paper. 'Here you go, the phone number for the advice centre. You never know, you might feel better if you speak to them.'

Hugh reached out and took it. 'Thanks.'

'I'm taking Robbie to school. See you soon.'

Roisin called from the bottom of the stairs, 'Robbie, come on, you'll be late for school.'

'Mummy, I can't come down. There's a spider on the stairs.'

Roisin took a deep breath and hesitated before climbing the stairs, remembering her recent spell in hospital and the spiders that infested 8 Goldfern Road. At the top of the stairs, on the banisters, there was a spiderweb upon which sat a small house-spider. She couldn't see any other spiders.

The spider crept along its web and pounced on a housefly trapped in the silky fibres. Roisin held her breath as she watched the arachnid. It appeared to paralyse the fly, which stopped moving. It was eerie to witness. She turned her attention to Robbie. 'Darling, I don't have time to deal with the spider now. I have to take you to school. Take my hand. That little spider won't hurt you.'

'But the other spider killed your baby.'

Roisin opened her mouth to speak, but didn't know what to say. It had been difficult telling Robbie the baby had died, but she'd imagined that Robbie had come to terms with it, and that perhaps at his age it would be easier for him to deal with. She began to question whether his recent moods and behaviour might have more to do with losing his sister than not seeing George.

'Darling, the spider didn't kill her. We told you that the angels needed your baby sister to help them, and that's why she had to go to heaven, remember?'

'But spiders try to kill people. The other one tried to kill you.'

'It didn't try to kill me. Mummy was allergic to the spider bite. Spiders are scared of us too, you know. Imagine how you would feel if someone as big as me was standing next to you if you were as small as this spider. That other spider was a special one, it was poisonous. Spiders don't usually have poison. This one doesn't.'

'How do you know?'

'I just do, okay? Come on, we're late!' Roisin reached out her hand and took Robbie's. He began to cry. 'I'll take the spider into the garden when I get home. I promise.'

Somehow Rex knew he was a fly, but he didn't know how he could still think; he'd never have imagined flies could think. He still identified as Rex Weaver, a human. His eyesight was so blurred and patchy he could hardly focus; there were only shapes, light and dark. The feeling that he was flying came to an abrupt end, as if he'd collided with something. Within a few seconds he was unable to move, stuck. Sensing a body with wings, he made an effort to move them, but they were rigid, caught in netting... He recalled the words *"...you will be caught by a spider, and you will know what it feels like to be trapped in a web..."* A shadowy form like a black cloud descended, and then a sharp needle-like object entered his body. Darkness surrounded him, and he was wrapped in something, enveloped. At the same time he became weaker. He remembered what he had read about spiders liquefying their prey. Everything turned black.

As Roisin approached the school gates, Robbie let go of her hand and called out, 'Daddy! Daddy!'

George was standing at the entrance. He picked up Robbie and hugged him.

'G-George? What are you doing here?'

'I came to see Robbie.'

'He'll be late for school. Robbie, darling, give your daddy a hug and say goodbye.'

'Mummy, can Daddy pick me up from school?'

'Yes, of course,' said George, before Roisin had time to answer.

She narrowed her eyes at him. Taking Robbie from his hold and pulling him forcibly through the school gates, she turned to George and said, 'Wait here. We should talk about this.'

A few minutes later, Roisin returned.

'Why did you come here?'

'I told you, to see Robbie. I've missed him. It's a weekday, he should be with me—that was the agreement.'

'So that's the agreement when it suits you? What about when I was in hospital and you refused to take him?'

'I haven't been myself lately.'

'The amnesia? You should have called me to arrange to see Robbie, you shouldn't have just turned up unannounced. How's your memory, has it come back?'

'It was a mistake. I never had amnesia.'

'What? Well... how can you explain not going to work, and not knowing where the GP was?'

'I can't explain it easily, but there was a reason behind what I was doing. Maybe one day I'll tell you, but not now.'

'It doesn't make sense.'

'It really doesn't, but you don't know the whole story.'

'So tell me the whole story. I'm listening.'

'I can't.'

'How can I trust you alone with Robbie?'

'There is an explanation for the way I was behaving, but you'd never believe me if I told you.'

'Try me.'

'I'll collect Robbie from school today, and I'll make him supper and bring him over to yours by about six.'

'You're avoiding the issue. And I don't live at my mum's anymore. Me and Hugh have our own place.'

'Okay, I'll need the address.'

'Your boss was phoning me every day asking where you were. You were avoiding his calls, and then you told me you had amnesia. Now you're acting like nothing happened.'

'I wasn't myself. I'd rather not discuss it.'

'Fine. Have it your way.' Roisin found a pen in her handbag and jotted down her address. 'Make sure you bring him home by six.'

'I will. Don't worry.'

She shook her head and turned to walk away.

After visiting the school, George took the medical certificate to his workplace. His boss suggested he take the rest of the month off. He headed home in a much more positive mood, until he saw a police car parked outside the building where he lived. Two policemen were getting out of the car. He wasn't sure whether he should run away or face up to whatever he had to face up to. If he did run away they'd assume he was guilty.

Taking a deep breath, George approached the communal entrance door, avoiding the policemen. He placed his key in the lock.

'Mr Barnaby?'

The policeman's voice sounded close. He could hear the two men's footsteps on the pathway behind him, and turned around slowly.

'We'd like to ask you a few questions, Mr Barnaby. We can do it here or you can accompany us to the station.'

'Um. You can come in,' he said.

Once inside the flat the policemen sat on the sofa in the living room and invited him to take a seat. He sat opposite them and almost choked on his own saliva as he gulped, remembering there was a gun under his bed. What if the police had a search warrant? Was it the same gun that Rex had used to kill all those people?

'Mr Barnaby, can you tell us where you were last Wednesday.'

'Wednesday? I must have been at home. I've been unwell. I had amnesia.'

'Do you recognise this man?' The policeman showed him a photo of a man who appeared to be in his sixties.

'No, I don't.'

'This man and four other men were killed last week. A man matching your description was seen leaving this man's property. You sent Facebook messages to one of the men who was killed, and there is reason to believe that you sent letters by e-mail to four of the men who were killed asking them to meet you at this man's address; in addition, there are further e-mail messages to the four victims.'

'My Facebook account must've been hacked. I haven't used Facebook for ages.'

'How do you explain the messages sent from your e-mail address, and from your phone?'

'I... Whoever hacked my account must have got all my information from somewhere. Criminals have ways of sending messages from any e-mail address or phone number by hacking in, don't they? You should know more about that than I do, you probably deal with that sort of thing all the time in your job, don't you?'

'We'll need to take your phone, and do we have your permission to look at your Facebook account?'

'Of course. Whatever has gone on was nothing to do with me. I had amnesia. My GP gave me a certificate signing me off work, which is why I'm at home today.'

'Can we see the certificate?'

'I gave it to my boss this morning.'

'We'll look into that.'

'Are you going to arrest me? Only, I have to collect my son from school this afternoon, and—'

The policemen stood up. 'We will need you to accompany us to the station, Mr Barnaby.'

George followed the policemen out of his flat, trembling. His heart skipped a beat as the severity of what he'd been told sank in. Would he be locked away for the rest of his life? He got into the police car and held back the tears as the car pulled away from the kerb.

Chapter Twenty-Six

Once more Rex had returned to the place that was too dark and too hot. Without a body, floating, nowhere. *This is beyond a joke.*

'Come now, did you not enjoy your experience of being eaten by a spider? Let's call it revenge for the spider you ate when you were Rex Rodenbury.'

That wasn't even my fault, and the name is Weaver.

'Rodenbury.'

You've had your fun, please let me go; it's like a sauna here, I can't bear it.

'This is what humans refer to as Hell.'

Is there a way out? There must be.

'Not for you, Rex Rodenbury. When you possessed the body of George Barnaby and murdered five people, you left behind a legacy of chaos. The man might be sent to prison for crimes he didn't commit. We do have the power to help in exceptional circumstances. I think this is one of those. So far we've been able to make sure the police didn't arrest him immediately. However, we are bound by certain rules. If George Barnaby is sent to prison, you will pay the price.'

What does that mean?

'You will return to his body to face the consequences.'

I'm not in his body anymore. It's not my problem.

'I will keep you informed about how that works out. In the meantime, I need to entertain myself. How would you like to be a spider again, Rex Rodenbury?'

Weaver! Yes, I would love to be a spider again. Please.

'Your wish is granted. You will be a common house spider, and you'll live in George's flat.' The voice followed the statement with a laugh.

To be a spider is all I've ever wanted. Thank you.

'My pleasure.'

Why are you being nice?

'I'm not. The spider you will become has four legs instead of eight, due to a birth defect, and it isn't able to weave a web. This spider is defenceless and will be the prey of its prey. I'll see you again soon, Rex Rodenbury.' The booming laugh faded away.

Roisin found Hugh seated at the kitchen table with his head in his hands, a bottle of whisky beside him. She ran towards him and lifted up the bottle.

'I thought I got rid of all the alcohol in the house.'

'I didn't drink any.'

Roisin sat at the table and peered at him, checking for any signs that he might be drunk. 'Why is there a bottle of whisky on the table? You know I don't want alcohol in the house. I have my son to think about.'

'I wasn't going to drink it. Regretted it as soon as I walked out of the shop.'

'Shouldn't you be at work?'

'I called in sick.'

'So you could go and buy some whisky?'

'It's not like that.'

'You can't keep taking time off. We've got a mortgage to pay.' Still holding the bottle, she stood up.

'I'd been on the phone with that advice centre,' said Hugh, eyes down, 'the one you gave me the number for. They said I couldn't apply to court until I tried going to mediation with Abi. She'll never agree to that. I'm never going to see Liam again, am I?' He looked up at her. 'I can't concentrate. I couldn't face going in to work today.'

With a sigh, Roisin placed the whisky bottle down on the table and took a seat opposite him. 'There must be a way around it. Didn't you tell the person at the advice centre that Abigail won't agree to any mediation?'

'I tried, but they said I have to speak to a mediator and explain it to them. I don't have the energy.'

'I can do it for you. What's the mediator's number?'

'They gave me a website and a number that I can call to find a local mediator.'

'Don't worry. I'll phone them.' Roisin stood up and took hold of the whisky bottle. 'Where did you buy this? Where's the receipt? I'll take it back, there's no point wasting money.'

'I didn't get a receipt.'

'Which shop was it?'

'I stole it, okay!'

'You idiot! They have CCTV in shops. How could you be so stupid?'

'It's no big deal, it was from the off-licence on the corner. I know the owner. The cameras are dummies, only there as a deterrent. It's only a bottle of whisky, for God's sake.'

'Only a bottle of whisky? Theft is theft!'

'You're overreacting. I'll return it.'

He stood up and approached her, holding out a hand.

'No! *I'm* returning this to the off-licence.'

'How will you explain where you got it? No harm's done. If you go to the shop you'll be opening a can of worms.'

Roisin let out a sigh, opened the bottle and poured the contents into the sink.

'What did you do that for!'

She spun around to face him. 'How can I have someone like you living in the same house as my son? No wonder Abigail won't let you see Liam. You should be ashamed of yourself! I can't trust you. How dare you bring this into the house,' she held up the empty bottle, 'after everything I said?'

Hugh skulked over to the kitchen table and sat down again, head in his hands.

'What are we going to do, Hugh?' She walked towards the table.

'It's my fault.' He looked up at her. 'I'll try harder. Will you call the mediator for me? Maybe if I can see Liam...'

Remorse took hold as she noticed a tear in his eye. 'You have to make an effort. I can't keep carrying you like this.'

He nodded.

'I saw George today when I dropped Robbie off.'

Hugh responded with a quizzical stare.

'He was outside the school gates. I didn't know he'd be there. He says his amnesia has gone—no, actually, he said he never had amnesia. Must've been misdiagnosed. He asked if he could collect Robbie from school today. I agreed because Robbie was so happy to see him and I couldn't bring myself to say no. Do you think I did the right thing?'

After glaring at her for a moment, Hugh looked at the table. 'I'd be a hypocrite if I said you shouldn't have let him. I wish Abi was as understanding as you.'

She squeezed his hand. 'It will get better. I promise. Now, let me phone the mediator.'

George collected Robbie from school at 3.30 p.m. Robbie ran towards him, smiling. George's anxiety faded as he hugged his son. Even the encounter with the police, which weighed heavily on his mind, became insignificant for the tiniest of moments. He'd been taken to the police station and released on police bail quite soon afterwards. They hadn't charged him, but the threat hung over him, and he was told he would have to return for questioning when asked.

'Did you have a good day at school? I've got some of your favourite chocolate biscuits.'

Robbie wrinkled his nose at the packet of biscuits in George's hand. 'I don't like those.'

George wondered how long he'd been away. Had it been weeks or months? Robbie looked an inch taller than when he'd last seen him. If the worst happened and he ended up in prison, he wouldn't see Robbie until he was an adult. Catching himself, he pushed away the negative thoughts. 'I'm sure I have other treats at home, come on, let's go.'

'Where's your car?'

'We're walking. Daddy only lives around the corner.'

They arrived at the flat, and as soon as George opened the door Robbie ran inside and began to investigate the new surroundings.

George ran after him into the bedroom, remembering the gun. 'Robbie, go into the front room, please.'

'Daddy, can I stay with you? I don't like living with Mummy.'

'Robbie, why would you say that? Your mummy loves you.'

'I do love Mummy, but I don't like Hugh. He's smelly and lazy.'

'Robbie!'

'It's true. Mummy said.'

'Mummy said he's smelly and lazy?'

'No... Not smelly, but she said to him that he's lazy and doesn't help her. I heard them shouting. I don't like them shouting all the time.'

'All the time?'

'Not all the time. Daddy, can I watch TV?'

George began to wonder about Roisin and Hugh. The boy might be making it up, or maybe he'd mistaken their discussions for arguments. They'd lost a baby, that could be a reason why they'd be stressed and arguing.

Robbie ran to the TV. 'How do you switch it on, Daddy?'

'It might not be plugged in, darling. Let me have a look.'

George settled Robbie in front of the television and went into the kitchen to prepare supper. It occurred to him that Robbie's taste in food could have changed since he'd lived with him, especially after the biscuit incident, so he walked back into the room and asked the boy what he would like to eat.

'Daddy, I think there's a spider up there. I'm scared of it. Can you kill it?'

George recalled the time he'd killed a spider for Robbie at their old house before life had changed forever. He looked up to where Robbie was pointing; it was definitely a spider but had fewer legs. He remembered a game he used to play with his cousins when they were children, where they would pull the legs off spiders in the garden. He'd forgotten about that until now. Everything that happened with Rex flashed before him, and again he wondered about his culpability. Had he been targeted by Rex because of what he used to do to spiders as a child? *How ridiculous.* But his mind continued to whirr.

'Daddy, the spider's moving.'

'I'll get it,' said George. He went into the kitchen and found a broom, then returned to the living room and aimed the broom at the spider. The creature's lifeless body fell to the floor. George picked it up with a tissue and left the room, thinking again about the gun as he passed the bedroom. He couldn't risk it still being in the flat when the police returned.

Chapter Twenty-Seven

'I called the mediation service. They said you can each go to mediation sessions separately, so you don't have to meet up. Do you think Abigail would agree to that?'

'She's determined to stop me seeing Liam.'

'Apparently, they can arrange a session and if she doesn't turn up they'll give you a certificate explaining you tried mediation but it didn't work. Then, if you have to, you can take her to court.'

Hugh looked up from his seat on the sofa.

'Sounds good, right?' said Roisin brightly, trying to lift Hugh's spirits. 'I've got a phone number for a local mediator, so you can arrange an appointment. Here you go.'

Hugh took the piece of paper from her. 'Thanks. And sorry about earlier.'

'Don't worry about it.' She glanced at her watch. 'I hope Robbie's all right. I should go and collect him from George's.'

'Phone him if you're worried. Didn't he say he'd be bringing him back?'

'Yes, but... I keep remembering when he had amnesia. He changed his story today, said he never had amnesia. Maybe it was because he wanted me to agree to him having Robbie. I hope he's okay.'

The doorbell rang while George was serving Robbie's supper. His heart jumped; had the police returned to arrest him? He'd been worrying all afternoon, even while he was trying to concentrate on spending time with Robbie. Was it enough that he had a doctor's certificate? It didn't even confirm the amnesia.

Should he try to explain the truth? Would he come across as delusional? Insanity could be a defence for the murders. But then wouldn't he be committed to a psychiatric ward? The thoughts were incessant and he could find no answers.

He continued to serve Robbie's food, reluctant to answer the door any earlier than he had to. Perhaps they would go away if there was no response.

'Daddy, someone's at the door.'

'Yes, I know Robbie. I wanted to make sure you've got enough food on your plate.'

The doorbell rang for a second time.

George returned the pan of baked beans to the hob and walked to the buzzer, accepting that he'd have to face up to whatever was coming. He had no control over it. 'Hello.'

'George, let me in will you?'

Glen. He caught his breath and only then realised how tense his jaw had been.

'What took you so long?' said Glen as he walked into George's flat.

'I've got Robbie over. I have to take him home soon.'

'Would you prefer me to come back later?'

'I do need to speak to you, but it'll have to be after I take Robbie home. You can come in and wait if you want.'

'I came to check on you and make sure you're all right.'

'I'm far from all right. I'll explain later.' George went into the kitchen, where Robbie was playing with his food.

'Eat up, Robbie. I've got to get you home by six.'

Robbie continued eating his food, and George sat looking at him. He wished he could capture the moment, keep it somewhere safe. The police could knock on the door at any time. A heavy cloud hung over him that wouldn't shift.

Glen walked into the kitchen and sat down. 'Hi Robbie, remember me?'

The boy smiled shyly.

'You've grown so much since I last saw you.'

'I'm five.'

'Wow, already?'

Robbie nodded proudly.

George continued to stare at his son while Glen chatted with him. When Robbie finished his food, George took the plate away and announced that they had to leave.

'Glen, you can wait here, I'll be back soon.'

Half an hour later George and Glen were seated in George's living room.

'What's wrong, George? You hardly said a word when Robbie was eating his meal. It's like you were deep in thought. What's happened? I mean, apart from the possession. You ain't heard from Rex's ghost again, have you? Blimey, you're not Rex again, are you?' Glen moved away from him instinctively.

'No, no. I'm still me, and I haven't heard from Rex. This is potentially worse, though. The police came round earlier and I had to go to the station. I thought they were going to arrest me. I'm on police bail.'

'What? But it means the police ain't got any evidence against you, or surely they'd've charged you, right?'

'It's not as simple as that. They've got to gather enough evidence against me before they can charge me, and that's what they're doing now. There were Facebook messages from me to one of the dead men, sent by Rex, of course; he'd also sent letters by e-mail asking the victims to meet me at the house where he killed them. There were other messages too. I looked at my Facebook account when I got back from the police station; it's all there in black and white. Rex lured them to the house and then killed them. He didn't even bother covering his tracks because he knew I'd be blamed, obviously.'

'What did you tell the police?'

'I didn't tell them about the possession because I thought they wouldn't believe me, or they'd assume I'm mad. So I told them I had amnesia. Is that enough? It's been driving me crazy all day. Rex killed those men while he was in my body. Is amnesia a defence to murder? Your sister-in-law's a solicitor, would she know?'

'I'm not sure. I can ask her. I know self-defence is a defence to murder. Could you make up a story? Maybe say these men were attacking you, and you were defending yourself.'

'But the reason they were at the house was because Rex invited them using my Facebook and e-mail. If I claim self-defence, I'd have to admit I knew about the messages. Besides, I've already told the police I had amnesia; I can't change my story now. I don't want to go to prison.'

'Pet's been inside before. She can tell you about it.'

'Are you joking?'

'No, it's true, she went—'

'What I mean is, you're supposed to be supporting me, and now you're more or less telling me I'm going to end up inside.'

'I didn't mean it to sound like that.'

'What was Petula in jail for?'

'Nothing like murder. Just shoplifting; she was going through a tough time.'

George held his head. 'I don't want to go to prison.'

'Let me try ringing Penny, my sister-in-law.' Glen took out his mobile phone. 'Hi Pen, how are you? ... Yeah, all good thanks... Yeah, we should. Listen, Pen, I need a bit of advice for a friend of mine. He had amnesia for a couple of weeks and he might have committed murders during that time and doesn't remember a thing, but the police have evidence that it was him... Yeah, I know what it sounds like... No, he's never been in trouble with the police before, this is totally out of character... No, I didn't think it was... Right. This is going to sound even weirder, but my friend believes he was possessed... Yeah, by a dead man,

94

and this dead man committed the murders while he was in my friend's body... I know... No, he's a good friend... He's not mad... I see, insanity might be a defence... Hospital treatment. Yeah... Right, could you help him if he's arrested? ... You don't... Okay... Yeah... Thanks, Pen. Say hi to your mum for me... Bye.'

'Well?' asked George. 'What did she say?'

'If you use the possession story, you've probably got a better chance of avoiding prison, I reckon, from what she said. Insanity can be used as a defence. The amnesia just means it makes it harder for the police to prove you were capable of planning the murders. I'm not sure it would be a defence, though. There are those Facebook messages.'

'I know. There's no way out of this.'

'Don't panic. Penny's gonna send me a list of criminal lawyers you could call if you're arrested.'

'I'm going to prison, aren't I? Or at least to a mental hospital. What am I gonna do?'

'Think positive.'

'I have the murder weapon. Rex left a gun. I hid it under the bed.'

'Bloody hell, George.'

'Can you get rid of it?'

'Me?'

'You once said you knew where to get guns, couldn't you take it there?'

'No, I'm not getting involved.'

'Thanks for nothing.'

'I'd help if I could, but it's risky. What if I'm caught with the gun?'

'Do you know anyone I could contact to get rid of it?'

'No, I used to know this criminal, that's all. I don't wanna get in touch with him, though.'

'What can I do with it?'

'Bury it, somewhere. Throw it in the Thames. You've got to get rid of it.'

Chapter Twenty-Eight

'I've booked an appointment to see a mediator next week,' said Hugh.

'That's great,' said Roisin. 'Cheer up, what's wrong?'

'I'm not sure Abi will agree to anything.'

'Do you want me to come with you?'

'No. I'll go alone.'

'If you're sure.'

'I am. Thanks.'

'I'm taking Robbie to school and going to work after that. See you later.'

'Is George having Robbie today?'

'No. But it would be good if he has Robbie every other weekend, and maybe he could collect him from school one day a week. It was nice having time to ourselves yesterday evening, wasn't it?'

'It was, but are you sure he's all right now?'

'He seems fine.' She blushed again.

Later that afternoon, when Roisin returned from collecting Robbie from school, she found Hugh asleep on the sofa.

'Robbie, go upstairs and play until I make your supper.'

Robbie ran upstairs to his room.

He's drunk again. The words taunted her. *No, perhaps he's just fallen asleep. He's been a nervous wreck since the baby died, and worrying about not being able to see Liam.*

Taking a couple of steps towards him, she smelt the alcohol before even noticing the glass next to the sofa with the almost-empty bottle of vodka; some of its contents had spilt onto the carpet.

She closed her eyes, wanting to erase the scene before her. *No wonder Abigail left him. He was probably like this the whole time.*

Hugh rolled over and woke up abruptly, appearing startled when he saw her.

'How could you?'

'I—'

'No excuses. I know you've had a hard time with losing the baby, but so have I. And how do you expect to get access to your child when you drink so much? You're an alcoholic. You're constantly blaming Abigail, but I should've known—there's always two sides to every story.'

'I'll get help,' he slurred.

'Yes, you should. Pack your things. I want you out of here tonight.'

'What? Where will I go?'

'I've warned you enough times. I said stop drinking, speak to your GP. I told you I didn't want an alcoholic around Robbie, but you didn't listen, did you?'

Hugh stumbled to his feet and faced her, 'This is my house too, you can't fucking chuck me out. I have rights.'

'Look at you, you can hardly even focus. How much did you drink? I remember the first time we were together and you were plying me with drink, I wondered whether you were an alcoholic then. Why didn't I go with my gut? I was such a fool! This is why Abigail left you, isn't it? You're a loser. I won't have you staying here. Where are your keys?'

'You can't do this. I own this place too.'

'Where are your keys?' The words left her mouth in a scream. Roisin ran into the hallway and fished in Hugh's coat pockets. Pulling out his house keys, she held them up and then faced him as he stood in the living room doorway, holding on to the jamb in an apparent attempt to prevent himself falling over.

Roisin crossed her arms. 'Do you think you can pack a bag, or should I do that? I'm serious, Hugh. I'll call the police if I have to.'

'Police?'

'Yes.'

'I'll go. But if I leave I'm not coming back.'

'Fine.'

'Are you sure?'

She looked into his eyes, the eyes that had lured her to him and kept her hostage. 'Just go.'

She watched him leave, knowing this would be the end of their relationship. Even if he did get help for his addiction, there was a part of her that had given up on him, and the rest of her was slipping into sync. Had losing the baby been a catalyst for it all? Perhaps she was wanting to rid herself of all the reminders.

Chapter Twenty-Nine

Hugh headed straight for the off-licence and then, after taking a bottle of whisky, making sure that the owner didn't see him, he went to the local park.

He found an unoccupied bench and watched as people walked through the park, some walking dogs, some jogging, some obviously tourists with their cameras at the ready to catch a photo of a passing squirrel or pigeon.

Wanting to forget what had just happened, he grabbed the whisky bottle and was about to open it, but stopped himself; for the first time in a while he questioned why he was going to drink the whisky.

An image of his first love came to mind, as it often did when he thought about why he drank alcohol.

He had met Madeleine at college when they were both sixteen. She became his obsession. Whenever he heard love songs on the radio, images of Madeleine would come to mind. She was the woman he wanted to spend the rest of his life with. Although quite shy, he somehow mustered up the courage to ask her out even though he thought she would reject him.

As Hugh reminisced, he wondered whether he'd been attracted to Roisin because she reminded him of Madeleine. They both had blonde hair and their eyes were a similar shade of blue.

In his early thirties, he'd bordered on becoming an alcoholic. When things went wrong, alcohol would make them right, or at least help him forget. The first time he'd reached for the drink to blot out his pain was after Madeleine left him. He'd only been an occasional drinker until she broke his heart. Hugh found solace in alcohol, and it was something that had become a pattern in his life. It was slow and steady at first; whenever reminders of Madeleine's betrayal threatened to disturb him he would reach for a beer. He'd found it hard to come to terms with what had happened. Not only did he discover that during their relationship she'd been secretly seeing someone else for at least a year, but he discovered that the man she'd been seeing was someone he'd considered a friend.

He'd worked with Rick after leaving college and they'd kept in touch over the years. Hugh's 25th birthday party was probably when the spark between Madeleine and Rick caught fire. Rick was always especially polite to Madeleine whenever he came to visit, but at the party Hugh noticed he was paying a lot of attention to her. Whenever he looked at Madeleine, Rick would be there somewhere in the background. It was a niggling concern, but he brushed it away. Back then he would not have suspected Rick or Madeleine. He'd been in a relationship with Madeleine for more than seven years at the time and they were engaged.

Two years later, a mutual acquaintance phoned Hugh to tell him he'd seen Rick and Madeleine at a local bar and they'd seemed quite close. The acquaintance asked whether he and Madeleine had split up. Hugh laughed it off. Madeleine told him she'd been out with friends that night; perhaps she'd bumped into Rick at the bar.

It came as a total shock when he eventually discovered what Madeleine and Rick had been up to.

He was on his way home from work on a bus, looking out of the window, when he saw them. The bus stopped at a red light outside the local supermarket. Madeleine and Rick were inside the shop, queuing up to pay. She was giggling, and he had an arm around her. As the bus pulled away from the traffic lights, Hugh blinked hard and turned his head to try to continue watching the couple.

He got off at the next stop and walked towards the supermarket, questioning his eyes, thinking maybe he'd imagined it. Round and round the thoughts taunted him. He stopped abruptly at the same set of traffic lights the bus had stopped at when he noticed a couple in a passionate embrace outside the supermarket. They were across the road, but even from that distance he could see it was definitely them. After their kiss, they held hands and walked towards the crossing. They both saw him at the same time.

Madeleine appeared suitably embarrassed, letting go of Rick's hand, while Rick had squirmed and given the impression he was looking for an escape route.

As Hugh approached them they remained on the other side of the road, like statues permanently fixed to the spot.

'How long has this been going on?' was the first thing Hugh had said, trying to remain calm.

'I bumped into Rick while shopping and we got chatting,' had been Madeleine's poker-faced response.

'So when you meet people in shops you end up snogging them... Is that a habit I should know about?'

'Hugh...' Rick interjected.

Hugh's temperature began to rise at that point. He wanted to tell Rick to go away, that this was between him and Madeleine.

'We didn't plan any of this,' continued Rick.

'We love each other,' said Madeleine, moving closer to Rick. 'I'm sorry, Hugh. It's best to be honest.'

Hugh watched on speechless, as Rick shrugged apologetically and took Madeleine's hand again. The couple walked away.

It was the last he saw of Madeleine. The last he'd heard from Rick.

She'd gone to stay with Rick, and had phoned Hugh the next day to say she would be collecting her belongings from their rented flat and leaving the key while he was at work. There was no explanation, no apology. She'd simply disappeared.

That episode left scars that were echoing throughout his life. He'd cleaned himself up before he met Abi, but when things started going wrong between them he'd reached for the alcohol, similarly with Roisin.

He squinted at the whisky bottle in his hands with disdain as fragments of the memory of Madeleine's betrayal floated around in his mind. As much as he knew the sensible thing would be to throw the bottle away, he also knew that when night fell he would need it. He could feel the descent of loneliness, and this liquid would help to drown out the negative thoughts.

He recalled how coldly Roisin had thrown him out of their home. It mirrored the way Madeleine had left him.

Was Madeleine still with Rick? He could go to Rick's house tonight and find out what had become of them. As the thought hit him, he opened the bottle of whisky and took a sip, savouring the taste on his tongue.

Chapter Thirty

The house had belonged to Rick's family and when his parents emigrated to Spain they'd given it to him. Madeleine had moved in with him back then.

Hugh was sitting on a wall across the road from the house and had been doing so for a couple of hours. No one had left or entered. He'd thought about knocking on the door, saying he was just passing by and was curious to see if they still lived at the same address, but he recalled the look on their faces the last time they'd seen each other. Any meeting would be awkward.

Just as he was thinking of leaving, he saw a man approach the front door and open it. In a flash he was inside. Hugh hadn't seen his face. It could have been Rick.

His curiosity heightened, but as he contemplated knocking the door he thought how foolish he would seem. For what reason would a fifty-year-old man revisit his ex-fiancée who'd cheated on him many years ago and never kept in touch?

The front door of the house opened again, and the man who'd entered was now standing outside. He lit a cigarette and sat on the window sill as he smoked. It wasn't Rick.

This man was older than Rick would be. Maybe about eighty.

Hugh wasn't sure whether he felt relieved or disappointed. The mystery surrounding what happened to Madeleine and Rick would not be solved tonight. Then the thought occurred to him that this man might know them.

It would be easier to speak to him than it would have been to speak to either Madeleine or Rick.

He stood up and approached the house.

Standing at the front gate he called out to the man, 'Hello, sir. Sorry to disturb you.'

The man appeared slightly perturbed, but he stood up and walked towards Hugh. 'How can I help you, son?'

'My friends used to live here many years ago. Rick and Madeleine. I was just passing by and wondered if they still live here. Did you know them?'

'Rick's my son. Madeleine was his first wife. He's remarried.'

'Oh, I didn't know they'd split up.'

Hugh wondered why he wasn't more elated at the news. It hadn't worked out. Isn't that what he was hoping to find? Somehow it left him numb. Maybe it was because he'd not heard from Madeleine or Rick in the years since. Surely if either of them had still cared about him they would have got in touch after they split up. They'd been friends before the betrayal, but neither of them had attempted to look him up and see what had become of him.

'They didn't split up. Gosh, it would have been easier on all of us if they had, that's for sure.'

Rick's father's comment jolted Hugh from his musings. 'I thought you said he remarried.'

Rick's father looked up at the sky for a moment and seemed to be deep in thought. He furrowed his brow and turned to Hugh. 'Madeleine died. It happened soon after she had their daughter. There were complications with the birth. Rick lives in Spain now. He had a hard time coming to terms with what happened.'

Hugh opened his mouth to say something, but no words came out.

'We were all shocked,' continued Rick's father. 'It's not an easy thing to come to terms with. We're just glad that he's managed to pull himself out of it for Mia's sake—their daughter. She's beautiful. Just like Madeleine. His new wife, Angie, has helped him get over the loss, and she's a great mum to Mia.'

Hugh could only nod, unable to find any words, still trying to get his head around what he'd heard.

'I'll tell Rick you called to see him. What's your name?'

'No. Don't worry. He probably wouldn't remember me.' Hugh turned to leave, but was stopped by the old man's words.

'When tragedy strikes, sometimes the best thing that can happen is meeting up with a friend from the past. It can help to put things in perspective. I'm sure Rick would be thrilled to know that you remembered him, and it's nice that you knew Madeleine too. I think it would comfort him to hear you were looking for him. There's always a reason for everything that happens. You turning up here today, it could be because Rick needs his friends. There's a higher power looking out for all of us. What's your name?'

'Um... I'm Hugh. Please send him my best wishes. Tell him I'm sorry for his loss.'

'I will, and thanks for coming. If you give me your phone number I'll pass it on. Good friends are hard to come by, and we should never take them for granted. Rick needs his friends more than ever now.' The man took his mobile phone out of his pocket and asked for Hugh's number.

Hugh gave a made up number; his intention had never been to rekindle a friendship.

As Hugh waved goodbye he reflected on the conversation and regretted saying: *Tell him I'm sorry for his loss*. What would that sound like to

Rick? It was usual for a person to express regret when they were offering condolences, but the circumstances were awkward. Would his words come across as sarcastic? After all, Hugh had "lost" Madeleine to Rick.

Hugh couldn't help the rush of memories that filled his mind. He'd been happy with Madeleine for so many years. Her sudden and unexpected disappearance from his life all those years ago had left a gaping hole. His plans for their future had been erased. The hollowness had never really left him, he now realised. She'd left him with questions and no answers, and now Madeleine was dead he would never get any answers.

Hugh pondered Rick's father's words of wisdom: *'When tragedy strikes, sometimes the best thing that can happen is meeting up with a friend from the past. It can help to put things in perspective.'* He thought about his own predicament and how he had believed nothing could possibly be worse. The meeting with Rick's father had definitely put things into perspective.

Chapter Thirty-One

George could get no peace. His thoughts churned over the same images and consequences, again and again. The doorbell might ring at any time, the police waiting outside to arrest him. After a trial, there'd be the inevitable commitment to prison or a mental institution. As hard as he tried he could not change this pattern of thinking; his own mind had created a prison for him. He contemplated changing his identity, leaving the country, going on the run; but what kind of life would that be?

George recalled the time when he had been floating, a non-entity, without a body. Was that the afterlife? If he killed himself, would the experience be worse for him? These kinds of thoughts had become part of his daily thinking because he needed a way out and could not see one.

His heart skipped a beat when the doorbell sounded and he simultaneously remembered that he still had the gun.

He lifted the door entry phone. It was Glen. He caught his breath and let him in.

'Shouldn't you be at work?'

'I've taken a couple of days off,' said Glen, pushing past George and eyeing him with a concerned frown. 'Are you okay, George?'

'What day is it?'

'Wednesday.'

'I've lost track of the days. Probably because I'm not working. It's hard to keep up.'

'I was worried about you. Have you heard any more from the police?'

'No.' George closed his eyes.

They went through to the living room and sat on the sofa.

'George. I've been thinking. You should give serious thought to changing your identity and going on the run. I know it sounds drastic, but it might be the only way to avoid prison. I know someone who can get you a fake ID and passport. You can leave the country and disappear.'

George shook his head. 'How do you know these criminals?'

'It's through a contact I met at the pub years ago. They can get it sorted really quickly. We don't know when the police might come knocking again. What d'you say?'

'But what about Robbie?'

'Roisin probably wouldn't let you take him, and it would complicate matters.'

'No, I mean, I'd never see him again.'

'Yeah, but what are the chances you'd ever see him again if you're locked up? You murdered five men, for fuck's sake.'

'I didn't murder anyone. Surely there must be a way to prove it.'

'He used your body, mate. For all intensive purposes it was you who did the killing.'

'Intents and purposes.'

'What?'

'You said intensive purposes.'

'I know.'

'That's wrong. The correct phrase is *for all intents and purposes*.'

'Is it?'

'Yes.'

'Fine, but it doesn't change the fact that you're in deep shit. Think about my offer, but don't take too long making up your mind. You don't have the luxury of time. The sooner you get away, the better.'

'This criminal, can he help to get rid of the gun?'

'I'm not getting involved in that. It's too risky. Seriously, think about my offer.'

Later that evening, Glen met his old friend, Scott Morefield, at The Red Lion. They'd become friends years ago after playing a game of darts together. Morefield ended up in prison shortly afterwards for fraud. Glen knew that Scott had many acquaintances in the black market who could get him whatever he asked for. After his release from prison, he'd stayed with Glen for a day or two before being set up in a plush apartment in the city by a drug dealer friend of his. Glen had visited the apartment once and felt envious, but he didn't want to join Scott in criminal activities, so he'd kept Scott at arm's length as much as possible. He knew he was a good contact to have for last-resort assistance. George's latest problem definitely fell into the *last resort* category.

After buying drinks for both of them, Scott sat opposite Glen.

Glen noticed a face he'd seen in the pub the week before; the man had been there when he was with George and Petula. For a moment, paranoia took over; were the police keeping tabs on him as well as George? He peered at the man through squinted eyes and then turned to look at Scott.

Scott lifted his tumbler towards Glen. 'Cheers.'

Glen clinked his glass against the whisky tumbler and nodded. 'Cheers,' he replied.

'Good to see you again, Glen. How's life been treating you?'

'Quite well, actually. I have a new girlfriend. Well, an old flame who's become my new girlfriend. Life's good.'

'That sounds great, so why did you want to see me? You sounded like you needed help.'

Glen couldn't help noticing that the man by the bar had looked at him a couple of times. It was making him nervous. 'Scott, wait a minute, I think I've seen someone I know. I'll be back.'

Glen approached the stranger. 'Hello, er... I saw you in here last week, right?'

The man's initial frown quickly changed to a smile. 'Yes. I've recently moved to the area. I come in for a drink now and then.'

'Where do you live?'

The stranger coughed and said, 'I don't mean to be rude, but we've only just met, and I'm not comfortable giving you that information. You could be a serial killer, for all I know.' He laughed, but his eyes were cold.

Glen gulped and wondered whether this was indeed a policeman under cover. 'I totally understand. Well, if you ever need help—'

'You might be able to help me, actually. I used to know a man called Del. He was recently killed. Did you know him?'

'Del?'

'Derek Cole?'

'No, I've never heard of him.'

'I thought you, or the man you were here with last week, may have known him.'

'Why?'

'I saw your friend leaving his house, and the next day I heard the news of Del's death.'

Sweat formed on Glen's brow. 'You must be mistaken.'

'So why were the police at your friend's flat on Monday?'

'I knew you were following us!'

The man stood up to face Glen and looked him in the eye. He, too, appeared nervous. 'Your friend probably knows about the gold. I helped Del break into a jeweller's years ago and he was the only person who knew where the gold was hidden. I've been looking for him for years. Please, tell your friend I only want to know where the gold is; half of it belongs to me. I don't want any trouble.'

'We can't help you. Leave us alone. None of us knew Del. The police thought my friend was involved in the murders, but he wasn't. They've not charged him.'

'Why was he at Del's house?'

'He wasn't.'

'I saw him with my own eyes.'

'It's complicated. There was a mix-up, and the police got involved.

They've realised he wasn't involved in the murders.'

'So where does that leave me? I have to find the gold. Your friend might know about it. I need to speak to him.'

'I told you to leave us alone.'

The man stormed out of the pub.

Anxiety swirled around Glen's brain. He would have to make sure George went into hiding as soon as possible. Clearly, it wasn't only the police who were after him.

Chapter Thirty-Two

'It's late, George, what are you doing here?' asked Roisin.

'I came to see Robbie. I'm going abroad for work, and I don't know how long for. I wanted to say goodbye. Can I see him?'

'I was going to read him a story. Do you want to do that?'

'Thanks.' He walked into the house and towards the stairs. 'Which room is Robbie's?'

'Directly ahead of you at the top of the stairs. The one with the dinosaur on the door.'

'Thanks.'

'How come you're going away?'

He turned around and looked at her from the landing. 'If I didn't take the position I was gonna lose my job.'

'Where are you going?'

'I'll contact you when I'm settled and give you the address.'

'When are you leaving?'

'Tomorrow morning.'

'What?'

'It was sprung on me at short notice.'

Roisin sat on the sofa waiting for George to finish reading the bedtime story to Robbie. How could this be happening? Just when she dared to believe that things might revert to normal, George was leaving. She'd been ignoring her feelings recently, pushing them away.

Hearing George's footsteps on the stairs, she stood up and waited by the entrance to the living room.

'He's asleep,' said George.

'You were always so good at getting him to sleep.' She walked over and touched his cheek.

He put a hand over hers, and for a brief moment it looked as though he was contemplating kissing her. She leaned in to encourage him, but he pulled away.

'I have to go now, but thanks for letting me see Robbie. I'll be in touch.' He turned towards the front door.

'Me and Hugh are over,' the desperate words reached out to him.

George turned to face her. 'I'm sorry to hear that.'

'When I came to help you, when you had amnesia—I'm not sure if you remember any of it—you kissed me, and I was cruel. I haven't been able to get you out of my mind.'

'I wasn't myself then. I can't remember a thing about it. I

wouldn't've kissed you because I knew you were with Hugh.'

'Things haven't been right with Hugh for a while, and I know I made the biggest mistake when I left you. You were so good to me, and you're the best dad for Robbie.'

'I'm sorry but... I'm over you. You left me. It was painful at first, but I got over you. We can't turn back the clock.'

'But—'

'Goodbye, Roisin.'

Tears threatened to fall as she watched him close the door.

As George walked away from the house, he thought about what Roisin had said. *Rex kissed her? The bastard.* He really had taken advantage of so much while in his body. He recalled, with sadness, Roisin's eyes pleading with him. He remembered how in love with her he'd been before her betrayal, but it seemed like a lifetime ago. So much had happened. The one thing he knew for sure was that he wasn't in love with her anymore. He didn't know when he'd crossed the line, but there was no turning back.

Chapter Thirty-Three

Bernard Parker. My name is Bernard Parker. I am Bernard Parker. George kept repeating the unfamiliar name over and over in his head. He held his fake passport open, staring at his new name, marvelling at how quickly Glen's contact had arranged everything. He'd been reassured that the passport was foolproof and would even work in the airport scanners. So why did he feel so anxious? The tension had turned into a headache an hour ago. He'd taken painkillers but they hadn't kicked in.

He'd been given a ticket for a plane that would take him to France, and from there he'd been instructed to collect a pre-booked rental car and drive to an address to await instructions. There were people there who would help him "go underground".

The train journey to the airport gave him too much time to think, and he dwelled upon what had happened since being captured by Rex. It had been an extended nightmare. Uppermost in his mind the whole time resided the dread that he might never see Robbie again. Robbie would think he'd died. A part of him wished Rex had succeeded in his mission at 8 Goldfern Road.

'Are you all right?' asked a female voice.

George, lost in thought, hadn't noticed anyone else board the train.

The young lady was seated opposite him. She took a tissue from her handbag and offered it to him.

Only then did he realise he'd been crying. He took the tissue and thanked her.

The woman smiled, a concerned frown fixed to her brow. 'I'm Julie, um... what's your name? If you don't mind me asking.'

'Bernard.' The name sounded odd spoken out loud, as he'd been repeating it in his head for the past half an hour.

'Nice to meet you, Bernard. If you want to talk I can listen. I'm not in any rush to be anywhere. Where are you going?'

'To the airport.'

'Gatwick?'

'Yes.'

'I was only going to the next stop, but I'm not in any hurry. I don't mind staying with you to make sure you get to the airport okay.'

'No, no, I'll be fine. I was upset because I'll be missing my family while I'm away, that's all. Getting sentimental in my old age,' he said with a fake laugh. Could she be a policewoman? What if he was being followed and they arrested him before he could board the plane?

Julie stood up. 'This is my stop. I hope you have a nice trip, and don't worry about your family. These days, what with FaceTime and Skype, you can see them every day. It'll be like you never left.' She smiled brightly and walked to the door as the train pulled into the station.

He breathed a sigh of relief as he watched her go.

Chapter Thirty-Four

'Did you hear about the terrorist attack at Gatwick Airport?' asked Petula as she entered the kitchen.

Glen had returned home from work a few minutes earlier; his conscience had given him no peace all afternoon. He felt worried, culpable, and a whole host of other emotions.

'Everyone was talking about it at the library,' continued Petula. 'We nearly had to tell people to leave because they were making so much noise. My manager said it was exceptional circumstances so for once the library wasn't as quiet as usual. It's not every day we hear such awful news, thank God. They've closed down some Tube lines and the Overground.'

'Gatwick? Are you sure?' asked Glen morosely.

'Lots of people died. They called it the worst terrorist attack this decade. That's why I'm late.' She glanced at her watch. 'Wow, I didn't realise it was that late.'

Glen hoped she would stop talking about it now, perhaps if he changed the subject, 'Yes it's late... Have you had dinner?'

She didn't hear. 'Hundreds, maybe thousands. Dead. Just like that. A bomb on a luggage trolley. But from the sound of it there must've been more than one bomb. It'll be on the news. Makes you realise how fragile life is. Why do these things keep happening? Why can't people live and let live?' She walked over to the kitchen table, picked up the remote control, and turned on the TV.

The news coverage showed a huge fire with headlines scrolling across the bottom of the screen. Glen heard snippets of what was being said, but couldn't concentrate as his mind whirred thinking of George, a sick feeling lurching in his stomach. "*Hundreds dead in terrorist attack at Gatwick Airport... No one has yet claimed responsibility... Panic at the airport as passengers watched friends and family die... Emergency services are at the scene... Chaos...*"

George woke up covered in what appeared to be dust. There was a lot of noise, people screaming, heavy footsteps as people ran past. He coughed and tried to move, but his limbs were sore and stiff. Slowly he sat up, holding himself up on his elbows. Before him was one of the most horrific scenes he'd ever witnessed. People were rushing towards an exit and saying that word a lot as they passed by: 'Where's the exit?'... 'Quick! The exit is this way...'

Fire, he kept hearing that word too, along with the sound of sirens blaring. 'We have to get out before more bombs go off,' he heard someone say.

Bombs? George couldn't remember what had happened before this, trying to recall was like reaching back through treacle. This looked like an airport... Gatwick. Slowly, it started to come back to him. Rex. The murders. He could not find the holdall containing the passport, ticket, and other documents he'd been given. Struggling to stand up, he searched the immediate area where he'd fallen. There was a wooden board next to where he'd been lying; he wondered if perhaps his belongings were beneath it. With some difficulty, feeling the pain in his limbs, he lifted the board. He was unprepared for what he found there. A lifeless body. A woman. A young woman. Maybe about twenty years old.

Blood.

Everywhere.

The young woman wasn't moving; her eyes stared ahead, devoid of expression. George couldn't hold the wooden board any longer; it was too heavy. He was unable to stop it slipping from his grasp, once more covering the woman. George puked and then stood up.

'The exit's over there!' shouted a man, pulling on George's arm. 'There's police and ambulances outside. They can help.'

Police. George watched as the man ran towards the exit. He knew that if he went out there and was taken to hospital, they would arrest him. He couldn't take the risk. The best thing that could happen would be for him to disappear now. Everyone would assume he'd died.

A way out.

His mobile phone vibrated in his pocket. He reached with a bloody hand and took it out. *Glen.* George leaned down and buried the mobile beneath the debris; he'd meant to leave it at home—police could trace mobile phones, he'd heard that somewhere.

He walked towards the exit. As the paramedics rushed past him, he thought about alerting them to the woman under the board, but he couldn't risk being seen. He covered his head with his jacket, not wanting any CCTV to capture him leaving the airport. *They'll find her*, he reassured himself.

Sneaking out amongst the crowd, he hid behind a nearby bush in the car park. When the immediate area around him had cleared, he walked away slowly but surely, with aching limbs, as far from the airport as he could. Anyone noticing him would think he was a zombie, he mused. He hoped no one saw him.

There was an abandoned suitcase not far outside the airport. In all the chaos, no one else noticed it. For all George knew, there could have been a bomb planted inside. In desperation, he took the case, hoping it might contain clothes, underwear, toothpaste; some essentials to sustain him until he figured out what to do next.

After dragging the suitcase a mile or so from the airport, he discovered that its lock was passcode protected. He cursed his luck, and his immediate thought, born of frustration, was that he should just abandon it. However, it didn't take him long to guess the code. The first combination he tried, 1111, failed, but the next one—1234—worked straight away.

Disappointment knitted his brow as he opened the suitcase to find women's clothing. The blouses, which he wouldn't have minded wearing if only for the warmth they might provide, were of no use to him whatsoever; they were far too small. There were a few other clothing items in the case: a skirt and a couple of pairs of trousers—again, too small. Even the underwear was child-sized. He found a hand-towel, and a wash-bag containing useful items: a new toothbrush—unopened—and travel-sized containers of toothpaste, shower gel, and shampoo, which were small enough to fit into his jacket pocket. Thankfully there was also a packet of plasters; he'd noticed wounds on his arms that were still bleeding.

After patching himself up and finding that, actually, some of the clothing worked well as makeshift bandages, he saw there was a book in the suitcase: a collection of short stories that sounded interesting. At least reading would distract from his problems for a while.

On opening a small zipped compartment his spirit were lifted when he saw a purse inside. It contained over a hundred pounds in cash, and loyalty cards for a couple of supermarkets; he could use the points on those cards to purchase essential items. It was a chink of light in what had been a dark day. For the briefest of moments he dared to believe that perhaps his luck was changing.

Then he saw the owner's driving licence and this changed everything: there was a face to the faceless haul. Flora Murphy. Red hair, glasses, thirty-five years old.

He thought of the young woman who'd been covered in blood at the airport. But no, this couldn't be her; this woman appeared older. The injured girl's hair was brown. Injured. He preferred to think of her as injured, preferred to believe she may have survived.

Looking once again at the suitcase, a sense of shame fell over him. Flora would be searching for these things he had taken. It would ruin her holiday, after it had already been ruined by whatever had happened at the airport. The pink blouse he had wrapped around his wrist to cover an open wound hadn't meant anything to him, but to Flora it may have sentimental value; maybe it was a birthday present from a special person —her mother, boyfriend, or a favourite aunt. Some of these items of clothing that were now covered in his blood, Flora had probably saved up for and purchased excitedly in anticipation of her holiday. Seeing her face put a different perspective on what he had done.

Feeling like a criminal, he tucked the cash and cards into his pocket and zipped up the suitcase, leaving it by the side of the road.

Chapter Thirty-Five

Roisin opened the front door to find two policemen outside.

'Mrs Roisin Barnaby?'

'Yes.'

'May we come in?' asked one of the officers.

'Yes.'

Roisin remembered one of her friends telling her that when her sister died in an accident two policemen had turned up at the door to inform her parents. *Hugh.... He was in such a state. What if he's had an accident?* She'd thrown him out, hadn't heard from him since. She shook away the anxious thoughts as she followed the police officers to the living room. Once inside the room, she asked, 'Would you like a drink?' not knowing why, something to say.

'Please sit down,' said the shorter of the two policemen.

Reluctantly, Roisin sat on a chair beside the coffee table.

The two policemen sat on the sofa facing her.

'Mrs Barnaby, did you hear the news about the terror attack at Gatwick Airport yesterday?'

'I remember seeing a headline on a newspaper when I was on my way back from taking my son to school this morning, but...' She shrugged.

'We are aware that you are no longer living with Mr George Barnaby.'

'We're divorced.'

'We're looking for him, and as you have a child together we wondered whether you'd seen him.'

'He came over, not last night, the night before, said he was going to work abroad.'

'His mobile phone was found amongst the wreckage at Gatwick. We couldn't find a trace of any flight booking, though. We wondered if you might know where he was going.'

'What are you saying? Is he okay? I didn't know he was going to Gatwick airport. Oh, no.' She stood up, wanting to get away from the thoughts that were taunting her. *Did he die in the terror attack?* Trembling, not really wanting to know anything else, she uttered, 'Y-you found his phone... Is he all right?'

'We went to his flat today, but he wasn't there. We're questioning him in relation to a crime. Did he mention that to you?'

'A crime?'

'It's a coincidence he was going abroad so soon after we questioned him about an investigation. Was Mr Barnaby involved in any criminal activity when you were married?'

'No. Never. He's never even had a parking ticket. Oh, except once when he forgot to display the parking voucher on the car when we went shopping.' Roisin felt hot, unable to catch a breath. A thought invaded her mind: *The amnesia—did George use that as an excuse to cover up a crime?* 'I need some fresh air.' Almost tripping over her feet, she stumbled to the front door and opened it before emptying the contents of her stomach onto the concrete step outside. Wiping her mouth, she turned around to see the two policemen at the living room door, watching her with concerned frowns.

They walked towards her. 'We're sorry to have been the bearers of bad news, Mrs Barnaby. The phone has been found but there is no trace of Mr Barnaby. That doesn't mean that he was one of the casualties, of course, so please don't be alarmed. We're still making enquiries. He may have been taken to a nearby hospital. If he does get in touch with you, please let us know.' The taller man handed her a business card.

Roisin didn't like Glen. But she knew she'd have to call him. He probably knew where George had gone. Her head had ached with worry ever since the policemen left the house over half an hour ago. Taking a deep breath and putting aside her loathing of her once-husband's best friend, she keyed his number into her phone.

'Hello, is that Glen?'

'Yes, that's Roisin, right? I have your number in my phone. George probably gave it to me in case I ever needed to contact you.'

'Right. Do you know where he is?'

'He's gone away for work.'

'He said that to me as well, but I had the police round here this morning looking for him, they said he'd committed a crime.'

'First I've heard of it. He said he was going away for work. He didn't tell me where.'

'Are you sure? He tells you everything. You were a bad influence on him. Was this crime anything to do with you?'

'Roisin, I know we've never been friends, but it's pretty low for you to blame me for getting George involved in crime. You hardly know me.'

She sighed loudly. 'I'm worried about him. His phone was found at Gatwick after the terror attack yesterday. The police are looking for him.'

'Oh no. I tried calling him on his phone when I heard the news, I knew he was going to Gatwick.'

'I thought you said you didn't know where he was going.'

'If the police talk to you again, don't mention me. I'm gonna deny it anyway. He was in trouble. Big trouble. And he had to get away.'

'What sort of trouble?'

'Do the police think he was killed in the attack?'

'They're going to search the hospitals for him. So why did he have to get away so urgently?'

'It doesn't matter, does it, if he's been killed in the attack?'

'Don't say that!'

'Sorry, I didn't mean... But...'

'The police might find him.'

'That would be worse for him.'

'Worse than being dead?'

'Much worse. You have no idea.'

'No, I don't. So tell me. What did he do? Why was he running?'

'You won't believe me if I told you.'

'Tell me. I have a five-year-old who's going to be asking questions about his dad, for God's sake.'

'I can't tell you over the phone. Let's meet in The Red Lion.'

'At lunchtime then. One o'clock.'

Chapter Thirty-Six

George woke up and squinted against the sun, too bright for his tired eyes.

Not having anywhere to sleep the night before, he had taken shelter in the doorway of an abandoned shop. He'd not been able to find a way to open the door, and the windows were locked. He contemplated breaking a window and going inside, but feared there might be an alarm on the property.

He'd tried to sleep, against the odds. It didn't feel safe. He'd slept for maybe twenty minutes at a time, and each time he'd woken it was either to the sound of a car or other vehicle, a cat howling, fox shrieking, or other "outdoor" sounds too close for comfort now that he was in this vulnerable state.

After waking up for the third time in less than an hour, and seeing it was just after 1 a.m., he settled himself beside the nearest lamp post and tried reading some of the book of short stories, which he'd found in Flora's suitcase. The first story was quite entertaining and for a while he was able to forget about his predicament. It was all about a man who was hiding an affair from his wife. The second story, however, gave him the creeps. It was about a man who'd broken into a house and stolen a woman's purse. Unbeknownst to the burglar, the woman, who was in her eighties, had died that evening. He was cursed with the worst luck. It reminded George too much of his current situation, knowing that he had some of Flora's belongings and she might be dead. The man in the story had ended up dying after being lured by the dead woman's spirit. For some reason, George had been engrossed enough in the story to read it to the end, but regretted it when he did. He had discarded the book after that and was plagued by nonsensical dreams for the rest of the night, whenever he did manage to fall into a short slumber. Rex featured in the dreams in various guises. In one of the nightmares, Rex appeared as a spider the size of a house.

George made it through the night, somehow. He moved to stand up and found his bones ached from sleeping on the hard ground, and the injuries he'd sustained still caused him pain. He was curious to read a newspaper to find out what had happened at the airport.

The light of day brought home to him the reality that he was on the run. He thought of Robbie and wondered if he would he ever see him again.

As he turned the corner of the street an odd sensation swept over him. Freedom. No one knew who he was. He could start again. No expectations. Even if all he did was live on the streets, begging for the next bite, he'd be free. If he went back home he'd undoubtedly be arrested. Here he was anonymous. It would have been a perfect solution, a literal get-out-of-jail-free card, except every minute that passed took him a minute further away from Robbie.

He'd have to find someone to help him; someone who'd allow him to stay with them, in hiding.

He wasn't far from his parents' house, just a couple of stops on the Tube. He'd phoned them the night before he left home, almost like he was saying goodbye to them for the last time. They were both in their eighties, and he would be in hiding for the foreseeable future. He'd become tearful on the phone, but made an effort to keep his voice steady.

He'd told them he was going to work abroad, the same lie he had spun for Roisin. That way if they spoke to each other the stories would match up. He wanted to go to his parents' house, a safe haven, somewhere he could hide. But he couldn't imagine explaining to them what he was hiding from. They were already worried about him because he'd split up from Roisin; if they heard the police were after him, how would they deal with that?

He knew the police would probably question his parents sooner or later, and they would be told he was a suspect in a murder inquiry. Wouldn't it be better coming from him? He tried to imagine explaining what he'd been through, but there was no logical way to tell them what had happened. If he went to stay with them, they would lie to the police for him, but it would be stressful for them, and they would be wondering whether he had killed people. He could not decide what to do, but knew he'd have to find someone else to help him.

His thoughts turned to Roisin. He contemplated going to see her, to ask for help, but the same doubts came to mind. He had to find somewhere else to stay and then let Roisin know where to find him, and arrange to see Robbie every so often.

But could he ever tell her or his parents where he was? The police would be keeping a close eye on the people he knew. Anyone who helped him would be potentially committing a criminal offence.

An answer came to him then: Stuart Heldon.

Stuart was an old friend from back in primary school. They'd been close. George spent so much time at Stuart's house when they were children, that people used to think they were brothers. Stuart had criminal leanings, and that was one of the reasons the friends had drifted apart. It began with occasional shoplifting, and then progressed to burglary. George knew his friend often stole snacks from the local shop, but ignored it; however, when he discovered Stuart and his cousin planned to break into an old woman's house, he was alarmed. He began to make excuses as to why he couldn't see Stuart.

One evening, when they were seventeen years old, Stuart boasted about how much money he'd found in a house he and his cousin had broken into. He said George should join them on their next burglary. George didn't agree with what they'd been doing and he told Stuart he wouldn't be getting involved. There'd been an argument, which ended their friendship.

George heard through friends that Stuart spent time in prison for burglary in his early twenties, and started dealing drugs when he was released. He reconnected with Stuart a few years later for a couple of months. George discovered that jail time hadn't changed Stuart; he was as crooked as ever. When he'd told Roisin about him, she'd said it would be better if he didn't see him again. 'Criminals who've been to prison meet other criminals. It wouldn't be safe for you to get close to a man like that,' she'd said.

He'd agreed with her at the time.

Things had changed.

Stuart would have no qualms about breaking the law.

Chapter Thirty-Seven

Roisin walked into The Red Lion and saw Glen seated at the far end of the pub. The place was familiar; George had brought her here before. She'd always hated Glen's attitude and hoped he'd changed, hoped age would have made him wiser. Whenever she'd been in his company in the past, he'd always come across as a blatant male chauvinist, often making derogatory remarks about women's looks.

She sat opposite him, avoiding his eyes.

'Hi, Roisin. Can I get you a drink?' He wore a frown.

'Um... I need to know why George had to leave.'

'I'll get you a drink. This won't be easy for you to hear. White wine okay?'

'Yes, thanks.'

Roisin watched as he walked over to the bar. He didn't seem like the Glen she'd known in the past; the irreverent fool, forever cracking jokes, often at others' expense.

He came back to the table with an apologetic half-smile and handed her a glass of wine.

She almost wished Glen would go back to being the jokey obnoxious clown she had known, instead of this sober character who sat before her.

Glen held his forehead and then breathed a deep sigh. 'He had to leave because he was at risk of being arrested. He probably would have been.'

'Arrested for what?'

Glen leaned in and whispered, 'Murder.'

For a moment Roisin was sure she'd misheard, but Glen's face told her that she hadn't. 'Not George. That's impossible.'

'He's innocent, but the police won't believe him because there's evidence against him.'

'What sort of evidence?'

'Evidence of him getting in touch with the victims in the days before they were murdered, and asking them to meet him at the address where they were murdered. There's Facebook messages and e-mails, apparently. And someone saw a man fitting his description leaving the house.'

'I don't understand.'

'Do you remember when he had amnesia?'

'Yes.'

'That was when the murders were done.'

'He murdered people but he couldn't remember murdering them?'

'That's one way of looking at it.'

'He wouldn't kill anyone. I know George. *You* know George, for God's sake.'

'He didn't, but he can't prove it.'

'You seem so sure when you say he didn't. What else aren't you telling me?'

'You wouldn't believe me.'

'Just tell me, Glen!'

'Keep your voice down. Maybe we should've met somewhere private.'

Roisin looked around. The place was practically empty. The other people in the pub were out of earshot, as far as she could tell. 'Please tell me. I'm going out of my head with worry.'

'He was possessed.'

Roisin shook her head. 'But... He didn't mention not being able to keep up the rent payments. I only took what was mine in the financial settlement. And what does that have to do with him murdering people?'

'What?'

'Losing his home wouldn't turn him into a serial killer. Was he defending himself?'

'What are you talking about?'

'You said he was repossessed—'

'No, I didn't. I said *possessed*, as in his body was used by a dead man to commit the murders.'

Roisin stood up. 'Oh, for God's sake! I'd hoped you'd matured, but you're still behaving like a juvenile. I thought you would put my mind at ease, tell me where George might be, but you're using this opportunity to —'

'Stop, Roisin! Everything I've told you is true. I told you it was unbelievable. He's on the run because he's being chased by the police for murders he didn't commit. They were committed by a dead man using his body. The man told you he had amnesia because he didn't know anything about George's life. He told me that too. We were both tricked.'

She grabbed her handbag from the table and sneered at Glen. 'This is nonsense. When you're ready to tell me the real reason George fled without even telling me when he intends to see his son again, get in touch. You know, George spent too much time with you. Whatever the police are looking for him about, I bet you're involved.'

'No. Well, not directly.'

'Huh! I knew it. Next time you speak to him, tell him to call me.'

Roisin stormed out of the pub, not sure what to think. Her mind was full of absurd information. Questions that couldn't be answered were battling for attention. Why had George disappeared? Why were the police looking for him? Why had Glen made up that ridiculous story? What would she tell Robbie? Every night he cried for George. What could she tell him, and how long would she be kept in the dark?

Glen watched Roisin leave the pub. He wanted to go after her, but whatever he said she wouldn't believe him. One thing that stuck in his mind was her accusation: '*Whatever the police are looking for him about, I bet you're involved...*' Yes. If he hadn't convinced George to go into 8 Goldfern Road with him, none of this would have happened. He picked up his glass and downed the beer in one go, wishing he knew where George was.

Chapter Thirty-Eight

'Mummy, when's Dad coming back?' asked Liam while pulling on his school blazer.

'I'm not sure, Liam. His work is very demanding. The last time I spoke to him he said he hoped he'd be able to see you soon.' A tear came to Abigail's eye.

Lately, she'd become more aware that it was wrong to keep Hugh from seeing Liam, and the recent talk about going to mediation made things worse. There was a missed call on her mobile that morning, which she'd ignored. The number looked like the mediation service number Hugh had given her. He'd said they'd be contacting her. He'd sounded sad on the phone.

During the years they'd lived together she'd taken the lead, knocking him down when he asked to make any decisions, controlling his every move. This refusal to allow him contact with his son was an extension of that and she didn't feel good about it. The proposed intervention of a mediator had forced her to reevaluate her behaviour.

Abigail knew the reason behind her treatment of Hugh, and realised how unfair she was being. She was still hung up on her first love. That was the root cause of her behaviour. It had taken her a while to work it out and face up to it. Now, in her mid-forties with a son who'd soon be a teenager, it was a notion that would sound ridiculous if spoken aloud, but inside and within her deepest secret thoughts, it couldn't be denied.

Between the ages of sixteen and twenty, she'd spent practically every day with Tiko. He'd been the love of her life. He left her for a girl who worked at the local take-away restaurant where they'd often gone for late-night meals when returning from gigs and clubs. Tiko and the girl, Jennifer, had a good rapport. Abigail assumed the girl was being friendly as part of her job. Jennifer was pretty and intelligent, a medical student working nights at the take-away shop to pay university fees. It transpired that the real reason Tiko invariably chose the same restaurant for their chips and burgers and midnight snacks was so that he could see Jennifer.

Abigail later discovered Tiko and Jennifer had been in a relationship, behind her back, for at least six months.

It took Abigail years before she even considered entering into another relationship. There was an underlying mistrust and fear.

When she met Hugh and he asked about her previous relationships, she'd lied to him and said she was abused by her former partner. Then Hugh revealed, quite plainly and seemingly without

125

embarrassment, that his ex-fiancée had cheated on him. 'I'm better off without her. I can see that now,' he went on to say, a smile on his face. 'Trust is so important in a relationship. It's living a lie to think otherwise.' Despite Hugh's openness, Abigail still found herself unable to talk about what Tiko had done, worrying Hugh would think there was something wrong with her, a reason why Tiko would choose another woman. It was a genuine irrational belief she could not shake.

When she'd lived with Hugh, Abigail often wondered whether her tight hold and control in their marriage might be due to the experience she'd had with Tiko. She'd catch herself being particularly harsh with Hugh over the smallest thing, or trying to stop him getting close to anyone else.

After finding out about Hugh's affair with Roisin, she knew she'd overreacted by cutting Hugh out of Liam's life completely. It brought back dark feelings she had never confronted after Tiko's betrayal; they'd remained inside, and like anything dark that is allowed to fester, they presented themselves in other ways. She knew there was a bitterness to her exterior, which she often resented, but over the years she'd become accustomed to the person she had turned into, accepted it as her personality.

In recent months, looking inwardly, she could see that the way she'd treated Hugh would have been enough to make anyone look elsewhere for the love they were being denied within their marriage. She knew that Hugh suffered the same as her when his ex-fiancée left him for someone else, yet throughout their marriage she'd played the victim and complained whenever he asserted himself.

She wanted Hugh to see Liam, to make up for the past, but Hugh was an alcoholic. Part of her blamed herself for driving him to drink, but a bigger part of her knew it wasn't entirely her fault and she couldn't put Liam's safety at risk.

Abigail took Liam to school and returned home to find a message on her mobile phone: the mediation service again. She decided that the best way around this would be to set up a meeting with Hugh, on his own. Her new boyfriend Victor had helped her, allowing her to move on and stop holding on to resentment from the past. It gave her the motivation to try to put things right.

In two minds, but trying to do the right thing, she called Hugh.

'Hugh, we need to talk.'

'Hello, is that you?'

The slurring was obvious. He'd been drinking again.

'Roisin?'

She felt an unexpected twinge of jealousy. 'No, it's me: Abi.'

'Abi!'

He sounded almost ecstatic to have heard from her. Her brow wrinkled in confusion. 'Um... can we meet today? I have a proposal for contact between you and Liam. He wants to see you.'

'You said he didn't want—'

'I know what I said. It's a long story, but let's just say being apart from you has done me the world of good, and I mean that in the nicest way. I would like us to move forward and try to make sure Liam isn't affected by any of this. He misses you.'

'I miss him too.'

Was he crying? There were definitely sniffling sounds on the line.

'Are you all right, Hugh?'

'No.'

Silence.

'Hugh?'

'Roisin's thrown me out. I have nowhere to stay and... I'm ashamed to admit it... I'm drinking again. I am going to stop, I promise.'

Abigail sighed deeply. 'That's one of the things we need to talk about. I don't want you drinking around Liam. I don't want any mediators or courts involved. We can sort this out between us. Can you come to my house today?'

'I can't afford it. I lost my job.'

'I'll come and see you. Where are you?'

'I'm staying with a friend. I can meet you in a café maybe.'

'How about the Costa on the high street? I can get there in about an hour.'

'See you then.'

Chapter Thirty-Nine

Hugh noticed the battery power on his phone was down to eleven per cent as he finished the call with Abigail. He'd spent the past couple of nights sleeping in a sleeping bag given to him by a volunteer from a homeless charity who'd noticed him outside the town hall.

His jeans were covered in stains, and he'd been wearing the same underwear for over a week. He was on his way back to the house to try to convince Roisin to let him collect some belongings and clean himself up. He couldn't meet Abigail looking like this; she would never let him see Liam. After living rough for over a week, with growth of stubble, and the smell of rain and sweat pervading his clothing, he was not a pretty sight.

Roisin opened the door and folded her arms, closing her eyes briefly. 'What do you want?'

Hugh raised a hand in protest. 'I don't want to argue. I've come to get my stuff, and I need a shower.'

'You don't live here anymore. Your clothes have gone to a charity shop.' She started to close the door, but he pushed it open and charged into the house.

'I thought Abi was heartless, but you take the prize for that! How the fuck did you think I'd survive out there?'

'You stink of booze!'

'I haven't had a drink for two days. I can't even afford food. I've run out of cash. I only had a tenner on me when you told me to leave.'

'I told you to pack a bag. It's not my fault you were too drunk to do that, is it?' Roisin held on to the front door, as if still waiting for him to leave, and looked him up and down. 'Where have you been staying?'

Hugh rubbed his forehead. 'Staying? On the night bus, the Underground. I found a hostel one night and managed to charge my mobile there, thought it would be safe, but I ended up being threatened by one of the other residents. He said he'd kill me if I didn't give him my money and phone. I managed to sneak out the next morning before he could see me. It's been hell.'

'I thought you'd find a friend to stay with.'

'As if you give a shit.'

'I'm not completely heartless. Go and have a shower and get your things together. You can use the computer to find somewhere to rent,' she said, closing the front door.

'But I lost my job, I can't afford to rent anywhere.'

'Whose fault is that? I can't afford to help you out, if that's what you think.'

'But I own part of this house. You're not being fair. At least give me some money if you're going to expect me to survive out there.'

Roisin closed her eyes briefly. 'I've given you so many chances.'

'Why are you being like this?'

Roisin stared at him. 'What did you expect? Sleep rough for a couple of days—'

'It's been over a week!'

'So? Did you think if you came back and begged, I'd feel sorry for you and let you stay? It doesn't work like that, Hugh! You're an adult, and you've got to start taking responsibility. I already have one child living here, I don't need another.' Her face paled after she said that. She took a seat on the stairs holding her face in her hands.

Hugh knew she would be thinking about the baby and regretting her choice of words.

He sat beside her and put an arm around her.

When she sat up there were tears in her eyes.

Closing his eyes, Hugh mumbled, 'I've messed up. I always mess up.'

Roisin stood up holding her nose and said, 'You stink. Use the shower. Sleep here tonight, but you have to look for a job and somewhere to rent.'

Hugh walked upstairs slowly, then turned to face her. She was watching him from the foot of the staircase. 'I really am sorry, Roisin. I'll take a shower and get my things. I won't hang around. I'll only sleep here. I'll come back when Robbie's in bed so I don't disturb you.'

'I didn't want it to end this way.'

'I know.' He turned back around and looked up the stairs as he ascended, holding back tears. He'd held out so much hope when they bought this place. It had been his home for a brief time, but he had lost it all.

Blinking out a tear, he went to the bedroom and opened the wardrobe to see that his clothes were in there, hadn't been given to a charity shop. He wondered whether there was anything left to recover from this relationship. He hated how he had left such bitter disappointment in his wake.

Chapter Forty

George looked up at the house. There were steps leading to the front door. He'd last been here over twenty years ago. It was Stuart's parents' house. Stuart no longer lived here, but George hoped his parents still did. He climbed the steps hesitantly, knowing he was supposed to be on the run. Would talking to Stuart's parents mean there'd be a trail the police could follow to find him? He couldn't risk anyone knowing his whereabouts. He preferred people to think he'd died at the airport. He rang the doorbell and waited, anguished thoughts giving him no peace.

A young woman answered the door. George knew Stuart had a sister, Melody, but she'd been older than him and had left home many years before he'd cut ties with Stuart.

George coughed, then said, 'Hello.'

The woman frowned at him and asked, 'Are you all right?'

George knew he must look pretty dishevelled having spent the night sleeping rough. He forced a smile. 'Yes, I'm fine. Um... I'm sorry to bother you, but do Mr and Mrs Heldon live here?'

'Heldon? Oh yes, Rita and Bob; they're the lovely couple who sold the house to us.' She smiled. 'Do you know them?'

'I knew their son, I was hoping to see him.'

The woman's expression changed again and her smile faded. 'I don't mean to be rude, but what happened to you?'

'I'm fine, I just fell over. Thanks for your time.' He turned to walk away but then wondered whether this woman might still be in touch with the Heldons, or at least have a forwarding address. Turning back to face her, he said, 'Can I just ask if you know where the Heldons moved after they sold this house.'

'They were moving to the countryside. I did stay in touch with them for a couple of months and I had a mobile number for them but haven't used it for ages. I'm not sure if they still have the same number.'

George hung his head.

'I do have their daughter's phone number. She came here last year to show her children where she grew up. We spent a few hours together and became good friends; we keep in touch. Would you like me to call her?'

George had never really known Melody. He and Stuart were about ten years younger than her and had little in common. Would she even remember him? He shrugged and said, 'Um... yes, okay, thanks.'

'I'll close the door while I phone her. I hope you don't think I'm being rude.'

'That's absolutely fine,' said George.

George stood outside the house wondering what to say to Melody. One more night sleeping on the streets of London would be more than he could handle, though. He had to try.

The woman returned to the front door. 'You didn't mention your name.'

'George Barnaby. I used to play with her brother Stuart.'

He watched as she put the mobile to her ear, 'Hi Mel, he says he's George Barnaby, one of your brother's old friends.'

The woman held the phone towards him, smiling. 'She remembers you.'

'Hi Melody... Yes, it has... I'm okay... Well, no, I'm not. That's the reason I wanted to see Stuart... He is? When? ... Oh... Why? ... No, don't worry. I'll find someone else. Thank you.' He handed the phone back to the woman.

She frowned at him. 'Not what you wanted to hear?'

'She says Stuart's in prison.'

'Now you mention it, I remember her telling me. Armed robbery, wasn't it?'

'Yes. Um, thanks for your time.'

'Wait George,' called out the woman as he descended the steps.

He turned to face her.

'Would you like to come in for a cup of tea? You look like you're down on your luck.'

'I-I wouldn't want to impose.'

'Don't worry, you won't be. It's a couple of hours until the kids get back from school.'

George followed her into the grand house. The entrance hall led off to rooms on both sides. A wide staircase graced the centre of the large hall. Nostalgic thoughts of when he and Stuart were children, chasing each other around the house, hiding in nooks and crannies, came to mind.

The new owners had redecorated. It was thoroughly modern looking. The psychedelic wallpaper that had been in the house since the '70s had gone; the walls were bright and airy with magnolia paint. Expensive-looking hardwood floors replaced the old swirly carpet he remembered from his youth. 'It's a lovely house.'

The woman turned to face him and crossed her arms. 'Yes, it is. I got it in the divorce settlement. The kids wanted to live with me. My ex-husband is always abroad. He's a pilot. Rich. Women flocked to him and he gave in to temptation. Long story short, we're divorced and I got to keep the house and a tidy sum in settlement. I deserve it after what he put me through.' She waved her hand. 'Sorry, I'm sure you don't want to hear my life story. Wow, I'm surprised I blurted all that out. You've got a friendly face, George. People are probably always telling you their problems, right?'

They walked into the main reception room; a large room with windows spanning most of the front of the house. George remembered the windows as being much smaller in the old days and wondered whether his mind was playing tricks on him. He marvelled at the length of the luxurious-looking curtains.

He sat on the sofa. The leather sofa, with a unique curved design, had probably been made to order.

'How do you like your tea?' asked the woman.

'White, no sugar.'

'I'm Lily, by the way. I don't think I introduced myself.'

He watched Lily leave the room.

On the large coffee table in front of him was a newspaper. The front page headline glared out at him: *"Gatwick Terror Attack - Hundreds Dead, Many Injured, Many More Missing"*.

Terror attack. The words filtered through George's mind as he recalled the debris and the panic within the airport terminal. He'd heard people say there'd been a bomb, and had suspected a deliberate attack, but a part of him had hoped the explosion was caused by maybe a faulty electrical item. Every time there was a terror attack it caused him to despair for the future. The idea that groups of people could get together and deliberately plan an attack that would harm, injure, and potentially kill many innocent people was a reality he didn't want to acknowledge.

George noticed the photos on the front page of the paper, faces of the victims. He picked up the newspaper and began reading. One of the photographs looked familiar. He held it closer and read the name beneath the photo. Flora Murphy. The story said she was missing. He thought about the suitcase he'd found. Grief and shame consumed his thoughts when he realised he'd taken the belongings of a woman who may have died in the attack.

Lily returned to the room carrying a tray. She placed it on the table, and George put the newspaper back onto the table, folded in half, the front page hidden from view.

'Very sad about that terror attack at the airport,' said Lily.

George hung his head and then looked up at her. 'I was there.'

'Oh, dear. Is that why you look so rough? I was wondering if you'd been in a fight.'

'That's part of the reason why I needed help from Stuart.'

Lily's hand went to her mouth. 'But Stuart's a criminal. Why would you need his help?'

'The police are after me.'

Lily backed away. 'I think you should go. I don't want to be done for harbouring criminals.' She walked out of the room.

George stood up and followed Lily out into the passageway. 'Why did you call me a criminal?' he demanded.

Lily turned pale. 'You said the police are looking for you. I don't want any trouble. My children will be back from school in about an hour.'

'Lily, I want you to know, I'm not a criminal. I'm on the run.'

'Do you know how many people were killed in that attack? Do you have no shame? There were children killed too!'

George shook his head. 'The terror attack? You think I was behind that—'

'You said you were there and on the run from the police.'

'I was caught up in it, that's what I meant. I was meant to leave the country under a new identity, because the police are looking for me, but then the attack happened and I lost everything, all my fake ID. I had to sleep rough last night. I thought Stuart might be able to help me.'

'Why are the police looking for you?' The colour had drained from Lily's face and she was holding on to the banisters, as though fearful she would faint.

'It's a case of mistaken identity. I'm innocent. You said I had a friendly face. I don't look like a serial killer, do I?'

'Get out!' The scream seemed to emanate from Lily's mouth involuntarily. 'Get out! If you don't leave I'll call the police.'

He backed away towards the front door. 'I'm going. But please don't tell anyone about this visit, especially not the police.'

'Why should I help you? You're a murderer, for all I know. Get out!'

He stood with his back to the front door. 'The truth is I didn't kill anyone; I don't even like killing spiders.' An image flickered in his mind but he blanked it out. 'I'm an innocent man; I have a five-year-old son who I'll probably never see again. I've been framed.'

'I don't want to get involved in this.'

'I have nowhere to go. Please, I'm begging you, don't tell the police you've seen me. I'm trying to stay underground. I will find a way to prove my innocence, but until I do I have to keep running.'

'I won't tell anyone, just go.'

He turned around and opened the front door.

Lily allowed enough time for him to step outside and then slammed the door. The sound startled him and he almost fell down the steps. He steadied himself. She'd looked so scared and hysterical, he was sure she would call the police straight away. He needed somewhere to hide. He imagined a searchlight sweeping the area; sooner or later it would catch him in its sights.

He began to run as fast as he could, as far away as his legs would carry him, not even thinking about where he was heading.

Chapter Forty-One

Please, I'm begging you. What can I do to get back to some sort of life? I'll do whatever you ask. You've proved your point. I know I was a bad man and I'll make up for it if you let me get back into a body.

'We don't bargain with evil,' came the reply.

Rex's energy was fading fast. *Please. I'm a changed man.*

'You're not a man. You're nothing, and soon even the nothing that you are will be obliterated, and it will be as though you never existed.'

One chance is all I am asking for. Help me live again and I will be a force for good.

'It's far too late. You have ruined a man's life.'

George?

'He's on the run because the police are investigating him for the murders you committed.'

I'll go into his body and face the consequences. You said I could do that, right?

'My, my, we are getting desperate aren't we, Rex Rodenbury?'

I don't mind admitting I'm desperate. I need you to help me.

'Help you, so that you can kill again?'

I won't.

'What about your spider obsession?'

Of course I still want to be a spider, but right now I just want to leave this place. I want a chance to right the wrongs I have done.

'Those you murdered are dead. Their families are grieving.'

You can do so many things, can't you turn back time? Take me back to before the murders?

'That's not possible.'

I can help those families. I can own up to the murders and they will have someone to blame. They can get closure.

'You are basically asking me to bring you back from the dead, and that can never happen. But there is a possible solution.'

Please. What is it? Rex's energy waned, and he doubted he would survive long enough to hear the reply.

'There is an evil murderer, Trevor Staines, who has managed to evade any conviction. His youngest victims were twin boys, aged nine, lured into his house and poisoned. Over the course of about fifteen years he killed seventeen people when he was living in America, but he was never caught. His first victims were his own parents.'

Rex sensed despair. In his faded thoughts, he imagined he would now be sent to be killed by this serial killer.

You win. I've had enough. Let me fade.

'No, you want to help George, right? Well perhaps you can. You will enter the body of Trevor Staines. His soul is beyond help because he has killed so many. His soul will come here. You will swap places. In Trevor's body, you will confess to the murders of your old school bullies, and George will then be free.

'You will, of course, spend time in prison. That cannot be avoided. However, when you come out you will be free, however, we will still be keeping an eye on you.'

But if I go to prison for five murders, I will be in there for life.

'Yes, but even if you die in prison, your soul will then be reborn into a better life. A win-win for you, Rex. The alternative is fading away. We don't often get to see the end of a malevolent spirit. Your kind usually live forever. It's only because you ended up here that we've been able to control your fate and deplete your energy. We're taking a risk by offering you this way out.'

What risk?

'That you may revert to your old ways, kill again. However, we are now in complete control. Be aware that if you step out of line there are no more chances. I hope you accept our offer, as it gives you a chance to change if that's what you really want to do. Evil lurks within your soul, as it does within the soul of every man, woman, and child. The individual decides whether or not they will follow its command. Everyone has good in their soul too. Even Trevor Staines. Nothing is impossible.'

But when I asked you if I could go back into my old body, you said that wasn't possible, so you obviously think some things are impossible.

'Nothing is impossible, but just because something is possible it doesn't mean we will attempt it. There are rules we must abide by.'

But if you want me to be a good person, why turn me into a man who is a serial killer by nature?

'It is Trevor's soul that is malevolent. His body is merely a shell.'

What about the other murders? The murders Trevor committed? Is there any way they can pin them on me if I'm in his body?

'That is a risk, yes, but unlikely. The last murder he committed was ten years ago in America; he fled to the UK and his appearance has changed considerably. He assumed a new identity once in the UK with the help of his criminal friends. In the US he was called Ted Barnes. He hasn't changed, though, and would still commit murder if the opportunity presented itself, but his lust for it has somewhat diminished over the years.'

But if you kill in America isn't there capital punishment?

'Not in every state.'

But if he was extradited, I could, in theory, end up on death row.

'There's a possibility. Although you wouldn't normally be sent to a state where the death sentence still exists, if you are being extradited from the UK. There are human rights issues that would usually be considered. It can't, however, be completely ruled out.'

I don't want to be him.

'You won't be him. You will be you, but you will be in his skin. As you were in George's. And what is the alternative? If you cease to exist there'll be no opportunity for you to help George and make amends for your sins.'

Will I be aware that I'm me...? I mean, Rex? Or will I think I'm Trevor? Will I have his memories, you know, the murders?

'Your memory as Rex Rodenbury will stay intact because you must help George reclaim his life. However, you will learn everything about Trevor's life before becoming him.'

Rex felt himself fade completely for a moment, but then found enough energy to say, *Okay, I'll do it.*

Chapter Forty-Two

'Please don't hurt me.' Trevor watched as the man lay prone on the floor before him and recalled an event from many years before.

He'd been living in America. An older man spat at him when he pushed past him to get into a taxi. Trevor remembered how he'd grabbed hold of the man and pulled him into the taxi beside him, holding a gun against his waist before shouting out a destination to the taxi driver. The man's face had completely changed. Gone was the bravado that had enabled him to spit on him. He appeared truly fearful.

'Listen, man, you can have the taxi. I need to get to work. Let me out.'

'You okay back there?' shouted the taxi driver over the rush-hour sounds that could be heard through the open windows.

Trevor kept hold of his victim as the taxi pulled away from the kerb.

'Where are we going?'

'I haven't decided yet.'

Trevor recalled the scene, in awe of his old self. He couldn't afford to be as brazen anymore. He had so much more to lose. It would be harder for him to get a new identity. He'd built a new life in the UK. He was a businessman; it didn't matter if the business was illegal. He was known locally as a successful above-board businessman. No one suspected the darker side. He had a wife, Rhonda, and two children, none of whom knew about his past life in America. He'd told Rhonda that his parents died in a car accident. It was partly true, he told himself. He'd run over them both with a truck. He'd forgotten why he decided to kill them, only remembered the desire to kill them.

No one knew he'd driven the vehicle. The truck driver was asleep in the front, and Trevor (or Ted, as he was then known) saw an opportunity to break in. It was easy enough for him to get into the truck, and the keys were still in the ignition. His parents were standing together, waiting for him to return from the toilet. He could still see their faces, lit up, startled, looking into the bright headlights. They didn't stand a chance.

The truck driver stood trial for the murders.

Trevor gave evidence at the trial, saying he'd been a witness and thought the driver had fallen asleep at the wheel. The driver denied starting the vehicle, claiming he had no idea how it had moved, as he was on a break—sleeping. He said he woke up in the passenger seat when the truck jolted to a stop and was sure he saw someone jump from the vehicle, but by the time he'd managed to get out and take a look there was no one there: *'That's when I noticed the smell; I can still remember it. Blood. Then I looked and saw something under the wheels of the truck; at first I thought it was an animal, maybe a dog, but on closer inspection I saw the couple. I climbed back into the truck to sit down... I was feeling light-headed. And then I called the police. I'm innocent.'*

The prosecution said that he must have started the truck while asleep, or perhaps he'd passed out.

Trevor found it interesting listening to the various theories of what might have caused the accident. So many legal minds, none of them with any clue.

In the end, the driver was found guilty of involuntary manslaughter. There were no other witnesses, and no CCTV.

Trevor went on to kill many more. He literally got away with murder and it amused him, made him believe he must be invincible. Remorse was not an emotion he was familiar with.

Looking down at this squirming man in his bedroom, Trevor wondered whether he would be lucky enough to get away with murder one more time. He'd found out that this man was having an affair with Rhonda. In the past, much lesser things had caused him to kill. For example, he'd once murdered a man who accidentally sneezed over his coffee.

Trevor's relationship with Rhonda was sour and they hadn't slept together for at least two years. He hated her, and the only reason he hadn't killed her was because he hadn't thought of a good enough plan that would ensure he would get away with it. Besides, he admitted to himself occasionally that he did love his children and wouldn't want them to lose their mother.

Rhonda had screamed when he entered the bedroom, and she'd covered herself up with the bedsheet, which he found ridiculous as he'd seen her naked body many times and had no desire to see it again. The man held up his hands as though expecting an arrest to take place. He even said 'Sorry'.

Trevor found the whole scene farcical and had had no intention of doing anything other than walking out of the room again, until he'd seen their reactions. He'd slept with many other women while married to Rhonda, hardly bothering to try to hide it.

He decided to have some fun, so shouted at the man, 'Get out of my house, you creep! What the hell do you think you're doing to my wife?'

Rhonda interjected then: 'Trevor! For fuck's sake. I'm hardly your wife anymore.'

'Then why do you look so guilty?' he'd roared.

'You sleep around all the time!'

'Do you know what this could do to our children? You're their mother. You're not supposed to be a whore!'

'Well, what sort of role-model are you? You're never around.' She got out of bed, no longer bothering to cover her nakedness, and approached him, glaring.

Rhonda's lover had got out of bed and was getting dressed quickly, fear and humiliation colouring his cheeks red.

'I should kill you,' said Trevor, staring directly at the stranger. Hearing those words coming from his own mouth filled Trevor with nostalgia.

'I didn't know she was married, she—'

'Fuck your excuses!' He'd walked over to the man and kicked him in the shin. That's when he'd fallen over and Rhonda had pushed Trevor away.

Trevor had whacked Rhonda and she fell, landing on the floor, hitting her head on the wooden leg of the bed. She passed out.

The man stood up, but Trevor had kicked him down again.

That's when he'd made the plea, 'Please don't hurt me.'

Trevor took a moment to imagine killing him, it brought a smile to his face, but knew he should leave him alone. He couldn't afford to be questioned by the police if this man went and squealed, and he couldn't kill him, because his children were in the house. 'You've got five seconds to leave this place: Five... Four...'

The man ran out of the room and out of the house at close to the speed of light.

Chapter Forty-Three

Hugh walked into the Costa coffee shop and saw Abigail seated at a table near the rear wall, a cup of coffee in front of her, reading a book. It crossed his mind that this might not have been the best choice of meeting place. Would they have an argument? As he approached, he noticed she appeared relaxed, which reassured him. He took a seat opposite her. 'Hi Abi.'

She lifted her eyes towards him. 'Hi. I was miles away. Thank you for meeting me.' She placed the book in her bag, which lay on the chair beside her. 'You look well.'

He recalled how he'd looked an hour or so ago and laughed drily. 'Thank you, so do you.' It was true; there was a peaceful aura about her. Being away from him had evidently done her the world of good. He lowered his eyes.

'Liam wants to see you, and I think it would be a good idea to agree an arrangement. I know you wanted to involve a mediator, but we don't need that.'

'I was only going to use a mediator because you wouldn't talk to me.'

Abigail sighed and nodded her head, closing her eyes briefly. 'I've had a lot of time to mull things over since we parted, and I've changed my mind. You weren't the only one to blame. But, and it's a big but, you must prove to me that you're not addicted to alcohol. Liam's safety is the most important thing.'

Hugh closed his mouth, which had fallen open in surprise. If he didn't know better he would have thought this was a different person masquerading as Abigail. 'Abi,' he started, then reached for her hand across the table.

She pulled her hand away and said, 'I'm only doing this for Liam. This isn't about me and you. I've moved on.'

'Is there someone else?'

'Why should that be any of your business?'

'Because you live with my son. I should know if you have a man living there.'

She thought of Victor. 'There's no one else. But that doesn't mean you should get any ideas about us. I'm sorry Roisin has thrown you out, but I think it would be a mistake to try to salvage something from the wreckage of our relationship just because you're lonely or desperate.'

Hugh looked down at the table, her words reminding him how cold she could be.

'The distance will be an issue,' she continued. 'It takes half an hour or so to travel between our homes. I don't want Liam using public transport on his own.'

'I'll buy or rent somewhere nearer to you.'

'On your own? So you and Roisin have split up for good?'

'Why should you care?'

'Fair enough. It's none of my business.'

'It's been difficult coping with the loss of our baby. Things haven't been right between us.'

Abigail narrowed her eyes as if contemplating whether to comment, then said, 'Losing the baby must have been hard.'

A lump came to Hugh's throat. He couldn't be sure if she was being sincere or sarcastic, but she seemed different somehow; softer.

'It's good that you'll be moving closer to Liam, but until then, what sort of arrangement should we have? How often do you want to see him?'

'Every other weeken—'

'But hang on, if Roisin has thrown you out, where will Liam be spending his time if he comes to see you? Where are you staying? Is it suitable for him?'

'I went to see Roisin today and she said I could stay at the house until I find somewhere to rent.'

'Right.'

'I could collect him every other Saturday and bring him back to yours in time for supper on Sunday, around six?' He held his breath, anticipating a scathing response.

'Hmm. Yes. That's fair.'

Hugh raised his eyebrows.

'You seem surprised.'

'No, um... All right, yes, I suppose I am. I really thought you wouldn't let me see him.'

She shook her head. 'You're his dad. He should see you. You can collect him at about ten-thirty in the morning on Saturday. I'm staying with my parents at the moment but have found somewhere for me and Liam, I'm waiting for the purchase to go through. A nice garden flat near the station—convenient for school. So, you'll pick him up on Saturday at about ten-thirty, yes?'

'Thank you. You have no idea how much this means to me.'

'Liam's intelligent. He'll know if you've been drinking. If I find out you're drinking again, I'll stop the contact.'

'I was drinking because I was going through a tough time. I'm not perfect but—'

'You don't have to explain yourself to me. None of us are perfect.

If we were, we wouldn't be in this situation, would we?' Abigail stood up. 'I haven't touched that coffee. Feel free to drink it. I have to go.' She picked up her handbag. 'I'll see you on Saturday. Liam will be looking forward to it. Don't let him down.'

Hugh stood up. 'You've changed. You seem like a different person. Thank you, Abi.'

'I'll take that as a compliment.'

'It is. I mean, I didn't mean—'

'I know what you meant. Let's try to make sure Liam's happy.'

He watched her leave, and sat down again. The smile she'd worn when they parted remained with him. He picked up the coffee. It was obviously bought for him; Abigail didn't like coffee. He sipped the drink and thought of a time when they had been happy as a couple. There'd once existed a small window of happiness. Could they ever revisit it?

Chapter Forty-Four

'I want Daddy to read me a story,' said Robbie as he climbed into bed. He turned around and Roisin pulled the blankets over him.

'I told you, Robbie, Daddy has to work.'

'He's not coming back ever, is he?'

Roisin's eyes widened. After the police visit she'd been out of her head with worry, and the meeting with Glen had only served to exacerbate her concern. Murder. She'd never imagined George would be capable of killing anyone. The police hadn't mentioned murder.

The familiar sense of guilt about having an affair rose to the forefront of her mind. Maybe whatever had ensued was a result of her betrayal.

Like the death of her baby.

She shut out the black thoughts that threatened her sanity. 'I'm sure Daddy will be back.' The words were spoken to reassure herself as much as Robbie, although she hated lying to her son, giving him false hope.

'If Daddy can't read to me today, can Hugh?'

Roisin heard the front door shut. That would be Hugh returning. 'Hugh is busy, darling. Mummy will read to you. What story would you like?'

'I want Hugh to read a story. Hugh!' Tears were forming in Robbie's eyes.

Roisin stood with her hands on her hips. 'You have to listen to Mummy, darling.'

'I don't want you. I want Daddy!'

'Well Daddy's gone, so all you've got is me! Get used to it.'

She trudged downstairs to the sound of Robbie sobbing into his blanket, feeling like a bad mother.

'I'm making a cup of tea,' said Hugh, catching her eye as she entered the kitchen.

'Fine,' she mumbled, taking a seat at the table.

'Is everything all right?' He approached her and stood beside the table.

She looked up and noticed he appeared relaxed. There was an air of peace about him, reminding her more of the man she'd fallen for. His eyes shone with the brightness that had first caught her attention.

'Robbie asked if you could read him a story. Well, he asked for George, but obviously George isn't around. Then he asked for you. I'm not enough for him, am I?'

Hugh sat next to her as the kettle clicked to indicate the water had boiled. He placed a hand on her arm.

She shook him off. 'Go and make your tea. Leave me alone.'

'Do you want me to go and read Robbie a story?'

'No!' She shot him a piercing look.

He held up his hands and stood up. 'Sorry, I was—'

'It's not you. It's me. No, it's you. Oh, for God's sake, what are we doing, Hugh? Are you back in my life, are you leaving? What's going on?' Tears fell onto her cheeks.

He sat down again and put an arm around her. This time she allowed him to hold her, lost and in need of support.

'I thought you wanted me to leave. That's why I was leaving.'

Her eyes met his, doubt clouding her mind. Would he be able to stay sober? 'Have you had a drink today?'

'No. I did have a coffee when I met Abi.'

Jealousy tugged at Roisin's heart. 'You... You saw Abi? Where?'

'In the Costa. We were talking about when I could see Liam. She was being nice. She said I can see him whenever I like. We've agreed every other weekend for now. Hey, it'll be nice for Robbie and Liam to spend time together again, won't it?'

'What made her change her mind?'

'I'm not sure, but she seems to have had a personality transplant. Maybe she's got a new man. She acted cagey when I asked her about that. She said Liam misses me.'

Roisin nodded. She'd contemplated leaving Hugh because of his drinking, had even thought briefly about getting back together with George. Was Abigail thinking the same way about Hugh?

'You and Abi.' She shrugged. 'Would you...'

'There is no me and Abi. That's in the past. I love you.'

Roisin smiled wearily.

'So, are you saying I can move back in?'

She closed her eyes briefly. 'It's your house too. I was being selfish. Even if we split up, you should still be able to sleep here. I'm sorry you had to sleep rough. But you know what my concerns are: you have to stay off the booze. Perhaps it'll help, now that you'll be seeing Liam.'

'Yes. I feel happy, Roisin, and you've made me even happier.'

He kissed her and she held him close, unable to dispel the nagging blackness that had crept into her mind and lodged there ever since George's disappearance.

Robbie walked into the kitchen as the two of them were caught up in an embrace.

'Mummy, can you read me a story?'

Roisin pulled away from Hugh and dried her tears. She put on a happy face for Robbie. 'Of course, darling. What would you like me to read?'

Robbie reached out and she took his hand, following him away from the kitchen and up the stairs.

Chapter Forty-Five

Rex had spent some time analysing the man Trevor Staines. He'd been given the opportunity to watch Trevor's past, like a movie. The invisible force that held him locked in this abyss said he had to learn as much as possible about Trevor before possessing his body. There would be no repeat of what had happened when he possessed George. This time it would be done in a way that ensured he knew everything he needed to know.

He'd witnessed flashbacks of all of the murders Trevor had committed, in gruesome detail, along with feeling exactly what Trevor had felt. Surprisingly, Trevor hadn't felt much; Rex learned that the man found murdering easy and that it gave him a "high". Trevor showed signs of being assuaged or calm after each murder; he appeared to have replenished his energies from the unspeakable act. This drew Rex closer to the man; he too had sensed retribution and relief after ending the lives of Terence and the gang. He shrugged these thoughts away, as he was aware that the voice would be able to read his mind and was no doubt keeping a record of his every reaction to Trevor's murders.

I don't want to be this man.

'Why the change of heart? I got the impression you were in awe of his behaviour.'

He's despicable, he has no conscience; he kills without remorse.

'That's an interesting observation coming from a cold-blooded killer,' came the sarcastic response.

I've changed.

'We are not convinced about that. You're motivated by a desire to be set free, it seems. Your kind would do whatever was needed to ensure freedom. I know you can easily switch your emotions on and off. As soon as you have accomplished your goal, you'll most likely revert back to the dangerous man you once were. We are willing to take a risk, however, because your actions caused an innocent man suffering.'

George?

'That's right.'

He's hardly innocent. He killed me.

'Maybe you haven't changed, if you can't see it was you who drove him to do so.'

I...

'Think of this as a sacrifice. You will be doing an altruistic thing for once in your life.'

I will spend the rest of my days in prison.

'We've already discussed that. There is no alternative. If you don't, you cease to exist.'

Backed into a corner, he answered: *I'm ready. What do I have to do?*

'We will organise everything. Trevor's life story, every memory, will be available to you when you become Trevor. The information will be there in your subconscious. For all intents and purposes you are Rex, but living in Trevor's body. Everything will become clearer when you're there. Goodbye, Rex Rodenbury. The next time we meet it will hopefully be in better circumstances.'

What do you mean "hopefully"?

'We fear that you will revert to your evil ways. For your sake, we hope that doesn't happen.'

Rex woke up in Trevor's bed. Alone. He remembered the last scene he'd watched of Trevor's life, when Trevor caught Rhonda with her lover. The voice told him he would be waking up as Trevor the day after those events.

A sour smell emanated from the sheets, which made him question whether the bedclothes had been changed since Trevor discovered Rhonda with the other man. He put a hand over his nose and stepped out of bed. He would never get used to seeing another man's naked body as his own. He walked over to the wardrobe door. Opening it, he found it was a walk-in wardrobe filled with designer clothing, both men's and women's.

Rex remembered Trevor was a rich man. Trevor made a lot of money when he came over to the UK. Selling drugs. He'd bought a luxury mansion and had a lot of money in the bank. It crossed Rex's mind that he could use the money to formulate an escape plan. He hadn't revealed this when he was on the other side for fear of jeopardising his chances of getting into a body, any body. When in oblivion, he'd been frightened, frightened enough to agree to anything. Now, however, things were different. He had a life again, and didn't want to waste it locked up behind bars for crimes he thought were justified; all he'd done was settle the score. Surely, if a higher power existed, he'd be understood. The niggling fear remained, though: the voice had given him clear instructions; he was to confess to the crimes to save George. If he didn't, he'd have to return to the state of blackness and uncertainty he'd been stranded in.

It occurred to him that he could try to work a way around this, with the riches Trevor possessed; concoct a way to get out of prison after he'd been convicted and sentenced. Surely there was a crooked judge somewhere willing to take money to allow an appeal against his sentence. Alternatively, if he found some of Trevor's contacts there was bound to be someone with enough standing in the criminal community to help him out.

He walked out of the wardrobe and over to the window in the bedroom, took the key which hung there, went into the en suite and unclipped one of the ceiling tiles. He used the key to open the inbuilt safe he'd learned of when receiving information about Trevor's life. There was a lot of money in it, and the keys to a lock-up containing more of Trevor's ill-gotten gains. He went into the bedroom and spotted a wallet on the bedside cabinet. He flipped it open and found Trevor's bank cards and other ID. Looking in the drawers in the bedside cabinet he found Trevor's passport. His memory told him Trevor owned a red sports car and the keys were kept on the table in the hallway.

Rex went back into the large wardrobe and found a pair of trousers, a shirt, and underwear, and returned to the bedroom. After getting dressed, he took a suitcase from the wardrobe and filled it with various items of clothing. He knew he wouldn't need any of the clothes in prison, but it made him feel better to think he would be a free man for at least a short while, until he had planned what he could do to secure a way out of jail. He wasn't ready to confess to the murders yet.

The bedroom door creaked open.

Rex walked out of the wardrobe and saw Rhonda standing in the middle of the room. She looked nothing like the glamorous woman Rex had seen when he'd been privy to the goings-on in Trevor's bedroom the night before; her hair was unkempt and there was a large bruise on her face. Her left eye was swollen almost shut and badly bruised. He remembered how Trevor had knocked her over during the scuffle that ensued after he'd caught her with her lover.

'You bastard.' The scowl on her face was deadly.

'Rhonda.'

'Why so formal?'

Ronnie, oh yes, Trevor calls her Ronnie. 'I'm sorry, Ronnie.'

A laugh burst from her mouth and she clutched at her chest, doubling over, obviously in pain.

The fall must have caused more injuries than he could see. When she straightened up, he saw the frown on her face.

'You could never be sorry for anything, Trev. All you fuckin' care about is yourself.'

'Ronnie, I'm a murderer.'

The confession caused Rhonda to take a sharp intake of breath. She then grabbed at her ribcage and exhaled, indicating that it was painful, and sat on the edge of the bed.

He sat down beside her.

Fixing her gaze on the carpet, she asked, 'Why did you say that?'

'Because it's true, and you need to know.' Rex was still getting used to having a southern drawl to his accent. He'd only heard the accent on TV, having never been to America.

'A murderer?'

'Yes.'

'Who did you kill? W-when?' She held a hand over her mouth, then stood up and folded her arms. 'Do I know the person you killed? Was it—'

'No, don't worry, lover boy is alive, as far as I know. I killed a few men a couple of weeks ago.'

'You said that as if it's normal. What's wrong with you? You're winding me up, right? It can't be true.' Rhonda began to laugh, but when he didn't join in with the laughter she stopped. 'Please tell me it's not true. I'm not stupid, Trev, I know you deal drugs.' She waved a hand at him, indicating she didn't want him to protest. 'I've known for years, but I figured if you're making all this money to look after the kids and keep us in this house with all the luxuries, I wasn't going to argue. To be honest, I don't care what you do, haven't cared for some time. Our marriage is in name only, as you're well aware. But murder? Please tell me you wouldn't get involved in that. What if the kids hear about it? Why on earth are you telling me this now?'

He nodded solemnly. 'The reason I'm telling you is because I'm leaving today.'

'You're going on the run?'

'Not quite. I have to confess to the crimes, or I'll die.'

Rhonda shook her head. 'I don't understand this, Trev. Did you get into a fight with a dealer, or with a drug addict? Were you defending yourself? I know you're a bastard, and you shoot your mouth off and have the worst temper I've ever seen, but a murderer? I—'

'You don't know me, Rhonda. Believe me when I say that.'

'You haven't called me Rhonda for years. It's like you're a different person.'

'Maybe I am.'

Rhonda took two steps backwards, as if afraid of him. 'What's happened to your eyes?'

He thought about the times they had turned black when he was in George's body. Joy floated over him as he contemplated turning into a spider, escaping this dead human existence.

'They turned completely black. Even the whites. Was I imagining it?'

'Must be the lighting.'

He stood up, and zipped up the suitcase, while Rhonda watched him with a startled expression on her face.

'Goodbye, Ronnie,' he said, as he walked past her and left the room. He decided he would find a local bed-and-breakfast to stay in until he had made contact with Trevor's more criminally minded friends to find out how they could help him.

Chapter Forty-Six

Roisin watched from a deck chair as Robbie and Liam played with their water pistols. Although still early spring, the sun shone, bringing with it a gentle warmth.

Hugh had been a changed man these past few days. They were getting closer with each day that passed, and this was the first time he'd seen Liam in months. Hugh hadn't stopped smiling, and the boy appeared happy.

Robbie and Liam were good friends when they used to live next door to each other, and it was as though they'd never spent a moment apart when they met again today. It warmed Roisin's heart.

She could not just relax and carry on, however. There was still no news about George. As time went by, her worry and concern heightened. She kept telling herself that one day, soon, there would be a knock at the door, and George would be standing there. For Robbie's sake, she did her best to maintain this mindset and to give the outward appearance of someone who wasn't completely devoid of hope. A numbness prevailed.

Robbie ran towards her. 'Mummy, when is Daddy coming back?'

Roisin sat up straight, her eyes widening at the unexpected question. He'd not mentioned George for a couple of days.

'I told you, sweetie, he's working.'

'Liam didn't see his dad for ages, and now he is seeing him. Am I going to see my dad too?'

Roisin couldn't help the tears making their way to the corners of her eyes. She put on a bright smile. 'Darling, your daddy loves you very much, and if he could be here he would.'

'I'm going to tell him about Liam when he comes back. Liam has been teaching me how to count in French.'

'That's nice, darling.'

'Do you know how to count in French, Mummy?'

'Yes, I do.'

'Does Daddy?'

'I think he does. You can ask him when he gets back.' She stood up to avoid any more questions, wondering whether she was wrong to give Robbie hope when she didn't know what had happened to George.

Robbie ran back to Liam, and Roisin breathed a sigh of relief.

George woke up on a park bench. Taking in his surroundings, he mused upon how he had become one of those people he would often see and ignore. Living in London, he passed homeless people every day. Whenever he did, it caused him to feel discomfort, unsure whether to smile at them, or avoid looking at them for fear it would make them feel self-conscious. He never stopped to give them money or talk to them. Homeless people had become symbolic to him of his own prejudices and sense of entitlement. He would counter his negativity by reminding himself of the sum he gave to a homeless charity by direct debit each month, but then he wondered if the money would actually benefit anyone who really needed it. He questioned the integrity of charity workers who stood on the same street as a homeless person, ignoring them, while simultaneously asking passersby to donate to the cause.

He'd never appreciated there were many ways a person might end up destitute: it wasn't necessarily their fault. To acknowledge that this was a world where anyone could end up on the streets, was something he hadn't dared to contemplate. He preferred to believe there was a reason behind it; the person might somehow have been the cause of their own downfall, or maybe chosen that way of life. Or the person begging wasn't homeless, but trying to make a bit of money.

The reality was, he realised, no one is immune to their whole world unexpectedly crumbling and falling to pieces before their eyes.

His perspective was forever altered.

He found himself with endless time, no one to talk to, nothing to do, and nowhere to go. Too much time to think. Too much.

He reminisced nostalgically about the life he had shared with Roisin, before events spiralled out of control bringing him to this point. He'd once had it all, but now he counted himself lucky to be given a cup of coffee or a sandwich by a passerby who took pity on him. Whenever it happened, he'd remember how insular and selfish he'd been before, totally ignoring those in need.

In addition to the stress of living on the streets and finding relatively safe places to sleep at night, a real concern persisted that the police would catch up with him. As a homeless person he stood out like a sore thumb to any police officer who happened to see him. He would doubtless be asked questions: his name, where he used to live, and why he'd ended up living on the streets of London.

His options were running out. He thought about getting back in touch with Glen; maybe his criminal friends could help to get him a fake ID again. But he didn't have any money.

Questioning his sanity, straining to remember what day of the week it was, he became more of a risk taker, not caring about where he settled down to sleep each night. Leaving himself open to being found.

A man had approached George a few days before and warned him to get off his patch. He'd stared at George through dead eyes, appearing inebriated, or under the influence of drugs. George avoided the area after that. He'd heard about the camaraderie that existed amongst the homeless community but was yet to experience it. Perhaps the vibe he was giving off indicated that he could go back to a privileged lifestyle whenever he wished. Whatever the reason, it made day-to-day life unbearable for him.

The night after he'd run away from Lily's house, he'd bought a bottle of whisky with the few pounds he'd collected from strangers, and had drunk most of the bottle hoping to die. Blissfulness followed, which lasted for all of ten minutes before he puked. The bottle was stolen from him by a group of teenagers who saw him lying by the side of a road.

As everything slowly fell to pieces, he became more and more obsessed with the life he'd had before. Roisin and Robbie. With every hour that went by he attempted to drum up the courage to return there, even knowing he risked being arrested.

Chapter Forty-Seven

This wasn't the deal, Rex Rodenbury.

The voice shook him awake and he looked at the clock. 4 a.m. He'd read somewhere once that spirits were around between 3 and 4 a.m. It would appear to be true.

He sat up in bed.

You have been living as Trevor Staines for days and have yet to confess to the murders. Perhaps you doubted our power. If you don't confess within the next twenty-four hours, you will cease to exist. There is no way out. Defy us at your peril.

Rex recalled how he had taunted George when he was a spirit, and felt the irony.

'I am planning to confess,' he said to no one in particular. 'You know everything, so you should know that,' he huffed. 'Oh, how I hate this accent. Can't I have my own voice back?'

You're in no position to bargain with anyone, Rex Rodenbury. You have already been given one more chance. Don't waste it.

'I beg you, give me a bit of time so I can find out if there's a way I can get out of prison once I'm in there. Trevor had many acquaintances who—'

That wasn't the deal.

'The deal was I had to help George. George will be free. Job done. Can't you let me be now?'

You have learned nothing, Rex, and you're trying my patience. Remember, the reason you're even in this predicament is because you murdered people. Serve your time, and then maybe we will rethink your fate.

'You don't scare me.'

A sharp pain pulsated through Rex's head, as if a needle had entered it. The spear-like sensation proceeded to tear through his torso, and caused him to writhe in agony as it passed along his legs. It was as though a bolt of lightning had passed straight through his body, entering his head and exiting through his feet. He collapsed back onto the bed gasping for breath.

Twenty-four hours, Rex Rodenbury.

Chapter Forty-Eight

Rex approached the police station reluctantly.

After being given the ultimatum by the voice the night before, Rex had looked up the contacts on Trevor's mobile. He first tried "Uncle Jim", because he remembered from the information he'd learned about Trevor's life, that he had an uncle who was a hardened criminal. He was the only family member that Ted Barnes, aka Trevor Staines, had in his contacts. He knew that Trevor felt a connection to this uncle because there were rumours in his family circle that Uncle Jim killed many men when he was a soldier and went on to become a criminal when he returned to the US. Trevor's parents had hated Jim, and this was one of the other reasons Trevor liked him.

Jim eventually moved to England, and he was the first person Trevor contacted when *he* moved to England. He'd stayed with his uncle for a couple of weeks before getting a new identity and going underground, however, he'd kept in touch with him over the years by sending Christmas cards and phoning him occasionally.

Perhaps the man could help. He had been willing to help Trevor when he first arrived in the UK. He soon realised, however, that he hadn't been paying attention when being told about Jim. Jim was unaware of Trevor's criminal past, and still referred to him as Ted. Jim scolded him for calling late at night when there wasn't an emergency. The man then went on to tell him that he was eighty-five years old and in poor health, listing his ailments and the medication he was taking. He then spent twenty minutes talking about his wife's funeral. Jim was annoyed at Trevor/Ted because he hadn't attended the funeral.

Rex managed to end the call eventually by saying he had to use the toilet.

The next number he called was a solicitor, whose services Trevor had used when he'd last been arrested. Rex was hoping this solicitor was crooked.

The solicitor initially thought Trevor might be calling him from a police station, so at first was interested in hearing from him. Rex used the opportunity to ask for advice: 'If, for example, I killed five men, what is the likely sentence?' It sounded stupid even to himself as he asked it.

'Are you telling me you've killed five men, Trevor?' came the response.

'No.'

'You're planning to kill five men?'

'No.'

'Good, because my advice would be *don't*. You'd never get out of prison.'

Rex hung up, realising this solicitor would be of no use. After the call, Rex scrolled through the names in the phone. There weren't many more, a dozen or so. He attempted one more, calling the number for a Huntley Page. The name struck him as familiar and he was sure he'd been told Huntley was a criminal.

The call was answered by a gruff-sounding man. 'Trev, how much do you need?'

It was late, he'd hardly slept, Rex wondered if he'd misheard the question.

'I have other customers waiting. How much?'

'I just want to speak with you.' Rex began to imagine that this man was perhaps a drug dealer. He tried to remember, but much of the information he'd learned about Trevor seemed to be distant and hard to recall.

'I'll meet you in the den in half an hour,' said Huntley.

Rex did remember he'd learned that "the den" served as a meeting place for Trevor and his drug dealer friends, located downstairs at a local nightclub where he knew the owner. But how much would Huntley be able to help with his current predicament?

'It better be worth my time, or you'll pay,' Huntley added.

The threat sounded ominous. 'Um... okay, let me run it past you now so—'

But Huntley had already hung up.

When Rex arrived at the den, a burly man greeted him at the door. 'Hello, Trev, good to see you mate. Keeping yourself out of trouble?' He followed with a hearty laugh.

As Rex walked down the stairs to the meeting place. The darkness of the stairs reminded him of the descent to the basement where he had kept those people captive at 8 Goldfern Road. He yearned to return to that simpler time, when he was in control of his fate.

The door at the bottom of the stairs was opened by a large man. Rex assumed the man must be Huntley Page.

'Trev. We meet again.'

Rex hovered beside the square table in the middle of the room.

'Sit down,' said the man, who took a seat at the opposite side of the table. The only light in the room came from the desk-lamp on the table, giving the room the feel of an interrogation suite. There were dark shadows all around, so it wasn't entirely clear if they were alone.

Rex sat down and gulped, out of his depth.

'You said you wanted to speak to me,' growled the man.

'Yes. I'm in trouble.'

'And you need my help?'

'Er... Yes. I would be grateful for any assistance.'

'Spill. I haven't got all day.'

Rex took a breath, intimidated by this large man whose eyes gleamed in the light of the desk-lamp and gave his face a sinister appearance. 'I'm going to confess to a handful of murders, and I want to avoid a lengthy prison sentence. Do you know a crooked judge we could pay cash to, or anyone on the inside who could help me?'

'I knew you were more than a ten-a-penny drug dealer, Trev. Murder is part of your DNA. You reek of it. I can smell these things from a mile away. You get the nose for it in this business, and I've been in the business a long time.

'I always knew you were a killer. My guess would be you've been killing people for years and getting away with it. My instincts have never failed me. That's how I survive in this game.'

The man seemed congratulatory of Trevor's murder spree.

Rex cleared his throat before saying, 'I killed when I was in the states, but that's history, and I got away with them. It's the recent murders I'm confessing to.'

'Why confess?'

'I won't get away with these; they're already on my tail.'

'I see.' Huntley rubbed his chin where there was an unkempt growth of beard.

'Well, do you think you can help?'

'As you're aware, my help comes with a price tag.'

'Yes, yes, I'll pay whatever. Money isn't a problem.' Rex nodded.

'Not money. I'd require you to assist with my shadier deals.'

'Wh-what kind of deals?'

'The ones that no one else will do. Murders and the like. But of course, you're skilled at all that, and I'm sure you'd be happy to help in exchange for your freedom, no?'

Rex shrugged and nodded, despite wanting to run. 'So, do you know any judges who could help?'

'Judges have to uphold the letter of the law. Stuffy individuals, difficult to sway them. Now, juries are a different matter; we can sometimes infiltrate them.

'I know people in many prisons who can help you escape: wardens, guards, police, you name it. If you pay the right price. It's a game to them, and one we play together. You know, police and criminals have always been friends. It's a tale as old as time. One needs the other. Like when we used to play cops and robbers at school; we have a kinship. They love us because we keep them in a job. We don't love them as much, of course, but they know that they owe us, so they're open to doing business. I've never had a problem with it in the past. Give the police a cut in a drug deal, for example, and they'll keep their mouths shut. As I say... a tale as old as time.'

'So you could help me?'

'Without a doubt. But I will expect you to help me too.'

'Of course.' That was the part Rex wasn't as happy about.

'Go and confess, if you must, and I will keep an eye on the news and will keep abreast of developments through my contacts in the police. As soon as we have information, such as where your trial is being heard, which prison you're likely to go to, etc., etc., we can plan further. Make sure you don't tell anyone about this conversation. If you do, you can kiss your life goodbye.'

'I won't tell anyone. Thank you.'

'Go in peace. I'll see you when you're out of prison, and we'll talk business.'

'Thank you.'

Rex left the place feeling as though he'd made a deal with the devil.

Rex parked Trevor's red sports car outside the police station knowing his next stop would be prison. Would he ever see this car again? It would remain here, battery running down, tyres going flat. They'd notice a luxury car in a place like this; it stood out. Someone might steal it.

He held onto the words he had heard from Huntley in the darkness of the den. Perhaps he would be free soon, and then he could come back and reclaim the car. But what would happen if Huntley helped him get out? He'd be released only to become one of Huntley's lapdogs. He didn't want to be under someone else's control. Maybe he would find a way to get rid of Huntley.

He thought about the poisonous spiders and this gave him hope. *One step at a time, one step at a time.*

Chapter Forty-Nine

Roisin came to the door a minute or so after George rang the bell. He saw fear in her eyes. 'Roisin, it's me.'

Her eyes widened and she turned so pale he thought she would faint.

'Are you okay? I'm sorry I startled you. I know I must look a mess. You should sit down, take a deep breath. It's the shock.' George knew Robbie would be at school, so at least he wouldn't see him in this state. It had been a while since he'd shaved, and his clothes were creased and dirty and still quite damp from last night's rain. He was wearing an old hat he'd found on the side of the road, probably discarded by its owner many days before; he hoped it made him less recognisable, concerned that police might be surveilling the area.

He found out about free shower facilities when he'd overheard a homeless man talking to a friend the day before. He'd followed them and found out where to go to get free food. For a short time he dared to believe that being homeless wouldn't be too bad. But when night fell it rained. He had been sure he'd die from pneumonia as the clothing stuck to his skin and became cold in the chill wind of the night. He'd never been forced to sleep in the rain before, having always had a home or office to run to; and he usually had an umbrella to fend off the worst of any downpour. After such a soul-destroying experience, he decided anything would be better than his current living conditions—even if it meant risking being sent to prison for life; that's when he'd decided to risk visiting Roisin.

She put a hand to her forehead. 'George? What happened to you?'

'Can I come in? The police are probably watching the house.' He stepped inside and closed the door.

'What have you done? Glen told me you were on the run.'

George walked towards the stairs. 'I'm in trouble,' he said, without turning to face her. 'If the police find me, I'll go to prison. They think I killed some people.'

'What?'

He looked at her. 'I know it's a lot to ask, but can you make me something to eat, please? I'll explain everything.'

'I'm not sure I want to know.'

'I have to tell you so you can explain it to Robbie when he's older.'

'Are you going on the run again?'

'What else can I do? I'm a wanted man.'

After a pause that seemed to last forever, Roisin shook her head and said, 'I am not sure what you've got yourself into, George, you're scaring me. I suppose I should at least hear you out.' She took a breath and signed. 'I'll make you a sandwich. Go upstairs and shave, and have a shower. You can use Hugh's shaver, and you'll find his clothes in the big wardrobe.'

'Hugh still lives here? I thought you two—'

'We're back together.'

'Right.' He nodded and turned towards the stairs.

George sat opposite Roisin at the kitchen table. He had acknowledged the sandwich and cup of coffee when he took his seat but hadn't touched them, feeling obliged to say something first, to try to explain. His mind attempted to formulate explanations, but they sounded crazy even as he thought of them, so his rational self prevented those thoughts from escaping through his mouth. It would not be easy to explain what had happened. He'd never spoken to anyone about Rex or the house, or the possession, other than Glen—and they'd suffered through a lot of the same things so it was easier to offload to him.

Roisin broke the silence, 'George, if I'm getting this right, you killed a few men when you had amnesia and are wanted by the police, is that right?'

His mouth fell open and he took a moment to think about what he'd heard her say.

'George?'

He didn't want to tell her. Once spoken out loud, it would be real, and she'd be involved. 'There are repercussions. If you know what I've done... well, what the police think I've done, will you be able to keep quiet about it?'

'I can't answer that question without knowing what all this is about.'

'Well, first and foremost, I'm innocent.'

'Right. So why are you a wanted man on the run?'

'The police have got it wrong.'

'So tell me and I might be able to help you figure a way around it.'

'About this time last year, Glen and I decided to go into that house on Goldfern Road.'

'The one I bought with Hugh?'

George nodded. 'We thought it had been abandoned, and Glen thought we could make money from it. It turned out the house hadn't

161

been abandoned. There was a man living there, just not obviously.'

'The serial killer?'

'I don't even know if he actually killed anyone, but he was planning to. He was keeping people in the basement. We ended up in the basement.'

'When you had amnesia you said you'd been captured... When did all this happen, and how on earth didn't I know about it?'

'Remember the night I said I had an injury at work?'

'When your hand was burned?'

'Yes. The injury to my hand was caused by an acid that this madman, Rex, sprayed at me.'

'This is all news to me.'

'I didn't tell you about it because I didn't want to involve you.'

'How did you get out?'

'We basically fought our way out. We called the police. Rex was arrested, but he got out of prison, or the mental hospital, or whatever—I was told he was treated in a psychiatric ward—I'm not clear on the details. He was rich. We wondered whether he'd paid his way out. I think he might even have left against doctors' orders, because he obviously wasn't well when we saw him again. When we met him at one of the neighbours' parties he agreed to sell the house to us. Then he tried to kill us again.'

'Party? What party?'

'We got to know the neighbour who lived next door. Theo.'

'You did? He spoke to me and Hugh when we went to view the house. Seemed like a nice man. I had no idea he knew you. When did you go to his party?'

'It was his eightieth birthday. He invited me and Glen. It was around the time you announced you were pregnant.'

Roisin looked at the table. 'Why haven't you told me any of this before?'

'I didn't want to involve you. It was a stupid money-making plan that went wrong.'

'I knew Glen would be behind this.'

'As much as I'd love to put all the blame on him, I know I went along with everything.'

'So what happened?'

'I killed Rex. I had to.'

'You killed him?'

'In self-defence, yes. And I burned the house down.'

'So that's why they're after you?' She held her forehead. 'So that's why you were having nightmares.'

'They never knew I'd killed him. They thought he died in the fire along with his criminal friends who were helping him.'

'There were more people in the house when you burned the house down?'

'Only the two criminals who had helped him capture us.'

'Do you even know what you're saying?' She stood up. 'How can you be so calm? You killed three men, and the police have found out and you're going on the run. What are you, some kind of psychopath? Don't you have any feelings, any remorse?'

'It was self-defence, they could have killed us.'

'If it was self-defence, why on earth would you be going on the run? Why not simply explain it to them?'

'You don't know the whole story.'

Roisin took a step back. 'I don't need to hear any more. You're a murderer.'

'No! It was self-defence. Aren't you listening?'

'You killed people, and now the police are looking for you.'

'There's more to it than that. They're not looking for me because of that. I'll try to explain. Please sit down, you're making me nervous.'

'I'm the one who should be nervous, I don't know what you're capable of.'

'Stop being dramatic. You've lived with me for years.'

'Yes, and evidently there is a lot I didn't know about you.'

'Please, sit down and I'll tell you why the police are looking for me. I'm innocent, by the way.'

Roisin sat on the chair opposite him but not before moving it further away from the table, as if she were afraid of being too close to him.

'Rex was stalking me from beyond the grave.'

'Beyond the grave? He was a ghost? You expect me to believe this?'

'I knew you wouldn't believe me. You've watched enough of those ghost-hunting programmes, I thought you believed in ghosts.'

'I'm curious about stuff like that, but it doesn't mean I believe it. What proof do you have?'

'Proof? That's the problem. I don't have any proof, except what Glen saw and heard too. He kept threatening me—'

'Glen?'

'No, the ghost.'

'Threatening what?'

'He ordered me to find him a poisonous spider so he could possess its body, because he always wanted to be a spider. I found him a spider. I put it in the house, and Rex possessed it, and then Hugh killed the spider.'

She stood up. '*You* put the poisonous spider in the house? It was you. Hugh said it was. But when I asked you, you lied, said you had amnesia.'

George stood up to face her. 'That wasn't me. Rex possessed my body.'

'Rex put the spider in the house?'

'No. I did, but then he possessed my body when Hugh killed the spider.'

'This is something you and Glen came up with, isn't it? He told me this crazy possession story. That man has always been a bad influence on you. How can you try to get away with murder? Don't you see that the longer you go untreated, the more chance there is that you will kill again.'

George hung his head. 'The longer I go untreated? I'm not going through some kind of mental illness. I'm telling you what happened. It all happened. It was real. This is why I didn't tell you before, because I knew you wouldn't understand!'

'I understand all right. I understand that you killed three men and then started hearing voices in your head and thought Rex was talking to you. Maybe it was the guilt. You're a good man, George... Well, you *were* a good man. You've changed; you're different. You should have gone for therapy if you weren't well. But you didn't, did you? You believed this man was talking to you, but he wasn't. It's madness! That spider killed my baby. The spider that you put in the house. Can you see that now, or are you still delusional? Your actions caused a tragedy. *Your* actions, George, not a dead man's. Do you see that? You need help.'

'I knew you'd think I was mad. Anyone would. That's precisely why I haven't told the police.'

Roisin began to cry. She took a tissue from the box on the table and wiped her eyes. 'I should hand you in to the police myself.'

George sat down and looked at the sandwich in front of him, which he had not yet touched. He began to eat, although he'd lost his appetite. He picked up the cup of coffee, and took a sip to find it was cold.

Roisin sat opposite him again. There was extreme tension in the air.

George knew he couldn't convince her he was telling the truth. Even he was struggling to believe what had happened. 'Please, don't go to the police. Let me explain. After the spider was killed, Rex appeared to me again. He was dressed as a spider, in a hideous spider costume he used to wear, and then the next thing I knew I was somewhere else—in darkness without a body, floating somewhere. Rex said he wanted to use my body. That must be when he possessed me. It happened so fast.'

'Your madness killed my daughter. My beautiful daughter. I've been thinking it might be karma because I had an affair behind your back. My beautiful baby is dead because of your madness, George. How could I ever forgive you?'

'It wasn't me, it was The Spider.'

'You put the spider there!'

'He possessed it—that's what he used to call himself: *The Spider.* He's dangerous! He possessed me and killed five men. The police want me for those murders.'

Roisin stood up and pushed her chair towards the table. 'There's something wrong with you. You need help.'

'Roisin—'

'There is no dead ghost spider-man, for God's sake. And I should be bringing charges against you for putting the spider in the house. It could have killed me or Hugh or Robbie.' She held her throat, let out a breath and said, 'I feel sorry for you, I do; whatever illness has taken over your mind, it's dangerous. Who knows what you're capable of? Finish your sandwich. I'll give you some money so you can find somewhere to sleep tonight, but I want you to stay away from me.'

'But what about Robbie?'

'You could have killed him by putting that spider in the house when you knew we might go there. I don't want you to see him. Not now.'

'You can't stop me seeing my son.'

'It's not forever, but you have to understand, the way you've been lately... I can't.'

'But—'

'I've told him you're working abroad. If you get help for your condition, whatever it is, then we'll talk again. You killed eight men. *You.* Not a ghost. *You* killed them. For all I know, you might kill me.'

'I won't... How could you say that?'

'I have to admit, I'm scared of you and what you're capable of. You obviously have no understanding of what you've done or how serious it is. You have to get help. Please leave after you have your sandwich, or I'll call the police.'

'But—'

Roisin walked out of the kitchen.

Her reaction to his story made him appreciate how unbelievable it sounded. There was no way out of this never-ending nightmare. He began to doubt his own mind. Had he imagined everything? The haunting, the threats, the visions of Rex. Maybe he, and only he, had killed those men. It didn't bear thinking about.

Chapter Fifty

George knew that the police could be watching Glen's flat. He made the decision to visit Glen under cover of darkness, but not too late as he wanted other people to be around so he didn't stand out. He'd been on edge all day since leaving Roisin's house, waiting for that tap on the shoulder.

As he approached Glen's flat his stomach tensed and he imagined police jumping out of a car across the road and pointing guns towards him. He rang the doorbell and waited, checking his watch. It was just after 9 p.m.

He waited for nearly a minute without a response. Where could Glen be? Probably in the pub. But he daren't go there. The regulars knew him, and it was possible that the police may have been in there recently looking for him. His sense of being "on the run" became all the more real as he stood outside Glen's flat.

He tensed at the sound of footsteps behind him. Had they found him? They'd take him to the station, charge him with murder, lock him up and throw away the key.

'Can I help you?'

George had never been happier to hear Glen's voice. He turned around to face his friend.

'George!'

'Keep your voice down, police might be around.'

'Sorry.' Glen walked past him and put a key in the door. 'Come in, mate. Where have you been?'

Once inside the flat, Glen blurted, 'George, what's going on? I thought you died in that terror attack. Why didn't you get in touch? I've been going out of my mind.'

'You knew where I was going. I'm supposed to be on the run, remember?'

'I know, but when that attack happened at the airport I tried phoning you—'

'I had to get rid of my phone or the police would've been able to trace me.'

Glen was quiet for a moment, then sighed and said, 'I suppose.'

'Oh, and I lost my fake ID.'

'Well, I'm glad you're okay, but you have to be careful, this is one of the first places the police would come looking for you.'

'I know that, but I can't live on the streets anymore.'

'On the streets?'

'I've been sleeping rough for the past week or so. Not sure how long. I want my life back.'

'You don't look like you've been sleeping rough.'

'I went to see Roisin earlier, had a shower and a shave. These are Hugh's clothes.'

'Hugh lent you his clothes?'

'Roisin said I could take them. He wasn't there. I was desperate, okay?'

'What did Roisin say?'

'She doesn't believe I was possessed. I thought she was gonna call the police. She doesn't want me to see Robbie.'

Glen shook his head. 'I'm just glad you're alive. Go into the living room; I'll make some coffee.'

Ten minutes later they were both seated in Glen's living room.

'I hope you remembered to boil the kettle this time,' said George, with mock humour, in an effort to lighten the mood.

'Ha. That joke's wearing a bit thin.'

George took a sip of coffee and smiled. 'It's good to see you again.'

A key turned in the front door and it creaked open.

The conversation ceased temporarily as they waited.

George wondered if it might be the police. Did they have a key for the place? Wouldn't they crash through, knocking the door off its hinges, like in TV cop shows? He held his breath, and then watched as Petula entered the room with a bright smile on her face, which soon turned to a frown when she saw him.

He lowered his eyes.

'George? I thought you were—'

'On the run, yes.'

'I— Sorry, George. Glen, can I have a word?' She left the room.

Glen shrugged as George caught his eye. 'I'll be right back.'

Glen returned to the living room a few minutes later. George had tried to listen in to the couple's conversation, but had only managed to catch a few words.

'Pet's worried that if you stay here the police will come and we'll be in trouble. It's an offence, apparently—harbouring a criminal, or perverting justice. She has a criminal record, doesn't want any trouble.'

George stood up. 'I'll leave if it's gonna be a problem. The last thing I want is to get you or Petula in trouble.'

'Sit down, mate, Pet's making a cup of tea. She wants to hear more about what the police said before she decides what we should do.'

Petula walked into the room and sat opposite George, next to Glen on the sofa. 'George, forgive me, I didn't mean to be rude. I—'

'No, really, I understand. You don't want a criminal in your house.'

'No. You've got me wrong, I'm not exactly innocent myself. I've been to prison.'

'Glen did mention something.'

'Glen? What have you been saying about me behind my back?'

Glen gulped. 'I only mentioned it because George was worried he would go to prison and—'

Petula giggled. 'I'm pulling your leg. That's ancient history, and I'm not planning to repeat it.' She looked at George. 'It was before I met up with Glen again, I was in a bad way. My life's completely different now.' She smiled.

George nodded.

'It wasn't as serious as murder, of course. Shoplifting. But still, I'm in no position to judge.'

'What's it like in prison? How long were you there? Um... if you don't mind me asking.'

'I hated it. I was only there for a week and was so glad to get out. It was a women's prison, though. Women can be horrible to each other. I don't know what men's prisons would be like.'

'Men's prisons are much worse than women's ones,' said Glen.

'And you would know that, how?' said George.

'I saw a documentary once, and I've heard from people who've been inside.'

'You're not helping,' snapped George.

'You're not going to prison, mate,' said Glen, calmly. 'Relax.'

'You're sure about that, are you?' sneered George. 'Five bloody murders, that's what they think I've done.'

'When did you last hear from the police?' asked Petula. 'You might have a defence.'

'We've discussed that, ain't we George?' said Glen.

'Yeah, but whatever story I go with, the amnesia or the possession, it sounds unbelievable. I really don't know what to do.' George let out a breath. 'When I told Roisin today, she didn't believe me, and now she won't let me near Robbie. I don't stand a chance with the police and the courts, they'll see me as a delusional serial killer.' He held his head.

'I've just had a thought,' said Glen.

'God help us.' George rolled his eyes.

'Charming. I'm trying to help you.'

'The last thought you had is what caused this chaos. If it wasn't for you—'

'Stop it.' Petula held up a hand. 'There's no point blaming each other, we have to find a way out. What was your thought, Glen?'

'I could give evidence for George. There's enough evidence that we were captured by Rex. We were questioned by the police at the time. I could mention what we saw: when he turned Roisin and Hugh into spiders.'

'No one's gonna believe that,' George huffed.

'But if both of us say the same thing—'

'They'll think you're lying for me because you're my friend.'

'That would be perversion, wouldn't it?'

'Perverting the course of justice,' corrected Petula.

'It's not lies, though,' said Glen. 'It happened.'

'I know, but it sounds ridiculous,' sighed George. 'What do you think of it, Petula? Doesn't it sound crazy when I say I was possessed, and wouldn't it sound ridiculous if Glen gave evidence that he saw a ghost turn my ex and her new man into spiders?'

'I... I don't know what to say. It's possible they would take it seriously and look into it,' said Petula, shrugging.

'Huh, you're just being polite,' blurted George. 'It sounds absurd and no one will believe it.'

'It's a lot to get your head around that's for sure,' said Petula.

'You have no idea,' said Glen.

'So these five people you're meant to have murdered, why hasn't it been on the news?' she asked. 'Who were they?'

'It has been on the news. It was a house in Brimstown Avenue. The dead bodies were found in the—'

'Garage!' Petula exclaimed.

'What?' said Glen and George together.

'Why did you say it like that, Pet?' Glen peered at her.

'I heard about that on the news but wasn't really paying attention and somehow didn't link the two. But it's good news, George.'

'How?'

'A man has confessed to the murders. Let me look it up online, hang on.' She practically ran out of the room while Glen and George looked at each other, bemused.

Petula returned shortly and passed her phone to George. 'There, look, there it is. Looks like you're in the clear.'

George began to read from the news story: '*Yesterday afternoon a man walked into Kent Road police station and handed himself in, confessing to the Brimstown Avenue murders...* Hang on this article was written on Monday. So I've been stressing out for no reason for the past few days.'

'What does it say, George? Who handed himself in? It doesn't

169

make sense.' said Glen.

George read on, '*Trevor Staines, a businessman, stated that at the time of the murders he was going through mental health issues due to the stress of working long hours. In a four hour police interview, Mr Staines described in detail how he killed the men, giving information that only the killer would have known. The police are not looking for anyone else in connection with the murders. Mr Staines will be remanded in custody until his trial.*'

'Good old Mr Staines,' cheered Glen.

'But... How?'

'Who cares?' said Glen. 'Come on, mate, this calls for a celebration. Let's go for a pint. Wanna join us, Pet?'

'No. I'm having an early night, the late shift at the library took it out of me.'

'Okay, love, see you in the morning. Come on, George.'

'I don't understand.' George's brain felt fuzzy. Could he be dreaming? Who was Trevor Staines? *Too good to be true*, was a thought that sprung to mind, and he couldn't help wondering if it was a joke. He expected to wake up at any moment on a park bench in the rain. He pinched himself discreetly.

'Stop questioning it, George. You're a free man.'

They headed to The Red Lion, George's mind in a whirl.

Chapter Fifty-One

'That man. No, don't turn around. He was snooping around a couple of weeks ago, asking about you. Something about gold.'

'What man?' George was tempted to turn around but was put off by what appeared to be fear in Glen's eyes. His mind grappled with an image of Rex dressed in the spider costume sitting on a bar stool behind him, eyes as black as coal. 'Is it anything to do with Rex?' he blurted.

'Yes,' said Glen, still peering over George's shoulder.

The colour drained from George's face. Would he ever be free of that man? Just when he thought his luck might be changing, the black cloud of doom that represented Rex hovered close by, yet again. 'Is he in here?'

Glen wrinkled his brow and turned his attention back to George. 'Yes, I just said—'

'Rex is here? Oh, my God!'

'Not Rex. What are you on about? Rex is dead.'

'You said it had something to do with Rex and you're looking at someone.'

Glen looked him in the eye. 'George, the person I'm looking at is alive and well. Rex is dead.'

'That didn't stop him before. Death isn't as simple as it's made out to be. There are lots of things we don't know. I've experienced it.' George was again tempted to turn around and look at what Glen was looking at, but a subtle fear stopped him.

'You didn't die, George.' Glen picked up his pint of beer and took a couple of sips.

'No, but I'm sure where I ended up when Rex possessed me was where dead people end up.'

'What was it like?'

'Complete blackness. It was scary at first, well, not so much scary, more unsettling. I had no idea where I was and couldn't feel my body.'

'Maybe because Rex had your body.' Glen chuckled.

'Everything's a joke to you.'

'Put yourself in my shoes; imagine if it was me saying this to you. Would you believe me?'

'Yes, I would, but I've been there. We don't just die. There were angels, and they said there are malevolent spirits that never die. They said Rex is a malevolent spirit.'

'What like Angelina Jolie in that film?'

'What?'

'Malevolent. That was the film, wasn't it? She was an evil fairy.'

'That was *"Maleficent"*, and this has got nothing to do with fairies. Rex is an evil spirit.'

'Rex has gone. I really think he's gone for good, so let's forget him.'

'How can you be so sure?'

'We haven't heard from him for ages.'

'Huh, you're not the one who was possessed. What were you saying before about a man in here asking about me and gold, something to do with Rex?'

Glen lowered his voice and leaned towards George. 'The man behind you, knows one of the men who was murdered when Rex was in your body.'

George twisted in his chair.

Glen put up a hand. 'No, don't look, he'll know I'm talking about him. He seems to be some sort of criminal. He saw you leave the house after, you know.'

'But Rex didn't murder anyone. The real killer confessed—'

'Loonies confess to crimes they ain't done all the time, don't they?'

'What are you saying?'

'All I'm saying is, people confess, and then years later they get released. The case ends up being reopened.'

'This isn't making me feel any better. I thought we were here to celebrate me being a free man.'

'We are. I'm just saying, this man who's confessed, he's obviously not the killer, is he? We know that.'

George took a quick glance around to make sure no one was listening to the conversation. No one was in earshot, and most of the people were having loud conversations, not showing any interest in anyone else. He breathed with relief and continued in a half-whisper, leaning towards Glen: 'Look, I didn't murder anyone. I don't give a flying fuck who this bozo is who's confessed to the crime. He might have done it. I have no recollection, so let's change the subject.'

'Okay, but that man, I'm wondering what he's doing here. And I'm sure I'm not imagining it, he keeps looking at us. He might still be after you.'

'After me?'

'As I said, he thinks you know about the gold.'

'What gold?'

'The last time he was in here he said he thought you might know where some gold is being hidden. He'd helped one of the dead men steal gold years ago and he wanted his share. Seemed frustrated and angry.'

'Great. Why don't we go back to yours for a couple of drinks?'

'We can't keep avoiding the pub forever. It's our local. He's the one who should be leaving if anyone is.'

'Are you gonna ask him to leave?' asked George flippantly.

'Maybe I should.'

'Glen... No, Glen, I was kidding.'

Glen had already stood up and was approaching the man. George kept his head down while surreptitiously watching what was happening.

'We meet again,' the stranger said as Glen approached him. 'Does your friend have any information for me?' He stood up to face Glen.

'Mate, you can't keep stalking us. I told you the last time, he wasn't involved, so I suggest you leave.'

'Firstly, I'm not your mate, and secondly, you're not the landlord of this pub. You can't tell me to leave. I've been waiting for your friend to show his face. I have questions for him.'

'You should be asking Trevor Staines.'

'Who the fuck is that?'

'It was on the news. He's the one who killed Derek Cole. He's handed himself in. If anyone knows anything, he does.'

'I saw your friend leave the house.'

'My friend was in the wrong place at the wrong time. Trevor has confessed to the murders, so he must've been there at the same time. You missed him when you were stalking my friend.'

'Is there a problem, gents?' Craig, the landlord, was now standing next to the pair whose voices had been louder than they realised.

'Um... No, this man was about to leave, weren't you?' said Glen.

The man peered at him through narrowed eyes. 'If I find out you're lying to me, I'll be back, and next time I won't be so friendly.'

Glen noticed the deathly silence in the pub around him and began to feel self-conscious.

'Now, now, less of that,' said Craig. 'I won't have any threatening behaviour in my pub.'

'Don't worry, I'm leaving.'

Glen watched him leave and then walked back to where George was seated.

'Blimey, Glen, did you have to cause a scene?'

'So that's the thanks I get for standing up for you?'

'I know what you were trying to do, but if he's a criminal you were taking a risk. He could easily come back with his friends.'

'Don't worry, it's sorted. He won't be back. He'll be looking for Trevor.'

'I hope you're right.'

'I'd like to raise a toast to Trevor,' said Glen, lifting his glass.

'I'll second that,' said George. 'If I ever meet the man, I'll be sure to buy him a drink.'

'I doubt you'll ever meet him; he'll be in prison for the rest of his life. Five murders. They'll throw away the key.'

'I was so sure Rex killed those men.'

'Well, he obviously didn't. Maybe Trevor is one of Rex's criminal mates and he got him to kill them. Maybe Rex set it up. Who knows? None of it matters anymore. You're free.'

Chapter Fifty-Two

Rex lay in the prison cell staring at the ceiling. He could hear his cellmate, Johnny Dregs, snoring in the bunk beneath him.

The size of the man was intimidating, and it took Rex back to how he'd felt as a child when Terence and his gang would pick on him.

Johnny had mocked the American accent when Rex first spoke to him: 'Ha, ha. I can see why you came to England to commit your crimes. In the US you would'a been put in the electric chair, or given a lethal injection, right? They're soft on criminals over here.'

Johnny had introduced himself by announcing, 'Hi, I'm Johnny. You can call me Sir. I killed my wife, what're you in for?'

Earlier this evening, the man had told Rex the whole story about the murder of his wife, before falling asleep. He'd had the excited look of a child relating an adventure story when he described how he'd planned the murder and eventually killed her.

'Obviously, I've told the lawyers and the police that I didn't do it, but between me and you she was a fucking whore and I'm glad she's dead. Don't tell them, though. If you tell them I'll have to kill you, and I don't wanna do that because I think you and me could be good friends. I have a plan for when I get out, and you could join me. It will make us millions, and we'll live like kings.'

Rex had mostly ignored what Johnny said until he heard *"When I get out"*.

'Do you have a release date yet?'

'No, not yet, but there's no way they'll find me guilty.'

'How are you so sure you'll get out? And me. I've killed five men. Unlikely I'll get out.' Rex was holding on to the hope that this man might have a decent escape plan. He waited for the answer.

'They don't have anything to prove it, man. I'm denying it all. Did you deny it?'

'Um... No, I confessed.'

'Oh, man, it ain't looking good for you. But I know this copper. He was a fresh-faced PC when I met him, now he's a Super. That's one more reason there's no way I'll be convicted. We used to be close, y'know what I mean? He's in the closet, married, with kids—big Super. He wouldn't want his past coming out, he's scared he'll lose his wifey and reputation. I mentioned his name to my lawyer, and he's going to look him up.'

'But you can't choose which police officer investigates your case, can you?'

'No, but there's ways. All these coppers know each other. He'll get

175

the word across to his buddy who's working on my case.'

'That's not the way things work, though. Your trial will have a jury.'

'With any luck, it won't get as far as a trial.'

Rex was sure this man was living in cloud-cuckoo-land, to believe he could blackmail the superintendent, but a small part of him wanted to go along with his deranged fantasy. He remembered back to what Huntley had told him about the crooked prison wardens and police he knew. Rex had heard news stories about corrupt police officers, so he was aware they existed. It might be better for him to get help from Johnny's "Super" rather than Huntley's contacts. Huntley's set-up would mean he remained indebted to the man and would be entangled in a criminal underworld where danger would constantly be present. Perhaps this was an easier way out.

'Do you think your Super friend could help me?' he asked.

'That depends. If you're willing to help me out, I could help you out, y'know what I mean?' The man winked.

'You mean...?' Rex gulped.

'Yeah, man. It'll be painless, I promise. We could be good together, me and you. So much time stuck inside, a man gets restless. You can imagine I'm a woman if you like. Some men like to do that.'

Vomit rose in Rex's throat. He adjusted his pained expression and said, 'Give me time to think about it.'

'Take your time. But know this, I'm your sure fire way to get out of this shit hole; and let's face it, if you don't play with me, there are plenty of others who'll just take you. Not everyone is as considerate as me, and you're a good looking bloke.'

Johnny was now snoring so loudly, the sound reverberated off the walls.

As Rex stared up at the ceiling in the dying light, he contemplated what he'd been told by the madman. Johnny had enormous self-belief, so sure he'd get out. Rex had forgotten to ask him if he'd managed to blackmail that police officer before. If it had worked before, it would be more likely to work again. He baulked at the thought of what Johnny wanted him to do, but it was merely a means to an end: it wasn't even his own body that would be violated but Trevor's. Still, even the idea was revolting. He remembered Huntley's offer to help. The man in the den had presented as far more sinister than this man. Having more than one option was good. The idea that freedom was not an impossible dream fed Rex's imagination as he began to contemplate what he'd do if he got out of prison. The thoughts were enticing. The voice from the abyss, and all its warnings, seemed so far away, like a nightmare he'd once had. Eventually he drifted into a fitful sleep.

Chapter Fifty-Three

It was too late to go and see Roisin by the time George left the pub, so he headed home but vowed to himself to contact her soon. The day's events had motivated him. He knew she had concerns about his mental health after their recent conversation, but he hoped that now it was proven he hadn't been involved in the murders she would not be afraid of him. She would still have to be convinced about his integrity, however, as there was no easy way of getting around the fact that he had placed the deadly spider in the house.

As he approached the communal entrance door, he remembered he had no keys; they'd been lost in the debris at the airport. It panicked him to think of spending yet another night sleeping rough. Seeing no other option, he decided to ring the neighbours' doorbell and ask them to let him in; they shared the same communal door. He'd never met the couple who lived upstairs, only seen them once or twice entering or leaving their property. A thought occurred to him after he rang the bell, what if Rex had met them and had been rude to them?

A man's voice sounded through the speaker outside the door. 'Hello?'

'Hi, sorry to bother you at this time of night. It's George from downstairs. I've lost my key. Could you buzz me in, please?'

'Wait a minute, I'll come down,' said the man, whose voice conveyed a hint of annoyance.

George had almost given up on being let inside when the door was opened by a large man dressed in a dark-green towelling robe. His attire caused George to feel bad again for disturbing him.

'Hello,' said the neighbour. 'Lost your key, hey?'

'Yes, thank you so much for letting me in.'

'I haven't let you in yet,' said the man, who was large enough to block the front door.

George was caught off guard by the comment.

The man followed with a laugh and stepped aside.

George echoed his laughter, out of awkwardness.

'We haven't met properly,' stated the man extending a hand. 'I'm Peter.'

George shook Peter's hand, 'I'm George. I only moved in recently.'

'Yes, I know that much.' Peter laughed, causing George to wonder once again how much contact Rex had had with this man while living in his body. 'We've lived here, Lia and me—my wife—for about five years,' said Peter. 'It's a great place to live. You'll like it. Have you settled in?'

'I'm trying to. It's been a bit up and down.'

'Understood. Maybe we can go out for a drink sometime, or you can come up to ours for a meal?'

'Maybe.' George had no intention of getting to know this couple. He preferred to keep his neighbours at arm's length. In this type of set-up, living downstairs from the couple, it would be unbearable for him to be expected to have a conversation with them every single time he saw them. He preferred neighbours he could say hello to and politely nod at now and then.

After nodding politely and bidding Peter goodnight, he realised that he wouldn't be able to open the door to his flat. His plan to run inside and get away from the man had failed.

'Oh, dear,' said Peter. 'Lost your door key as well?'

'They were on the same keyring,' said George grumpily.

'I can change the lock for you,' offered Peter. 'I'm sure I have spares upstairs. I rent properties for a living, so it won't be a problem. I'm always having to change locks when tenants move in and out. I think I have a spare key for the communal entrance door too. You can have it.'

George began to warm to Peter. Perhaps it would be worth getting to know him. He breathed a sigh of relief and turned towards him: 'Thank you so much. That would be amazing.'

Peter smiled and headed upstairs.

Half an hour or so later, George was inside his flat. He'd invited Peter in for a drink to thank him for changing the lock.

They were seated on the sofa when Peter said, 'I hope you don't mind me asking, but I noticed there were police here recently and you haven't been around for a while. Is everything okay?'

'Yes, fine.' George tried not to choke on his whisky. 'It was a mistake. They were given this address, probably to do with the previous tenant.'

'Who? Old Miss Barnes? Unlikely,' said Peter, chuckling, and managing to splatter whisky on George's face in the process.

George discreetly wiped the spots of drink away. 'Well, they did say it was a mistake, they were looking for someone else. Can't remember the name.'

'Sometimes criminals give the police the wrong address, I suppose.'

'It was probably that,' said George.

'So where have you been this past week? Me and the missus thought you might be in prison.' He laughed.

George faked a laugh before replying, 'I've been working abroad.'

'Sounds good. Anywhere nice?'

'Just France.'

'You say that so flippantly. I'd love to go to France. Me and the wife have never been able to afford much travel. The furthest I've been is Dorset. But with the unrest, wars and the like, it's probably safer to stay at home these days. Did you hear about the terrorist attack at Gatwick airport? Scary times.'

George had a flashback to the disaster. 'It was terrible,' he said. The face of the young woman he'd discovered underneath the wooden board flashed before him, and was shortly followed by the face of Flora Murphy, whose luggage he'd taken. He took a deep breath.

'Can you imagine being caught up in something like that? You should look after yourself. Do you travel a lot for work?'

'Not really.' George stood up and yawned.

'It's late,' said Peter, finishing his drink. 'I'd better get back to Lia, she'll be wondering where I am.'

'Thanks again for changing the lock. How much do I owe you?'

'A pound of flesh.'

A frightening thought gripped George: Rex may have possessed this man's body. He gulped.

Peter's laugh soon brought him back to reality.

'It's a famous line from "*The Merchant of Venice*", you know, the Shakespeare play.'

'Right. Yes, of course.'

Peter laughed again. 'Me and Lia are part of the local am-dram. We're putting on a show next month at the church hall. You should come along.' He walked towards the door.

George had a fitful night. He fell asleep straight away after Peter left, but then had a vivid dream of Peter entering the flat and telling him that he kept a spare key in case he had to check for dead bodies. When George questioned him as to why he would have to look for dead bodies, he replied that he knew about the murders and demanded a pound of flesh. The imagery then shifted, and George found himself with Glen on the spinning spiderweb at 8 Goldfern Road. Peter threw something onto the web as it spun around; George became increasingly dizzier. Peter then took off a mask, revealing himself to be Rex.

George woke up and was unable to get back to sleep for hours. He feared falling asleep in case he dreamt more of the same. "Lullaby" by *The Cure* got stuck in his head on repeat, making it even harder for him to sleep.

He eventually got out of bed and made a warm drink, but all the while he had the sensation that he was being watched and kept expecting Rex to jump out or appear as a spider. On returning to the bedroom he noticed a small spider climbing up the wall, so he decided to sleep on the sofa in the living room, just in case.

The sleepless night had left George shattered. His head pounded like it was hosting a party to which he hadn't been invited. He decided to make a cup of coffee before committing to anything else. He'd planned on going to see Roisin, but wasn't sure he could convince her of anything in his current state.

After having a coffee, George regained some energy. He checked his e-mails. There was a three-day-old e-mail from his boss enquiring as to when he'd be going back to work. He remembered the chat he'd had with his boss when he gave him the medical certificate, and began to feel guilty for taking more time off when there was nothing wrong with him.

He replied to the e-mail saying that he was much better and would return to work the following Monday. That allowed him time to organise things beforehand. There was an element of fear and trepidation about going back to work. Would he be capable of holding down the job? So much had changed, and he was still coming to terms with a lot of the changes; but he could not afford to be out of work.

George became nostalgic for what he and Roisin once had, but realised the futility in his thinking: the last time he'd seen her she'd told him she and Hugh were still together.

He recalled how she'd tried to rekindle their relationship recently and regretted how easily he'd shrugged off her advances. Their marriage had been good for many years. It made him question whether he was the one who'd made more mistakes. Perhaps he'd driven her into Hugh's arms. Regardless of whether there was any kind of future for them, one thing was certain, he had to regain her trust if he was ever going to be able to see Robbie again. When he'd been living alone on the streets, the thought of getting his life back on track so he could spend time with Robbie was the main thing that had kept him going.

He decided to leave it for a few days, remembering how adamant Roisin had been that he couldn't see Robbie when he'd visited her the day before. If he went back so soon, she would surely throw him out, or even call the police as she had threatened to. She needed time to calm down. Once he had started back at work and his life was in some sort of order, he would go and see her, prove to her that there was no reason to fear him.

Chapter Fifty-Four

Rex was awoken by a loud crashing sound. On opening his eyes he found he was inside the prison cell, which he had hoped was a just a nightmare, not reality.

'You're awake.'

Rex heard the words and then caught a whiff of stale breath as Johnny leaned over the top bunk.

'Morning Trev. Have you had time to think about our deal?'

'Deal?' Rex remembered the conversation they'd been having the evening before. Looking at this man repulsed him, and he couldn't contemplate the idea of allowing him to even touch him. He sat up and pulled as far away from the ogre-like man as was possible in such a small confined space. 'Um... yes. I have thought long and hard about it, but I cannot betray my true love. You see, I have a lover who's waiting for me outside.' The excuse came to him without forethought.

'He'll be waiting a long time, Trev,' said Johnny. 'You're not getting out anytime soon, at least not without my help, if ya know what I mean.'

'He? It's a she. She's my wife.' His thoughts turned to Trevor's wife. He allowed himself the luxury of wondering whether he could maybe try to seduce her when he got out of prison.

'You're in the closet, Trev. It couldn't be more obvious.'

'I am not.'

'Keep fooling yourself. I can tell from a mile away. I feel sorry for men like you. Why not face up to it? Me and you could have fun.'

'I'll help you in other ways. I have useful contacts on the outside who will be helping me to escape. I could help you in lots of ways when we get out. There must be many others in here who would gladly satisfy your other needs. I could help you find someone, if you like.'

'I already have plenty of offers, thanks. I thought you'd appreciate a bit of one on one. I have a sixth sense for these things, and if I didn't know better I'd say you were a virgin.'

Rex was in awe for a moment. How did Johnny know? How could he tell from this limited time together? His defences then kicked in and he blurted, 'I'm a married man.'

'I know, but you've never been truly satisfied, have you? You're gay, Trev. You need me.'

The door to the cell opened and the two men were ordered to follow the rest of the inmates and join them for breakfast.

Johnny winked at Rex as they left the cell.

181

Chapter Fifty-Five

Abigail couldn't stop thinking about Hugh. When he'd told her he was no longer with Roisin and would be moving nearer to her, a seed was planted in her heart.

He'd changed. He'd given up the alcohol. When he'd brought Liam back on Sunday evening after the first weekend contact they'd had, she nearly fell in love with him all over again. It was wrong—she was in a new relationship now—but Victor didn't spark the flame that Hugh did.

She'd met Victor on an online dating site when in a low mood, convinced at the time that finding love would make everything better. He'd helped her to see things differently, having recently come out of a relationship similar to hers and Hugh's.

Victor was a quiet man, and she got the impression he'd been treated badly by his ex-wife and had lost his confidence. He'd opened up and appeared a lot happier recently. Leaving him would be akin to throwing him back into an abyss of gloom and doom.

Her growing obsession with Hugh, however, was something she couldn't ignore.

Her spirits had been dampened when Liam kept talking about Roisin and how the woman played a big part of the weekend he'd spent with Hugh. He talked of how tasty the sausages were that Roisin cooked for them, and how she'd taught him how to play a game on the computer.

Despite her reservations, the feelings refused to go away. The next fortnightly contact visit was looming. She took Liam to school that Tuesday morning and then phoned Hugh.

'Hello, Abi, nice to hear from you.'

Nice to hear from you. That was a good sign, wasn't it? Her mind was working overtime. 'Hi, Hugh. How did the contact go with Liam last weekend? I've been meaning to catch up with you.'

'It was fantastic. Thank you. Liam had a good time, I think. He loved seeing Robbie again. I'm looking forward to seeing him this Saturday. Same time, yeah?'

Her initial high spirits waned at the mention of Roisin's son's name. 'Yes. Um... I was thinking of a change of plan for this weekend. It would be nice if we all spent time together; me, you, and Liam. I've been reading up on these things, and it's best for the child of a separated couple to know his parents are getting on well. How about we meet on Saturday and spend the day as a family? We could go to the zoo or a museum.'

'I'll have to check with Roisin and see what we have planned.'

'Right. Um... I may have got this wrong, but didn't you say that you and Roisin had split up?'

'Yes, we had, briefly, but only because I was back on the booze. I was missing Liam, you see. All's good now, and I've been referred to a counselling group by my GP, so there shouldn't be any repeat of that.'

'I'm glad you're finding a way through.'

'I'll let you know about Saturday. It would be nice for Liam.'

'Yes.' Abigail put down the phone, feeling as if she'd lost in a battle of wills. *Why does Roisin get to have the clean, flawless version of Hugh, when I had to suffer with him drinking all the time?*

Maybe she could try to make Hugh see that Liam would be better off if his parents were together. But was she still in love with Hugh, or merely trying to prove a point and separate him from Roisin?

'Abi has suggested we meet and spend the day together on Saturday.'

'Um, I'm not sure I want to spend the day with Abigail. It'd be awkward.'

'No, not you and me, me and Liam. She says it's best for Liam to know his parents can get on together. What do you think?' Hugh smiled at her and waited for a response.

Roisin's eyes widened. 'Wow. That's surprising, isn't it? Didn't you say she was a dragon?'

'When did I say that? Anyway, she's changed recently. She's making an effort.'

Roisin looked down at her plate, not liking where the conversation might be going, already envious that Hugh and Abigail had managed to put their differences aside for the sake of Liam.

When Hugh came out with things like 'For Liam's sake', or 'It's in Liam's best interests', it made her feel like a terrible mother. Letting George see Robbie wasn't an option at the moment, and it was becoming increasingly difficult to explain her reasoning to the child because he would now be seeing Liam and Hugh spending time together. He constantly asked for George.

'Well? What do you think? Would you mind if I spend Saturday with Abi and Liam?'

'Do what you want,' she huffed, standing up and taking her half-full plate of food and dumping it in the sink.

'What's wrong?' asked Hugh, following her out of the kitchen.

Roisin spun around to face him. 'Be honest with me. What's going

183

on between you and Abi? All of a sudden she's this wonderful mother who knows what's best for her son. I thought you hated her.'

'I don't hate her. Maybe I used to hate the way she behaved but—'

'You're not helping yourself,' snapped Roisin, storming into the living room and slamming the door behind her.

As she slumped onto the sofa, her temperature soared; a sudden fury had taken over. Why was Hugh getting on so well with Abigail?

Roisin fought with her irrational jealousy; surely there wasn't anything to be jealous about. Hugh didn't love Abigail... or did he? This woman had come to represent a threat. One minute Abigail was the dysfunctional ex-partner refusing to allow Hugh contact with his son, but she now presented as picture-perfect and could do no wrong.

The door to the living room opened slowly and Hugh walked in. Roisin noticed he appeared hesitant. Still angry, she didn't speak.

'Roisin, you're the one who encouraged me to try to get contact with Liam, and it's helped. Look at me, I'm sober and I've got two job interviews lined up. I've never been happier.'

'I don't want you to spend time with Abigail.' Roisin couldn't meet his eye, instead she focussed on the coffee table in front of her.

'Why?' Hugh sat next to her and put a hand on her arm.

Roisin shrugged him off. 'Would you like it if I announced I was going to spend Saturday with Robbie and George? Think how you'd feel.'

'Abi says it would be better for Liam—'

Roisin stood up, incensed, 'Abi says, Abi says... For fuck's sake!'

'Now you're being childish. I'm thinking of Liam.'

Roisin turned around and saw that Hugh had stood up to face her. 'How can it be better for Liam? I thought you said that you and Abigail are always arguing. He'll witness that, if you spend time together. If you care so much about his best interests, you'll leave things the way they are. Plenty of children grow up in one-parent families and they're perfectly fine.'

'Are you jealous?'

Roisin let out an exasperated breath. 'D'you know what, I can't be bothered to argue with you about this. You seem to have already made up your mind. Why did you even bother asking me? Go and spend time with your ex if you want, but don't expect me to be happy about it. And how can that be healthy, huh? If we're at each other's throats, how is that healthy for Liam to see?'

'Why not grow up then, and stop acting like a jealous teenager? What do you think is going to happen, I'm going to see Abi on Saturday and fall into her arms? We weren't right for each other, but Liam shouldn't suffer because of it. Parents should communicate; it's better for the children to know their parents don't hate each other. It's a one-off, and then it'll go back to me seeing Liam every other weekend.'

'Do what you want.' Something told her Abigail would try to stir things. Recollections of the way the woman had treated her with disdain floated through her mind.

'I need to know you're okay with it,' said Hugh.

'I don't want to talk about it. I'm going to bed,' she spluttered. She faced him and said, 'You know I'm not okay with it, but it doesn't make any difference, does it?' She stormed out of the room before he could see the tears welling in her eyes.

At that moment the front doorbell rang.

'I'll get it,' said Hugh as he watched Roisin storm upstairs.

When he opened the door, he was surprised to see George standing outside. Roisin had told him a few things about George recently, but the man at the door didn't look as dishevelled as he would have expected. He'd heard that George was wanted by the police for murder, and Roisin said he seemed unhinged. Hugh held onto the door in case he had to close it abruptly.

'Hello. Is Roisin in?'

'She's just this minute gone up to bed.'

George looked at his watch. 'It's only seven-thirty.'

'She wasn't feeling well.' Hugh coughed.

'Right.'

Hugh heard a noise behind him, and when he turned around he saw Roisin on the staircase.

'Hello, George. Come in.' Roisin's voice was deliberately loud enough for Hugh to hear as he walked away into the kitchen. If Hugh was going to get cosy with his ex, she'd show him two could play that game.

She ushered George into the living room and closed the door behind her.

He sat on the sofa. 'I came over for a chat. I have to explain a few things.'

Roisin sat next to him and then recalled their recent conversation and that he'd practically confessed to killing eight men. Slowly, she stood up and moved to the armchair facing the sofa, so that the coffee table was between them. If necessary it could be used as a weapon. The situation, and her thoughts, struck her as absurd: George had always been as gentle as a puppy; he wouldn't harm anyone. Or would he? She struggled to put her fear to one side.

'What I told you when we last met up was wrong,' said George,

185

breaking into her thoughts, 'I didn't kill anyone. That is, the man who possessed me didn't kill anyone. The murderer has confessed. Did you see the news about the murders at Brimstown Avenue?'

'You know I don't watch the news.'

'I'm in the clear.'

Roisin straightened the hem of her skirt and said, 'I still have serious concerns about your mental health. You were so sure when you were telling me you were possessed by a dead man.'

'Whether it actually happened or was the result of a post-traumatic episode, I will never know. But I'm not dangerous. Robbie won't come to any harm if you let me see him, I promise you. Whatever anxiety I was suffering from, caused by being kept captive, I'm over it. I'm back at work now; I was just on my way home from work, actually. I'm feeling much better. Oh, and I have to give you my new mobile number; I lost my old phone.'

'I'm glad you're feeling better, but I'm still not convinced about allowing you to spend time with Robbie, sorry.' Then she had a thought and a smile curled on her lips. 'Maybe if I'm there whenever you see him. It would be good for him to know his parents are getting on well.' Quoting that last sentence broadened her smile further. She couldn't wait to tell Hugh her plans.

'I don't see why not. At least at the start until you're no longer concerned about my mental health.'

'Brilliant. Hugh is meeting Liam this Saturday and will be out for the day. Why don't you come over then, let's say around ten o'clock? You could spend time with Robbie in the garden. The weather is supposed to be nice on Saturday.'

After giving Roisin his new number, George walked away from the house in a buoyant mood. He'd sensed something was awry when Hugh opened the door; he'd seen Roisin sneer at Hugh. They may have had an argument. He'd known Roisin long enough to be able to tell when she'd been crying. Her eyes were puffy and cheeks flushed. The way she'd looked at him when she offered to supervise his visit with Robbie added to the intrigue. There'd been a definite smile on her face, as if she were keeping a secret. Perhaps there was hope for their relationship. He missed the closeness they'd once shared. Maybe he could give it one more shot.

Chapter Fifty-Six

Hugh opened the front door and turned back towards the house, shouting out, 'See you later, Roisin. Should be back by about eight.'

'Why so late?' she asked, emerging from the kitchen, then looked past him and smiled. Hugh turned around to see why she'd reacted in that way. He came face to face with George.

'George? What are you doing here?'

'I invited him,' said Roisin.

'I didn't know he was coming.' He turned to Roisin. The smile was still glued to her lips.

'Come in, George. Robbie's having breakfast. He'll be so happy to see you.'

'I'll go through to the kitchen then,' said George.

Hugh stepped aside to let him in, albeit reluctantly; his tolerance level was low, but he wasn't about to make a scene in front of this man. 'Can I speak to you for a minute, Roisin?' Hugh said, in the most high-spirited way he could muster.

'I should make sure Robbie's okay.'

'This is important.'

'We'll talk later when you get back—'

'No.' Hugh took Roisin's arm as she started to walk away from him towards the kitchen, and he ended up having to practically drag her into the living room. Once inside the room he shut the door.

'What do you think you're doing?' she huffed.

'Me? What am *I* doing? What the fuck are *you* doing?' He struggled to keep his voice down, knowing that George could be eavesdropping.

'You're spending the day with your ex, so I thought it was an opportunity for George to see Robbie. You know how much Robbie misses him. It's in his best interests to see his dad, wouldn't you agree?'

'That's what this is about! You're not happy with me seeing Abi, so you're doing this. I thought you were worried about George's mental health. Surely it wouldn't be safe for him to be around the child if he's suffering from a post-traumatic condition.'

'I'll be here the whole time.'

'You're jealous of me spending time with Abi, and you're trying to make me jealous?'

'So now *you're* jealous? I thought it was only teenagers who got jealous.'

Hugh could feel his temper rising and tried to keep his composure, aware George wasn't too far away. 'Do you know how petty you're being?'

187

'I could ask you to pack your bags again. You have no respect for me. I've put up with a lot from you, what with your alcoholism. You don't know how lucky you are to still be living here.'

'So you're going to throw that at me every time we have an argument?'

'Why not? It's true, isn't it?'

'There's no use talking to you when you're like this.'

'Like what?'

'You're not blameless in all this. You cheated on your husband, and you left your son in the house alone while you went next door to have sex with me.'

'So you were innocent, were you? You cheated on your wife and you didn't even see Liam for months, what type of dad does that make you?'

'You know Abi didn't let me see him.'

'Yes, and you know how it feels not to see your child. Why would you want me to stop George seeing Robbie?'

'I didn't say that, I just don't like the way you went behind my back. How many other times have you arranged meetings with your ex behind my back? You were oh-so-cosy with him when he told you he had amnesia. Are you sure there's nothing going on between you? You do have a track record.'

'Now who's being petty? George is spending time with Robbie, that's all. Go! You'll be late. Or maybe you don't want to see your son as much as you claim you do.'

Hugh grabbed the door handle, unable to speak. Anger buzzed around his mind. He hated Roisin at this moment and began to wonder about all the times she'd been telling him George had mental health issues, all the times she'd gone over to visit him saying she was helping him.

It was becoming clear, she was probably seeing George behind his back. He recalled the way she'd smiled at George when he'd arrived at the house.

With each step he took towards the train station Hugh left behind his anxious thoughts. He started to think about Liam and his mood improved. He thought of Abi and how different she'd been behaving recently, so relaxed and calm; a world away from the woman he used to live with. It did occur to him that he might be better off cutting ties with Roisin and trying again with Abi. He hadn't appreciated how challenging it would be with Roisin having George in her life because of Robbie. It would be wonderful if he could see Liam every day. Maybe he and Abi could have more children.

By the time he was at the entrance to the train station he began to feel as if he were betraying Roisin. However, he reminded himself that she was currently playing happy families with Robbie and George.

Chapter Fifty-Seven

George had spent the morning playing with Robbie in the garden. When the boy asked if he could watch television, Roisin saw an opportunity to talk to George and suggested they have a cup of tea and discuss the contact arrangements.

'Is everything all right between you and Hugh?' asked George.

George's question took her by surprise.

'Why do you ask?' she said, avoiding his eyes and stirring her cup of tea.

'He didn't seem very happy this morning. I hope I didn't arrive at a bad time.'

Roisin recalled how Hugh had practically manhandled her into the living room. She wondered how much of their argument George had overheard. Waving a hand, as if to dismiss his concerns, she replied, 'He was stressed because he was going to spend the day with Abigail, that's all. They had an acrimonious split, and he was worried about what he would say to her. He wanted my advice.'

George nodded. 'I see. Well, I can't say I'm not disappointed. I thought you and Hugh had split up, and then found you were back together again. I kind of got my hopes up that there might be a chance for us.'

Roisin looked down at the table. 'I don't know what to say.'

'I regretted my behaviour that night when you wanted us to get together again and I was telling you we're over,' continued George, 'I need to know you're happy with Hugh, I suppose, so I can move on. I thought things were rocky between you two. Are you being honest with yourself?'

Roisin recalled how she'd tried to stop him going abroad. Things had changed since then, in so many ways. Thinking about George's recent mental health issues, it was all slightly unnerving; what if he was somehow obsessed with her now? She shook away her paranoid thoughts. 'Wow, I never expected to be having this conversation, George. You do realise things can never be the same now I know what you did. After the way you behaved, I don't think I could fully trust you.'

'I'm better now. It was a post-traumatic thing.'

'I'm not sure. Is it that simple for someone to recover from trauma? Isn't there always a risk that you'll have another episode?'

'I'm fine. There's nothing wrong with me.'

'I don't understand why you kept it secret for so long, you know, the spider-man and all of that. If our relationship had been healthy back then, you'd have been able to talk to me.'

'I didn't want to get you involved. I was thinking of your safety, and Robbie's.'

'You weren't thinking of that when you put the spider in the house.'

'That's unfair. I've already explained that.'

'Have you, though?'

'We can keep going round in circles, and you can carry on blaming me for everything, but be honest, I'm not the only one who's thought about us getting back together recently, am I?'

Roisin remembered how desperate she must have seemed when he'd told her he was going abroad and she tried to stop him. 'Sorry. I never meant to lead you on. It's complicated. I'll always care about you— you're Robbie's dad—but I'm with Hugh, and we have our ups and downs but...' she shrugged.

'This morning, I got my hopes up again when I saw the way Hugh reacted when he saw me and when you smiled at me.'

She lowered her eyes, realising she'd used him as a way to get back at Hugh without thinking about how he would feel. 'Sorry. I was trying to make a point to Hugh, that's all. He arranged to spend a whole day with Abigail, and I was annoyed. That's why I asked you to come over today, I wanted him to understand what it felt like having the ex around.'

'So the only reason I was able to spend time with my son was to make your lover jealous?'

'It's not like that.'

'What's it like then? You can't blow hot and cold and use our son as a pawn in a game.'

Roisin took a deep breath before speaking again. 'Let's not argue. You're not exactly innocent in all this. It takes two for a marriage to fall apart.'

'You're the one who had an affair.'

'So much has happened since then. You're not innocent, George, so don't try to act as if you are. It wasn't easy for me— or Hugh—when I lost the baby.'

'You still blame me for that.'

'You're lucky I didn't report you to the police,' she sneered, raising her voice. 'The only thing that stopped me was remembering the man you used to be. I know he's in there somewhere. I was so shocked by what you did. But, I'm done with blaming and anger and hatred. It's worn me down. I have to pick up the pieces of what's left and move on. We all have to do that.'

'Maybe.'

Silence followed. Roisin let out a breath. 'It's like a few weeks ago when I tried to kiss you; I think you're just caught up, like I was then, remembering what it was like in the past. Things have changed. We've both changed. We can't go back.' She saw a sadness in his eyes and looked away. 'We should sort out the arrangements for you to see Robbie.' She forced a smile. 'With Abigail agreeing to Hugh seeing Liam, it did make me think about you and Robbie. It's wrong for me to stop you. Robbie misses you. You're the first person he asks for when he wakes up from nightmares.'

'Really?'

She noticed a tear in George's eye. 'I had an interesting conversation with a friend of mine recently, one of the mums from Robbie's school. She was telling me about her sister who split up with her husband and they'd ended up in court fighting over access rights. Her sister's solicitor said the law says it's best for a child to have a relationship with both of their parents. It's better for their development and mental health. You can imagine, after hearing that, I wanted to try to sort out contact for you and Robbie. I know he's missing you. He loves spending time with you. Today is a great example. You were good with him when you were playing in the garden.'

'It means a lot to me. Thank you. I know I'm not perfect, but Robbie has a right to know his dad.'

'I agree. I'm still not happy for you to take him out on your own, though. But you could visit sometimes. It could coincide with when Hugh is out with Liam, so you two won't have to have any awkward meetings.'

'Sounds sensible. I wish I could prove to you that I'm not a danger to Robbie. I'm still me. I used to take Robbie out on my own practically every day.'

'I know, but things are different now. Please try to understand. I'm doing this for Robbie, not for you.'

George drank the rest of his tea. 'I'll go and sit with Robbie and watch TV with him, if that's okay.'

'Yes, of course.'

Roisin became nostalgic for a moment, wishing she could find a way to recapture the past; but no matter how much she wished things could be different, the truth was George had changed. They could never go back to what they once had. She thought of Hugh, their row in the morning. He'd been so angry when he left the house. Would he find solace in the new, improved version of Abigail? All he did lately was sing her praises. Holding her head in her hands, Roisin resolved to try to make it up to Hugh when he returned home.

Chapter Fifty-Eight

After Robbie was settled in bed, Roisin put the finishing touches to the evening meal.

She'd seen the recipe on *MasterChef* a couple of years ago and had pretended to George at the time that she'd invented it; a delicious selection of fishcakes, with colourful ingredients to give the dish an original and appetizing appearance. The *MasterChef* contestant who'd thought it up had been an interior designer by trade, and took his inspiration from a wallpaper design, of all things. George wasn't much of a fish lover, though.

She'd made the fishcakes for Hugh one evening, a year or so ago, and he'd enjoyed them and praised her for her amazing skills. It had been one of his favourite dishes ever since and never failed to put a smile on his face.

As she took the fishcakes out of the oven a niggling concern caused her brow to crease: after tonight, this dish might come to represent something else to Hugh.

She shrugged off her concerns and placed the fishcakes onto a heated plate, covering them to keep them warm.

The oven's clock caught her eye: 8:15. Where could Hugh be? He'd told her he'd be back by eight. Had he decided to stay at Abigail's house? Roisin caught her breath and went into the living room to find her mobile phone, which she'd left on the sofa earlier.

There were no messages from Hugh. That was odd. He usually sent her updates every couple of hours when he was away, with lots of emojis.

Just then, she heard a key in the front door. Breathing a sigh of relief, she ran out of the room to greet Hugh.

He raised his eyebrows and hung his coat on the rack by the door. Without saying a word, he walked past her, into the living room, and switched on the television.

'What's wrong? Didn't you enjoy your day with Liam?'

'I enjoyed my time with Liam and Abi, thanks. We had a fantastic time. In fact, we've decided to make it a regular thing. Liam loves being with me and Abi. She's like a different woman now, she's changed.'

Roisin didn't like the way Hugh had said all of that while looking directly at her with a stern frown on his face.

'But the day with Abigail and Liam was supposed to be a one-off.'

'Things change. I'm seeing them again next Saturday, actually.'

'Your contact is supposed to be fortnightly.'

'I'm doing it for Liam more than anything else. Did you and George have a good time?' he asked, while switching channels on the television and picking up the TV guide, as if he didn't intend to listen to her reply.

'George came to see Robbie, not me.'

'Right, whatever.'

'What does that mean?'

'I'm tired. I've been travelling for an hour. Can I catch my breath before we have an argument, please?'

'Wh-why would you think we'd have an argument?'

Hugh sneered at her. 'Because, my dear, if you haven't noticed, you pick on every little thing and you try to make it into a big deal. You're so hard to live with.'

Roisin wanted to say, '*Well, go and live somewhere else, then*', but she suspected he was waiting for her to say that. Tears welled in her eyes. She'd spent over an hour preparing his favourite meal; the smell of the fishcakes must surely have been obvious when he'd entered the house, but he hadn't commented on it.

She left the room and went into the kitchen to serve a plate of food for herself.

Half an hour later Hugh walked into the kitchen and Roisin realised she'd eaten half of the food and then sat there staring into space while the rest of it went cold. She couldn't remember what she'd been thinking about whilst in a virtual trance.

'I ate at Abi's,' he said. 'She made a delicious curry.'

His words were spoken irreverently, with obvious deliberate disrespect; he could see the fishcakes in her plate.

He continued, seemingly oblivious to any pain his words might be causing, 'I had no idea she could cook so well. She said she's started cookery classes. Back when we were married, I'd be lucky to have a steak that wasn't burned.' He chuckled. 'I think I'll go to bed early. I'm knackered.'

Roisin listened as he climbed the stairs, a hollowness inside.

As he lay in bed, Hugh thought back to the kiss. He hadn't meant to kiss Abi, it had just happened naturally, as though they'd been transported back to a time when their relationship had been good. That was the problem. The kiss was like a wish for everything to be good again. They'd both said sorry to each other afterwards, but the kiss couldn't be erased.

The ecstatic sensation in his heart would not go away.

She'd sent him a text message. He found it when he got home, when Roisin was in the kitchen.

I had a lovely day. Liam was so happy. Thank you. I'll see you again next Saturday. I'm so glad we can still be friends x

She didn't mention the kiss, but the x at the end of her sentence served as a reminder. Was that deliberate, or was the x added out of habit? When he replied to her, he'd done so like a teenager looking around to make sure his parents weren't in the room while he sent a secret message to a love interest.

I had a great day too. Thank you so much. I'm looking forward to next week x

The kiss. Again. He'd added one too. Would she get the wrong impression? Did he still love her? Did he want to resume their relationship?

He thought of Roisin. He'd smelt the aroma when he walked in the door: she'd cooked his favourite meal. But he was caught up thinking about Abi. If he'd sat down for a meal with Roisin, it would have wiped away the memories, and he had wanted to hold onto them for as long as possible.

He'd lied to her so easily, saying Abi had cooked a meal for him. Everything he and Roisin did lately seemed to be a way of winding each other up. But she'd cooked the fishcakes; was that her way of trying to make amends? The thought made him feel worse about his feelings for Abi.

He'd made a decision to sneak downstairs when Roisin was in bed and eat the fishcakes. She was bound to have put the leftovers in the fridge.

He thought of the message from Abi. What if Roisin saw it? Should he delete it? He didn't want to. Abi had been nice today. She was softer and kinder, and in comparison Roisin seemed bitter. He recalled how she'd thrown him out when he needed her, and appeared so pally with George lately.

He knew it would be a mistake to make his mind up based on one day with Abi. One kiss.

He heard Roisin going into the bathroom. It was an hour since they'd had a half-hearted conversation in the kitchen. She'd be getting ready for bed. He decided to go downstairs. He took the spare duvet and a pillow from the wardrobe. He needed to sleep alone, to think over his options.

Thankfully, he managed to walk past the bathroom without having to talk to Roisin. He wasn't in the mood for conversation. He wondered whether he would have been in the mood for conversation if she'd been Abi, but he caught himself and blocked the thoughts that would inevitably lead back to the kiss.

He made a bed for himself on the sofa downstairs then went into the kitchen and pulled open the fridge door. He'd hoped to find the delicious fishcakes. Had she eaten them all? A thought struck him and he went over to the bin.

The sight of the colourful fishcakes in the bin brought a frown to his face, knowing she'd have cooked them for him and then been disappointed, jealous even, when he told her he'd eaten at Abi's. He shook away the negative thoughts and put a couple of slices of bread in the toaster. He took some cheese out of the fridge and, as he was about to close the door, saw a couple of cans of beer in there, which he'd bought a while back. He'd expected Roisin to have thrown them out.

The confusion in his mind made him want to grab the beer and drink it, use it to mask the painful thoughts. The truth was that he didn't know whether going back to Abi would be the best thing. What if she reverted to her old ways? But at least if he was there he'd be with Liam.

Would Roisin be upset? They'd gone through so much together, what with losing the baby. And he'd been like a father to Robbie for so long. He let go of the fridge door and watched it close slowly. The beer wouldn't help. It hadn't helped before.

Roisin appeared in the kitchen when he was seated at the table with his cheese and toast.

'I thought you ate earlier.'

'I did. I fancied a snack. Do you have a problem with that?' He hadn't meant to snap.

Roisin poured herself a glass of water and left the room without speaking.

Hugh knew he would have to make a decision soon. Abi or Roisin. This wasn't fair on anyone.

Chapter Fifty-Nine

Rex was hauled out of the prison cell early that morning by two wardens, who had taken him to an office within the building. He'd been glad they'd arrived when they did because Johnny was trying to convince him to let him into his bed.

The two guards sat opposite him. One skinny and the other large. They made him think of Laurel and Hardy. That comparison didn't last long though, as there was no humour here, just sneering glances as they looked from him to the paperwork in a file in front of them and whispered to each other.

'Why have you brought me here?' he asked when the silence, stares, and sense of foreboding forced him to speak.

'Trevor, we know you didn't kill the men in that house,' said the Oliver Hardy lookalike.

Rex raised his eyebrows. His brow then creased into a frown. What would this mean? The unknown forces in that terrifying land of nonexistence had told him to lie and say he, as Trevor Staines, committed the murders—to save George being convicted. What would happen if George was now in trouble, if DNA evidence proved he was to blame? Rex would be forced to go back to no-man's land and eternal Hell.

Breaking into the silence, the warden continued, 'A man has been arrested, and forensic evidence has tied him to the scene. We found none of your DNA, and the witness we spoke to said they had seen a dark-haired, much younger man, leaving the property. You don't fit the description. You had a lot of information about the murders, though. Where did you get that information?'

'I was trying to protect someone,' said Rex.

'Perverting the course of justice is a serious crime, however, in this case it seems you have a guardian angel. It's highly unusual for someone to be let off with what amounts to not much more than a slap on the wrist for something like this, which is why my colleague and I have been thoroughly checking this paperwork. In this case it appears that the powers that be have decided to overlook what you did because the real killer has been found and the case is wrapped up. For this type of crime, it's more usual to see someone locked up for years.'

The Laurel lookalike scratched his head as he continued to peruse the paperwork, making him look even more like the famous funnyman.

'So I can leave? I'm free?' asked Rex.

The Hardy double shrugged, 'Looks that way; after the paperwork has been sorted out. You're a lucky man.'

As Rex was waiting for the paperwork to be completed, he couldn't help wondering about what the prison officer had told him. The reference to a "guardian angel" brought to mind the faceless voice in the abyss that had given him strict instructions to save George. Or could it have been Huntley who'd arranged his release?

Rex breathed in the polluted London air outside the prison gates, and a feeling of indestructibility set in. He'd survived so much relatively unscathed; perhaps the spider that bit him all those years ago really had given him superpowers.

He looked up to the sky wondering about the place he'd existed in before going to prison. Had it been real, or a dream?

Noticing a Tube station across the road, he decided to make his way back to where he'd parked Trevor's car, and then drive to George's flat. He had to check whether George was the one who'd been arrested for the murders, if so, there could be more trouble ahead.

Chapter Sixty

'So how are things? Seems like ages since we last met up,' said Glen. 'Probably 'cos I'm used to phoning you all the time and I didn't have your number for a while.'

'Yeah, sorry, I had to change the number when I lost my old phone, and I forgot to tell you the new one. Anyway, I suppose you're busy with Petula.'

'I'm not gonna turn into one of those blokes who forgets his friends because he has a girlfriend, you know.'

'I didn't mean it like that.'

'I have news about me and Pet, actually, but I'll tell you later. We're here to talk about you. What's been happening?'

'It's Roisin. She's basically told me we could never get back together because of what happened with the spider.'

'So, what's the problem? That's great news; I was worried you were gonna say you and Roisin had got back together.'

'You've always hated her.'

'Not always, but for as long as I can remember. You have to admit, she wasn't your best choice of life partner.'

'Why? We were married for years; it was a good marriage.'

'Until she cheated on you with the neighbour.'

'Rex drove her to it.'

'You could use some therapy, mate. No offence.'

George began to eat his pie, ignoring the comment.

'You should find a girlfriend, then you'll feel better.'

'Really?' George rolled his eyes. 'Why did I think talking to you about any of this would help?'

'I know you loved Roisin, but she cheated on you, mate. You deserve someone better.'

'Seems to be a pattern, though. Belinda cheated on me too. Is that how it's always gonna be?'

'Belinda was a rebound, you can't count her. You were going through a mid-life crisis.'

'I'm not middle-aged.'

'It can happen at any age. You were stuck in a loveless marriage for years—'

'It wasn't a loveless marriage.'

'Okay, not always, but she cheated on you. That Belinda fling was a rebellion against that, mate. Even you have to admit she was too young for you.'

'She wasn't.'

'All I'm saying is, don't give up. Look at me, I was a hopeless case until I found Pet, and now we're getting married.'

'You're getting married?'

'Yeah, that was my news. Oh, and I'd be honoured if you'd agree to be my best man.'

George shrugged. 'I'd be happy to.'

'Fantastic! I can't wait to tell Pet.'

'I'm happy for you.'

'Thanks. And, listen, forget about Roisin.'

'How can I forget about her? She's the mother of my son.'

'I don't mean *forget* forget, I just mean, you know, forget about trying to get back together with her.'

'I wanted to try, for Robbie's sake more than anything else.'

'Mate, listen, she's already got a fella, hasn't she?'

'Yeah, but—'

'She's living with him, right?'

'Yeah, but I'd got it into my head that she didn't really love him. It was something she said to me that made me think she wanted us to try again.'

'Have you told her how you feel?'

'Yes. She said she can't trust me since she found out about me killing Rex and putting that spider in the house. It killed her unborn child. How could she ever forgive that?'

'It's over, mate, but an end is always a beginning.'

'What?'

'When we stare too long at a closed door, we don't notice the opportunities in front of us.'

'Have you been studying philosophy?'

'No, it's just something I saw online.'

'I can't see any opportunities. Doors keep closing.'

'You're focussing on the negatives. You're seeing Robbie now, right?'

George nodded.

'And you've got your job back.'

'Yeah.'

'Good, well, concentrate on what you have to be thankful for then. Remember, you didn't end up in prison for committing five murders, and you no longer have a criminal following you looking for gold. If I were you, I'd be counting my lucky stars.'

'Hmm... That's true but—'

'No buts, just concentrate on thinking positive. And you never know, when you go to my wedding you might get lucky with one of the bridesmaids.' He lifted his glass. 'Here's to the future.'

'To the future,' said George, clinking his glass against Glen's. For a moment, sitting there in the pub with his old friend, things didn't seem so bad.

Chapter Sixty-One

Ever since Ben Gibbons found out that Trevor Staines had confessed to Del's murder, he'd been frustrated, because he knew the man would be going to prison so he wouldn't be able to talk to him. He'd made enquiries through criminal contacts, but no one knew where Trevor was.

Ben was now back at George's flat. There was no doubt in his mind that George knew about the murders. That obnoxious man in the pub, Glen, had done his best to put him off the scent, but it was obvious George was somehow involved. The man was jittery, always looking over his shoulder as if expecting to be ambushed. It made him wonder whether George was taking drugs; perhaps that was why he appeared so highly strung and on edge.

From across the road, he watched as George entered the building just after seven o'clock in the evening. Ben had been sitting in his car, in the vicinity of George's apartment, for a few hours waiting for him to return.

Shortly after George closed his door, Ben noticed a red sports car turning into the street. Ben recognised the car straight away; it was unique and stood out amongst the run-of-the-mill cars that lined this residential street. He'd seen the car's owner walk up to the building earlier, in the afternoon; the man had rung the doorbell and then seemingly given up when there was no response. Ben couldn't be sure whether the man had been looking for George, because the building contained more than one flat. However, there was a familiarity about his face that sparked his curiosity. When he'd left, Ben looked up the recent news on his phone and it confirmed to him what he'd suspected: the man was Trevor Staines. He'd been kicking himself all afternoon for letting him get away. Seeing the same man approach the building for a second time now, it felt as though Christmas had come early. Here was the proof he needed, a link between George and this killer. But why had Trevor been released if he'd confessed to murdering five men?

Ben wondered whether Trevor had noticed him when he'd been there earlier. The man was a serial killer, so he knew he would have to be careful.

Perhaps these two men were going to be discussing the gold. There was no way Ben was letting these losers get their hands on the thing he'd spent half his life searching for. The gold was all he needed to give him the freedom he craved. These men held the information and he was determined to get it, no matter the cost.

Rex rang the buzzer for George's flat and waited.

There'd been no response when he was here earlier, and he'd hoped George had been at work, rather than at a police station being questioned about the murders.

He'd driven to a café near George's flat and had waited there for the rest of the afternoon.

All day Rex's sense of paranoia had been unshakeable, as if someone was following him, but couldn't see anyone around. It occurred to him that the formless voice which spoke to him when he was in the place they'd called "eternal Hell" might be watching him, sitting in wait for a time to pounce and take him back to the unknown.

He'd had too much time to think, sitting for hours in that café, and he began to worry about the deal he'd made with Huntley Page before going into prison. If the eerie disembodied voice didn't get him, Huntley Page and his gang would, expecting him to commit murders on their behalf.

George knew how to get a poisonous spider, so after he'd made sure George was not the person who'd been arrested for the murders, he planned to get the details from him and create a community of spiders where he could live and thrive. Anyone who came close would be killed. He would rule in his kingdom.

George's voice sounded through the speaker: 'Hello?'

'George Barnaby?'

'Yes, who is it?'

'I have a delivery.'

The buzzer sounded and Rex entered the building.

George greeted him at his door. 'Hello?'

'Hello, Mr Barnaby.'

'I thought you had a delivery?'

'It's about the delivery you received.'

'The delivery I received?'

The frown and then the look of almost fear on George's face brought a smile to Rex's lips. He had now realised he was talking about the spider.

They went inside George's flat. George held on to the door handle as if planning to let Rex out as quickly as he could. He said in hushed tones, 'I already paid your colleague, and it was much more than the price I was initially quoted for the spider. I've been out of work, and I can't afford to—'

'Please, relax. I didn't come for money, it's information I need. I'm an undercover detective,' said Rex.

George took a deep breath and blinked. He looked fearful.

'We're investigating the importation of poisonous spiders,' Rex continued.

'But how did you know...?'

'Don't worry; if you give us the information, you're in the clear. We want to stop the influx of these spiders into the country as there has been a recent surge of dangerous spiders being discovered in UK homes.'

'Hmm... I think I heard about that on the news. But aren't they usually brought over in bananas, and things like that?'

'I'm more interested in the illegal trade of spiders, rather than the accidental ones.'

George nodded. 'I see.'

'Give me a name, an address if you have it.'

'I don't want to get anyone in trouble. I had to get the spider for, well... for a project. It was all above board, I promise. My friend helped me without having any idea what would happen.'

'Your friend?'

'I don't want to get anyone in trouble.'

'If you don't give me the information, it could mean a prison sentence for yourself for up to two years.'

Rex revelled at the shock he saw in George's expression and struggled to keep a straight face.

'I-I... Would it help if I set up a purchase? Then you could track the spider and be here when they come to collect the money?'

'No. I need an answer today. Now.'

'But—'

'Give me your friend's name. He won't get in trouble. I will explain this to him as well.'

'It's a woman. She won't get in trouble... you promise?'

'The only people who will get in trouble are those who are importing the spiders.'

George closed his eyes briefly. 'Her name is Jess—'

'Um... can you write the name and address down for me, please?'

'Er... If there's any way you can avoid telling my friend that I sent you to her, I would be eternally grateful; we've been friends for a long time and... Perhaps you could say you're making enquiries and there's a lead you've found that came up with her address.'

Rex tapped his nose and said, 'Don't concern yourself, I will be as discreet as I can. No names will be mentioned.'

'Thank you.'

Rex took the piece of paper from him: Jess Robson. He remembered the text message he'd found on George's phone, and kicked himself for not following up on this contact earlier.

The address wasn't too far away. He hoped he had enough time.

When Rex exited the building he noticed a blue car across the road and a man sitting in it. The man had been there earlier, when he'd initially come to see if George was at home. His heart began to beat faster. Was this man one of Huntley's gang? It had struck him as too good to be true that he'd been released from prison so quickly. Rex remembered what Huntley said to him: *"I will expect you to help me too."*

Rex knew he had to try to keep his head down until he could get a spider. The plan was to become a spider again, but to make sure he owned a good supply of spiders to enable him to continue to live for as long as possible as a spider; when one died he would possess another. He couldn't help smiling when he thought about it. For now, though, he hurried to get away from the house and away from the man in the car.

Huntley's words haunted him: *"I'll see you when you're out of prison, and we'll talk business."*

As he speed-walked towards his car, he heard footsteps behind him... getting closer.

'Excuse me, sir.'

Rex turned towards the voice. It was the man from the blue car. For a moment he was stunned into silence, but eventually managed to sputter, 'I'm in a hurry.'

'I won't keep you long. I wanted to find out about that man in the flat you just visited. George. You did visit him, right?'

'Who wants to know?'

'Um... I'm Ben Gibbons. George used to know my old friend Del. Er... Derek Cole.' The man was waiting for a response.

An old friend of Derek's? So he wasn't one of Huntley's cronies. Rex couldn't help wondering if he'd crossed paths with this man back when Derek was seeing his mother. He shook his head. 'I've never heard of him.'

'Are you Trevor Staines, by any chance?'

'As I said, I'm in a hurry.'

'Trevor, do you know about the gold? I want to know where it is. Del promised me a share of it. I helped him steal it, years ago. He died before I could ask him. If you help me find the gold we could share the proceeds. I need to know where he stashed the haul.'

Rex turned to face Ben. 'Gold? What gold?'

The man said in a half-whisper, 'Del knew a rich family years ago. They owned a jeweller's. He fell out with them, and he had a plan to take gold and jewellery from their safe, but he didn't know how to break in. I helped. We stole the gold, and he hid it. Must've been worth at least half a million at the time, and I'm talking well over ten years ago. The price of gold has skyrocketed. Del said he was keeping it hidden, as the police would be sniffing around looking for it after the burglary. Problem is, I lost touch with Del, and when I finally tracked him down again I found out he'd been killed.'

Rex was fuming inside. This man had helped Derek steal the gold and jewellery from his family's shop. He'd known Derek had stolen the gold, but didn't know it was stashed away somewhere. Had Derek sold it and been bluffing Ben about it, or was it hidden somewhere?

'So, do you have any information? Does George? I'm not a greedy man, I just want what's mine. If you help me find it, I'd appreciate it, and would be willing to give you a share.'

Rex decided that this man, Ben Gibbons, would be his first victim when he became a spider again. He couldn't bear to look at him, let alone listen to the man's drawl.

'I don't know about any gold. I do, however, know a man who would be very interested that you burgled his family's jewellery shop. He has always wondered who got away with the crime. If you bother me or George again, I'll make sure he finds out, and I'm sure the police will be interested in the information.'

'You wouldn't.'

'I definitely would. I'm warning you, I am well connected with the criminal underworld, and I could phone someone right now who would make sure you're dead and buried in the next ten minutes, and like the elusive gold, your body will never be found.'

'Your eyes, man. How did you do that?' Ben began to back away at a speed that was dangerous for someone going backwards; he narrowly missed walking into the path of a car.

Rex began to laugh as he crossed the road to get into his car. His thoughts turned to the gold. It might still be out there, if Derek hadn't sold it. If so, he was determined to find it. As a child, he'd known Derek well; he knew many of Derek's favourite haunts. Perhaps the gold would be hidden in one of those places. The paranoid feeling of being watched hadn't gone away even though Ben was gone, so he knew he would have to leave as quickly as he could and try to find a spider before his time ran out. Everything else would have to wait.

Chapter Sixty-Two

George met Glen for lunch at The Red Lion.

'We should meet up with Jess and Tom again soon. Have you seen or heard from them recently?' said George.

'If I'm being honest, I ain't thought about them for ages. I'm surprised you'd even care, considering the way they behaved when they thought we had money.'

George had been unable to stop thinking about Jess and Tom since he'd given their address to the detective. The man was shady. His dark eyes appeared almost black and reminded him of Rex's. There was one point in the conversation when the man looked at him and said, 'I'm an undercover detective,' and George could have sworn the whites of the man's eyes had gone completely black. Brushing away his fear, he told himself it was yet another flashback. Why hadn't he thought to ask for the man's ID before giving Jess's address to him? What if he was a criminal? The questions went around and around in his head, giving him no peace.

'Since I hooked up with Pet I've been happier than I've ever been in my life. I don't wanna look back. Whenever I think of Tom and Jess I get negative feelings.'

'But I thought we'd put all that behind us. Remember when we met them and Jess gave you Pet's address. Without that, you'd never have got back together.'

Glen waved a hand. 'I would have found a way. We were already in contact on Facebook. It was a matter of time. We were meant to be together. Besides, I ain't seen Jess or Tom-Tom in here since then, have you?'

'Not in here, no.'

'If you wanna be friends with them, I'm not gonna stop you, but I don't trust them, and if they're not making an effort to keep in touch, why should we? They didn't even contact us to let us know their baby was born.'

'Maybe she hasn't had it yet.'

'She has. I've still got Tom as a friend on Facebook, for some reason. I thought I'd unfriended him when I unfriended Jess. He posted a picture of their baby and shared it publicly. Has he never heard about the paedos and all sorts that go on Facebook?'

'Seems too early for her to have had the baby. They only told us she was pregnant a couple of months ago, didn't they?'

'It was longer than that. Maybe she didn't find out she was pregnant until she was a few months in.'

'Come to think of it, she did look heavily pregnant the last time I saw her.'

'When was that?'

'When I went to see her about getting a spider for Rex.'

Glen stared off into the distance and smiled, seeming not to have heard what George had said.

'What are you thinking about?' asked George.

'Just thinking maybe me and Pet will have a baby. It would be nice.'

'I never imagined you as the paternal type.'

'Neither did I. Pet's changed me.'

'Maybe we should visit Jess and Tom and congratulate them. There comes a time to let bygones be bygones.'

'I don't wanna visit them. Anyway, they might've moved. Tom posted on Facebook a while back saying they were looking for a bigger place, gloating about the pregnancy.'

George's eyes widened. What if the detective went to the address and they'd moved? Would he be back asking more questions? He remembered, with relief, that he'd also given Jess's mobile number to the man, although he couldn't be sure she still had the same mobile number; he'd taken the details from an old address book he had, because he'd discarded his mobile phone at Gatwick Airport.

'George? Earth to George.'

George saw Glen's fingers clicking in front of his eyes, and only then noticed he had been lost in thought. 'Sorry, Glen.'

'What's up?'

'Nothing, I was just thinking. Um. Do you still have Jess's mobile phone number? I lost my contacts when I left my phone at the airport.'

'I've probably still got it. I copied your contacts when I lost my phone at Number Eight, remember? You can copy them back from mine.' Glen chuckled.

Glen scrolled through his phone. 'This is Jess's number.' He pointed at the screen. 'Copy it into your phone and then I'll delete it from mine. It's not like I'm ever gonna phone her.'

George took out his phone.

'That's a fancy phone. Let's have a look,' said Glen, taking the slim phone from him.

'Luckily, I had insurance on my old one. Got the updated model when I claimed,' said George.

'Hmm... I ended up having to buy a new one when I lost mine; didn't have insurance,' said Glen, handing the phone back to him.

George added Jess's number to his phone contacts, and took the opportunity to add other people's numbers from Glen's contact list. He was glad to see Glen had Roisin as a contact.

'I've got time for one more drink before I have to get back to work. You?' said Glen.

'No, I'd better be going. My manager keeps looking at the clock whenever he sees me come and go from the office. I think he might be looking for a reason to get rid of me because I took so much time off.'

'Why don't you look for another job?'

George shrugged. 'Maybe I will. But I can't afford to be fired because if I don't keep up the maintenance for Robbie, Roisin will have more reasons to stop me seeing him.'

'I thought she's been allowing you to see him.'

'She has, but only under her supervision, and she practically admitted she only let me see Robbie in the first place to wind up Hugh.'

'More proof that I'm right about her. She's a cow.'

'She's not, she's all right, but I get the feeling she still doesn't trust me.'

Chapter Sixty-Three

'Victor? What are you doing here?'

'That's a nice way to greet the love of your life,' he chuckled.

Abigail hadn't wanted him to find out her address, but on Thursday—after they'd been out for a meal together—he'd offered to walk her home. She'd had a few to drink, and it was late, so she'd accepted.

Hugh was due to visit in less than ten minutes for their planned day together with Liam. She'd been looking forward to taking Liam out for an early birthday lunch with Hugh.

'I've missed you, Abi,' said Victor, stepping into the house and putting his arms around her.

She held the front door open and said, 'I was about to head out, actually. Liam's birthday's on Wednesday, and I have to get a present for him.'

'Okay, let's make a day of it. On Thursday, you said we should arrange for us to meet—'

'I never said you should meet Liam, it's too early for that, we—'

'No, you said me and you should meet. I'm busy next week, so I thought we could get together this weekend. But I'm gonna have to meet Liam soon, aren't I?'

'Not yet. It's complicated.'

'His dad causing trouble?'

'Not at all. Liam is seeing his dad this weekend,' said Abigail.

'Oh, so he's not around?'

'He's upstairs, his dad's on his way.' She'd thought things over since Thursday and realised she still cared about Hugh. As she looked at Victor, it was clear that her mind and her heart had already made a decision: she didn't love this man.

'Great, so after he's collected him, we can spend the day together. The weather's beautiful. I can help you pick a gift for Liam's birthday.'

'I'm not sure.' She looked at the floor.

'You're not having second thoughts about us, are you?'

'I—'

He pulled her closer. 'I enjoyed our kiss on Thursday. I've been thinking about that ever since.' He leaned in and placed his lips on hers.

Abigail's mind whirred. *Why don't I just tell him how I feel?*

There was a knock on the front door. Abigail pulled away from Victor and instinctively wiped her lips on her sleeve. Her eyes widened on seeing Hugh standing outside the half-open door.

'Sorry to interrupt,' he said.

Abigail looked at him and then at Victor, who was smiling at Hugh.

'Hugh, um... hello. Er... Victor, this is Liam's dad.'

'Very pleased to meet you.' Victor extended a hand to shake Hugh's.

Hugh didn't shake his hand immediately, first asking, 'And you are?'

'I'm Abigail's boyfriend, Victor. We met a couple of months ago, didn't we, love?'

Abigail's cheeks reddened, mostly out of frustration with herself. She wanted to correct Victor—he wasn't her boyfriend—but instead gazed at her shoes, and then nodded and forced a smile at Victor. *What am I doing?*

'Nice to meet you, Victor.'

'You've come to collect Liam, right?'

'Yes.'

'Me and Abi are gonna find somewhere nice to spend the day, aren't we love?' He pulled her closer.

'So there's been a change of plan?' said Hugh, unexpectedly.

Here was her chance to tell Victor that she already had plans with Hugh. But Hugh had witnessed the kiss, and had been told that Victor was her boyfriend. Any hope of a reconciliation was slipping through her fingers. 'I'm sorry, Hugh, Victor came over unexpectedly, and—'

'And, she can't resist my charms,' interjected Victor, with a laugh.

Abigail found herself joining in with the laugh, mainly due to nervousness.

'But seriously, did you two have other plans for today?' asked Victor.

'We usually spend time together with Liam. It's good for him,' said Hugh.

A spark of hope. Perhaps he wanted to spend the day with her, after all. She opened her mouth to say something, perhaps find a way to get rid of Victor.

'But don't worry. I can see that the two of you would rather be together.'

'That obvious, hey?' said Victor, sniggering like a schoolboy and putting an arm around Abigail.

She stifled a scream. Her mind recalled the kiss she'd shared with Hugh and she wished Victor would vanish, but he was holding onto her. She excused herself so that she could fetch Liam.

Ten minutes later, Abigail watched from the front door with Victor as Hugh and Liam made their way to the high street.

Victor put an arm around her. 'It's hard, isn't it? I know. I hate seeing my ex-wife and son together, stirs up so many memories. I want to hate her, especially after what she did, but I can't. It's like she's burrowed into my heart. It's hard to shake away the times we spent together and erase it all, move on. I guess everyone feels the same. Don't get me wrong, I would never consider starting again with Serena, but thoughts of the good times haunt us when we're lonely, don't they? Which is why I'm glad I found you. I could see it in Hugh. It's a man thing. He still loves you, probably always will.'

Abigail forced a smile and said, 'Right, where shall we go today?'

Life had to carry on.

Hugh had packed a small suitcase and brought it with him. He'd been hoping to stay with Abi. Everything seemed so positive the last time they'd spoken. He'd made up his mind, he wanted to try again. For Liam's sake, but also because Abi had changed. Life with Roisin had been good for a while, but increasingly it felt like a broken thing that was crumbling and constantly being glued back together. He couldn't see a way back to what they'd had before losing the baby. And the way she had been behaving lately, showing so much interest in George and his life, was off-putting. He'd told her he was leaving her, going back to Abi.

He pulled his suitcase along behind him as Liam chatted happily. He'd missed half of what the boy had said since leaving the house.

'Dad, what do you think?'

'Sorry, Son, I was miles away. What were you saying?'

'Mummy said you used to drink a lot and you forgot things; she said you forgot about me too sometimes.'

'I've never forgotten about you, Liam.'

'Have you been drinking, Daddy? Is that why you weren't listening to me? Mummy said you used to be in your own world when you were drunk. She said you were hard to talk to because you didn't listen.'

'What? When did she say that?'

'When we moved to Gran's house. She said we had to leave because you were drinking.'

Hugh stopped walking and faced his son. 'I haven't been drinking, Liam. I was thinking about something and didn't hear what you said, that's all.'

'Okay.' Liam walked ahead.

'What were you saying?'

'I was asking you what colour shoes I should get to wear to the party. Mummy said you would buy me new shoes today and clothes for the party. But Mummy was supposed to be coming with us.'

'What party?'

'My birthday party.'

'Wait... what did you mean about Mummy coming with us?'

'She said we were all going shopping together and for a special birthday lunch. Mummy said it would be nice, and she asked me if I like going out with both of you.'

'So why did she change her mind?'

'She probably wanted to be with her new boyfriend.'

'Victor?'

'Today was the first time I saw him, but they always go out together. So, Daddy, will you come to my birthday party? My birthday's on Wednesday.'

Hugh's heart sank. 'Liam, I know that. I could never forget your birthday. Your birth was one of the happiest days of my life.'

'Why wasn't it the happiest?'

'Of course it was the happiest.'

'Mummy said you were only happy when you were drinking.'

'Did she?'

'Yeah.'

'Liam, listen, I didn't forget your birthday. I just didn't know you were having a party. Mummy didn't tell me.'

'Will you come to the party?'

'When is it?'

'Next Saturday. It's for my school friends, but I want you to come. If you don't, Mummy will bring that man.'

'The man who was at the house?'

'On Thursday, I was alone in the house with Gran and Granddad when she went out with him. They said she might get married and have more children.'

'They told you that?'

'No, they were talking when they thought I couldn't hear them. They said you wouldn't come to my party because there won't be any beer.'

'Is that what they told you?'

'No, I was listening from my bedroom. They were worried you would have a fight with Mummy's new boyfriend.'

'Liam. I don't fight.'

'Mummy said you can get angry when you have a drink.'

'I don't drink anymore, Son.'

'Do you think Mummy and her boyfriend will have more children?'

The dark clouds gathered more closely in Hugh's mind, blocking out the sunny day he should have been enjoying with Liam. This man, Victor, must be pretty settled into the family if Abi's parents were talking about marriage. Why hadn't Abi told him how serious the relationship was? Why had she let him kiss her last Saturday? She'd led him on, and he'd let himself get carried away.

Liam was talking again and he wasn't listening again, his mind so full of confusion. 'Let's go and get a coffee, Liam,' he said, needing a caffeine fix to take away the jumbled thoughts.

'I don't drink coffee. Mummy says it's not good for me.'

'How about a hot chocolate?'

'Okay, and then can we go and buy my clothes, because Mummy said we have to get them.'

'Right.'

'You have to come to my party, Daddy.'

'We're having a lovely day together today, Son. I will try to get to the party, but if I don't, it's only because I've got to go to work. Let's have a fun day today and treat it as an early birthday party.'

'It's not a party, though.'

'Yes, but we can go to the park. We could go bowling if you want. You decide.'

'Bowling.'

'Bowling it is then.'

Hugh smiled at Liam. He dreaded the thought of having to go to Liam's party and watch Victor smooch with Abi. He'd seemed like a nice enough man, but Hugh wasn't ready to contemplate such changes; after all, up until half an hour ago he'd been seriously considering rekindling his relationship with Abi. He would have to think of a good enough excuse for not attending Liam's party. It tore at his heart even thinking about that.

Chapter Sixty-Four

'Hi Jess.'

'George? Wow, it's been ages. How are you?'

'I'm fine, thanks. How are you and Tom?'

'We're fine.'

'Um, I heard you had the baby. Congratulations.'

'Thank you. We have a beautiful baby girl, Ophelia.'

'That's a nice name.'

'Yes, it is. Tom and I decided that as it was our love of Shakespeare that brought us together, we would name her after one of his characters. And, I've always loved the name. You should come and visit. Do you have our new address?'

'No.'

'Have you got a pen and paper? It's not far away.'

George wrote down the address. 'Thanks, Jess. I will try and visit soon.'

George looked at the piece of paper in his hand. Tom and Jess's new address. She was right, it wasn't far away. He'd driven past the street, and even walked past it a couple of times, unaware they lived there. He felt a sense of loss. If he hadn't spoken to Jess today, he would never have known where they lived. Years would have gone by and they would have become even more estranged. Despite this bittersweet nostalgia, George had no intention of visiting them. He hadn't spoken to Tom or Jess for months, hadn't even thought about them. In truth, he probably felt the same way as Glen did. He couldn't rest, however, knowing he'd given their contact details to the detective. It made him feel obliged to stay in contact with them.

He discarded the piece of paper into the top drawer of his desk.

The phone rang again and Jess assumed it must be George, as he had literally just hung up. Perhaps he'd forgotten to tell her something. She answered in high spirits, 'Hi.'

'Is that Ms Robson?'

'Um... yes, who's speaking?'

'I believe you know where I can get hold of a poisonous spider.'

Jess remained silent. It couldn't be coincidental that the call from

George had been so out of the blue and immediately before this call. Had he called her just to make sure she hadn't changed her number and then passed it on to this person?

'Ms Robson, are you still there?'

Jess cleared her throat. 'I don't know about any spiders. Goodbye.'

The phone rang again. A number she didn't recognise. She let it go to voicemail, as she usually did with unknown callers.

She rang George back. 'George, who have you told about me getting the spider for you?'

Silence followed.

'George!'

'I don't remember telling anyone. Um... actually, I told a detective.'

'A detective?'

'He said that they knew about the spider and asked for details of where I'd got it. He promised you wouldn't get in trouble; he was asking about the importers.'

'So you gave him my number? I was trying to help you. You promised you wouldn't tell anyone where you got it. How could you?'

'They're only interested in the people who are importing them.'

'One was imported because you ordered it! If anyone is to blame, you are.'

'Jess—'

'Tell this detective you got it wrong. I'm not answering any more calls. You didn't give him my address, did you?'

'No.'

'Good. Keep it that way, or I'll go to the police myself and tell them you asked for the spider.'

'But Jess—'

'Goodbye, George. And this *is* goodbye. Don't phone me again. You're not a friend.'

The line went dead and George stared at his phone. Thoughts of *The Spider* haunted him again. How would the detective have known about the spider at 8 Goldfern Road? No one else knew, apart from the delivery man and the importer. How did the detective find him? The only people who knew were Jess, Tom, Rex, and... Glen. Glen? But why would he? Then, like a sharp knife to his heart, it hit him: *Roisin. It must be her.* The last time they'd spoken she'd mentioned he was lucky that she hadn't called the police. He thought they'd reached an understanding and that she was willing to forget the past so they could concentrate on making sure he had a good relationship with Robbie. What if she'd decided to call the police after thinking things through? Maybe Hugh had coerced her;

or perhaps it was Hugh who called the police.

Obviously they hadn't forgiven him for putting the spider in the house. If it was one of them who'd reported him to the police, this wouldn't end well.

Now that Jess was refusing to give any information, the detective would no doubt be back. Anxiety caused him to panic, plan ways he could leave, get as far away from here as possible.

The Spider still had him in his web. Wherever he turned, a reminder flashed before him, risks and danger.

He was stuck, as if captured in one of those cocoons on Rex's wooden web, with no easy way out.

Jess found the voicemail message on her phone after she'd settled Ophelia down to sleep.

"Ms Robson, I'm a detective investigating the importation of dangerous spiders. Your assistance will be crucial, and a reward can be arranged. This is a temporary phone number. Please call me back as soon as you get this message with details of where you purchased the poisonous spider. Please tell your friend George he's in my web. It's an in-joke. He'll understand."

As much as she hated to do so, after having written him out of her life, Jess knew she'd have to contact George. She considered waiting for Tom to come home and asking his opinion, but decided it would be easier to sort this out alone.

George was surprised to see Jess's name flashing on his mobile phone. Cautiously, but without hesitation, he answered it.

'George, I didn't want to call you, but that detective's left a message on my phone asking me to pass a message on to you. He said you're in his web. He said it was an in-joke and you'd understand. He's asking for information about where to get the spiders. He didn't sound friendly. Honestly, I don't even know if my brother's friend still does that sort of thing. Please explain what's going on. This man's obviously a friend of yours if you're sharing in-jokes. Tell him to leave me alone; I have a young baby. This is scaring me.'

George had frozen after hearing Jess say *you're in his web*. He remembered Rex used to say, *'I've got you in my web'*. Someone was playing a practical joke. Would Roisin do this? But she didn't have Jess's number, and she didn't know Jess was involved in helping him find a spider. She also didn't know what Rex used to say to him. No one knew that Rex used to say he was in his web. Did anyone know? He couldn't recall telling anyone. Had he told Glen? But it didn't make sense that Glen would do something like this.

George thought back to the meeting with the detective. Goosebumps appeared on his arms as he recalled the man's eyes. The way they'd turned black. *But... Rex is dead.* The more he thought about it, however, the more likely it seemed. Rex could have come back from the dead and found him again. He'd witnessed enough weirdness over the past year or so to know anything was possible. But no one would believe him. He would be labelled insane if he even suggested it as a possibility.

'George. Answer me.'

'Jess. I don't know what's going on. I never told anyone about the spider. Only that detective. I don't know him personally. He came to see me saying he was a detective; I'd never seen him before.'

'He had an American accent,' said Jess.

'Yes, that's him.'

'What should I do, George?'

'Keep your head down. He doesn't have your new address and I won't be giving it to him.'

'You're going to see him again?'

Jess's question had popped up in his mind before she asked it. Rex would most likely be back. Would he ever be free?

Chapter Sixty-Five

George and Glen were sitting at the same table in The Red Lion that they'd been seated at when the discussion about 8 Goldfern Road had led to their lives being turned upside down.

'How's work going, mate?' asked Glen. 'You look tired.'

George noticed his friend seemed happy, happier than he'd ever been. He'd always seen Glen as the morose figure in their relationship, using dry wit to cover up a life of regrets, the typical clown who wears a smile to hide his sorrow. George had been the happy one once. The tables had turned. 'I'm fine,' he huffed.

'You don't sound fine,' said Glen in an upbeat tone, which George was beginning to find irritating.

'He's back.'

'Who?'

'Rex.'

Glen took a deep breath and frowned at George. 'You still ain't been for therapy, have you?'

'I know what it sounds like, but there's proof this time. He left a voicemail on Jess's phone, and he visited me.'

'Jess? What's she got to do with it?'

'He found out that she knows where to get the poisonous spiders and now he wants her to tell him where to get them.'

'Rewind. How... What...? I admit I've got no idea what you're talking about. This is nonsense. Dead people don't leave voicemail messages.'

'I'm being serious.' He leaned in towards his friend and whispered, 'You know what that man is capable of. You saw it with your own eyes: Roisin and Hugh, remember? He possessed my body, so why is it so hard for you to believe that he could possess someone else's?'

Glen paled. 'But... But why would he come back now?'

'He wants a spider.'

'You gave him a spider.'

'Yes, but Hugh killed that one.'

'I need another drink. Shall I get you one?'

'No, I'd better get back to work. But come to mine tonight.'

'Why?'

'We have to talk about this.'

'What can I do?'

'We need a plan.'

'You blamed me for everything that went wrong last time, why would you trust me with a plan?'

'I'm desperate. I keep thinking about when he possessed me, and I don't wanna go back there.'

'I'm going out with Pet tonight. Can we meet tomorrow instead?'

George's brow wrinkled in frustration. 'Tomorrow. Eight o'clock at mine.'

'See you then.'

Chapter Sixty-Six

There'd been a time when she held all the cards. Her life with George, thrown away for an affair that had caused pain and heartache, seemed idyllic in hindsight.

Tonight it had taken an hour to convince Robbie to go to bed. He'd been screaming for George. Then, when he accepted he wasn't coming, he'd screamed for Hugh. Nothing Roisin did could placate him. Reaching a state of complete desperation, she'd even considered phoning George and asking him to take Robbie, to keep him.

When Robbie fell asleep, she found a half-empty bottle of whisky, which Hugh had obviously hidden under the bed, or dropped under the bed in a state of drunkenness. After finishing off the bottle and then puking out the contents of her stomach into the toilet, she'd taken paracetamol for the pain.

Repeating the dosage after a couple of hours, when the pain persisted, she found herself unable to remember how many pills she'd taken, except that it may well have been more than the recommended amount. The pain was relentless, in her head, in her stomach. Unbearable.

Robbie began to cry. Roisin covered her head with a pillow to drown out the noise and wondered how much pressure would be needed to block out all air.

Her ensuing tears echoed the sound of her son's.

Hugh was gone.

He'd left on Saturday morning. Three whole days with no word from him.

His eyes had shown no emotion when he told her he was going to give it another try with Abigail, for Liam's sake. He'd even suggested she try to get back together with George, effectively wiping away the past year or so, all they'd shared together.

'It was like a storm, Roisin,' he'd said. 'Storms come to cause chaos and destruction. I think we're all getting back to where we're meant to be. It's painful, I know, but I've thought about it. It will be for the best in the long run for both of us, and Liam and Robbie. Who knows, if our daughter had lived things may have turned out differently. But you know, I think she was never meant to be a part of our lives. She left so we could get to where we need to be. That's what I think.'

She'd slapped him then. How dare he discuss the loss of their child so flippantly? How had he come to terms with the loss already? Then, as she withdrew her reddened hand and watched him rubbing his cheek, it was obvious: he didn't love her. Perhaps he never had.

In her state of desperation, lying in the darkness, sniffing back tears and listening to Robbie's sobs, thoughts of George filtered into her mind. She couldn't forgive him for leaving the spider in the house that killed her daughter. It would forever be there between them, an unspoken reason to hate. Robbie would pick up on it. But she couldn't deny that Robbie needed him around. 'I want Daddy, I want Daddy,' was a chant repeated by Robbie every evening as she tried to settle him to sleep. She picked up her mobile phone, which was on the bedside cabinet then realised she couldn't call George in her current state, he'd hear the trace of tears in her voice. A text would have to do:

Come and get Robbie. He needs you.

After pressing *send* she noticed it was after 10 p.m. Maybe she should have waited until morning. Robbie's tears had stopped, he'd fallen asleep at last.

Collect him from school. Tomorrow. I'll pack his things and you can come and take them. I can't look after him anymore. Sorry.

Robbie will be better off with George.

Chapter Sixty-Seven

George woke up to the sound of the doorbell and looked at the time with eyes squinted against the light coming through the thin curtains.

It was 6.30 a.m. Who could be calling at this hour? He thought of Rex, and shuddered as a black cloud descended and he imagined meeting the man again.

He got out of bed and glanced out of the window to see a parked police car and two policemen standing at the door.

His mind felt fuzzy from sleep and he was trying to remember what had happened about the murder enquiry. They'd caught the killer, hadn't they? A man had confessed. What if they'd found evidence that linked him to the murders? He still had the gun, and they would surely have a warrant to search the place by now. He began to panic, but there was no way to avoid answering the door. If he tried to escape through the back door, they would definitely think he was guilty. He pulled on his dressing gown and reluctantly walked to the communal door.

He opened the door resigned to his fate. Two concerned-looking policemen greeted him. They didn't appear stern as he would have expected them to if they thought he was guilty of multiple murders.

'Mr Barnaby, we're very sorry to disturb you at this early hour, but there has been an incident. Can we come in?'

'Yes, of course.'

The policemen entered through the communal door and then into his flat. As George walked into the flat behind them, he caught sight of Peter at the top of the stairs.

'Everything all right, mate?'

'Er... Yes,' answered George, head down.

'Got the wrong address again, have they?'

The man's sarcastic drawl caused George to grimace and slam his door behind him.

He walked into the flat to find the policemen sitting on the sofa.

They indicated to George to sit down.

He sat facing them, on an armchair.

'We have a few questions for you. When did you last see Roisin Barnaby?'

'Roisin? Um... it was about a week ago. Last Saturday, yes, I spent the day with my son at their house.'

'When did you last speak to her on the phone or on social media?'

'She sent me a message last night asking me to collect Robbie from school today. Why? What's happened?'

'Roisin was found unconscious this morning by your son. He managed to call an ambulance. She's in hospital.'

'Oh, no. Is she all right?'

'It appears to have been a suicide attempt. Do you know why she would have been upset?'

'Suicide? Roisin? She wouldn't do something like that. She—'

'Has anything happened recently that would cause her to feel desperate enough to do something like that?' asked one of the policemen.

'She lost a baby recently.' George remembered how Roisin had blamed him for that and he paled.

'Anything else?'

George felt as though they were interrogating him. Did they know about the spider, had Hugh said something about him placing the spider in the house? 'Have you spoken to Hugh, her partner?' he asked with trepidation.

'He was questioned. We managed to track him down, and your son is with him at their house.'

George felt the perspiration on his brow. 'I'm sorry, I don't know anything else. I never thought Roisin could do something like this. How is she?'

'She's alive. We don't have any updates on her condition yet.'

'I should go and collect Robbie.'

'Do you mind if we take a look at your phone?'

George gave the phone to the police officer, his hand shaking, wondering if there was anything on there that could incriminate him. Thankfully, the police were only interested in the text messages he had received from Roisin the night before. Now he had a chance to read them again, he was angry at himself for not calling her, or replying. He'd read them too quickly, not paying much attention. *I can't look after him anymore. Sorry.* Her words were a cry for help, he could see that now.

After the police had gone, George phoned his boss.

'I can't come in today, I have to look after my son. His mum's unwell, and he's not feeling up to going to school.'

'You've hardly been to work this month.'

'I know, but it's been beyond my control. I will make up the time.'

'I'm not sure we can give you many more chances. Make sure you're in tomorrow or we'll have to talk about this again.'

The phone call left George in an anxious state. If Roisin couldn't look after Robbie he'd have to find a way to make sure he didn't miss work. Belinda always came to mind when he thought about hiring a nanny, with all the dark thoughts associated with that relationship. He tried not to think about it.

George made his way to Roisin's house knowing that he would have to speak to Hugh. He'd never really spoken to him alone, except in the days when he was just a neighbour. Things had changed so much.

He rang the doorbell and waited.

'Hello, George.' Hugh looked relieved to see him.

'Um... hello. I've come to collect Robbie.'

'Yes. Er..., would you mind coming in for a minute?'

George followed him inside.

Hugh went into the living room and sat down.

'Where's Robbie?'

'Don't worry, he's upstairs. I wanted a word... about Roisin.'

'Right.' George avoided eye contact as he sat next to him on the sofa. 'Do you know what happened to her?'

Hugh covered his face with his hands briefly, then sighed. 'It's embarrassing, actually, but on Saturday morning I left Roisin. I told her I was going to try to work things out with Abi—my ex.'

'I see. So she was upset about that?'

'I don't want to speculate. So much has gone wrong lately. She changed when she lost the baby, and things have been difficult between us since.'

George stood up, not quite knowing where to look. He'd known it would be awkward discussing Roisin with her new lover but he hadn't expected to feel so disorientated. 'I should take Robbie now.'

'Wait George... did you talk to her yesterday?'

'No. She sent me a couple of texts last night, asking me to collect Robbie after school. She said she couldn't look after him anymore.'

'I do feel partly to blame, you know, leaving her, but I didn't think she was even capable of doing anything like that. I'm going to go to the hospital to see her after you take Robbie home.'

Something like jealousy reared its head. George wasn't sure why it should bother him, and the longer he stood there the more agitated he felt.

'I made a bit of a fool of myself,' continued Hugh. 'Abi's moved on. I'm thinking of staying with Roisin, at least until we can figure out if our relationship is going anywhere. She seems to need me around. If I'm being honest, I'm confused.'

'You're going to stay with her because your ex doesn't want you?

Isn't that dishonest? Wouldn't it be better for you to leave and let her heal on her own, rather than pretending and patching up the relationship for your own ends only to hurt her again when you get bored?' George could feel the heat on his face. He had no idea why he'd said any of it; the words seemed to just come out. He held a hand in front of his mouth instinctively, as if to avoid saying anything else.

Hugh stood up. 'You have to face up to the fact that she doesn't love you, George. You're living in the past. The only person who can make her happy again is me; that's why I would be staying, not for any selfish reasons. I suffered when we lost our child, and you were the one responsible for that. You're lucky the police weren't called. Roisin stopped me contacting them because she felt sorry for you, seeing as she knows you're clearly insane. Don't think I've forgotten the way you behaved when she was in hospital after losing the baby. In fact, thinking about it, you probably caused everything that went wrong, leading to Roisin trying to take her own life.'

George took a deep breath. 'I'm taking Robbie home now.'

'You do that.' Hugh walked out of the room and called Robbie's name. He handed a small suitcase to George. 'I packed this for him. Sort your head out, George, and keep your nose out of other people's relationships.'

George was fuming inwardly when he left the house but put on a happy face for Robbie.

'Daddy, are you taking me to see Mummy?'

'Not right now, Robbie. Don't worry, she'll be home soon.' He thought of Hugh going to visit Roisin at the hospital and the lies he would be telling her to wheedle his way back into her life after being rejected by Abigail. He pushed the thought from his mind, feeling foolish and embarrassed about the impromptu speech he had made in defence of Roisin. He shook his head at the memory, knowing Hugh would no doubt tell Roisin about it and they would probably laugh at his expense.

Chapter Sixty-Eight

Rex received the call shortly after 10 a.m. when he was hiding away at a bed-and-breakfast he'd booked to try to avoid being found by Huntley Page. Apparently they'd been tracking him since he left prison. He knew it had always been a possibility, because they wouldn't have gone to the trouble of getting him released unless he could be of use to them. He thought of running, going into hiding, but he acknowledged the futility. They could easily trace him.

'Meet me in the den at two o'clock. I have a job for you. Don't be late.'

That was it. No explanation.

Rex cursed his luck. If only he had a spider to possess. He held that thought in his mind. He would do this "job" for Huntley and then when he had the spider he planned to escape. They would never find him. In fact, Huntley could be one of his first victims. The idea of that made him smile.

Chapter Sixty-Nine

Roisin woke up to find Hugh seated beside her bed.

Hospital.

Again.

It hadn't been too long ago that she'd been in practically the same position, after losing their baby.

Hugh looked sad. Initially, she empathised; he had suffered too when the baby died, and he wasn't good at showing his emotions. Then their last conversation came back to her: he'd told her that he was planning to get back together with Abigail. It made her wonder if all she'd ever been to him was a safe harbour during his rift with Abigail.

She wondered why she was in hospital, her memory of the night before was hazy. She remembered taking pills, and then her concerns that she may have taken too many.

Their eyes met.

Hugh's face brightened. 'Roisin! You're awake. How do you feel? Shall I call a nurse?' He stood up and leaned against the bed.

'What are you doing here?' She made an effort to keep the emotion out of her voice.

'The police got in touch. Robbie found you. He's so clever, he called an ambulance. George has him now.'

George? 'George? Why?'

'The text you sent him, do you remember?'

She closed her eyes, feeling foolish.

'Are you okay?'

'I'm fine. You can go now.'

'But—'

'Go to Abigail. That's where you belong, isn't it?'

Silence followed.

Roisin opened her eyes, hoping he had gone, but he was still there, seated by the bed, a blank look on his face.

'Me and Abi are over. You're the one I love. I knew as soon as I left the house, but I was too stubborn to tell you. I went to see Liam, that's all. Besides, Abi has moved on. I met her new fella.'

'Aha, so that's why you came back, is it? She doesn't want you?'

'No. I knew about him before. I was being stupid when I said what I said to you. I was annoyed about you spending time with George. I was jealous.'

'Jealous? There's nothing going on between me and George. You know I can't trust him after what he did.'

228

'I know that. He doesn't seem to realise, though. He's stuck in the past. When he came to pick up Robbie this morning, he was trying to give me advice. Can you believe it?'

'What sort of advice?'

'He said I only wanted you back because Abi is with someone else. What does he know?'

'Sounds like George was trying to stand up for me.'

'He's a loser.'

'No. He's not.'

'I knew there was something going on between you two! How long, Roisin?'

'There isn't anything going on. But even if there was, it would be none of your business. There's nothing going on between me and you, either.'

'But... I know you need time on your own, but maybe one day... Please forgive me for... everything.'

Roisin sighed. She saw tears in Hugh's eyes. He looked older. Had time been responsible, or had she? 'We probably shouldn't get back together, but if it makes you feel better, you're forgiven. None of us are faultless.'

'We could try again.'

'No, Hugh. I'm done.'

'But what was all this about? You were obviously upset when I left, trying to kill yourself.'

'Don't flatter yourself. I didn't try to kill myself. I accidentally took too many painkillers.'

He stood up. 'I can't deal with all this blowing hot and cold. I'm going now, and I won't be coming back.'

'You need to take a long hard look at yourself. I gave you too many chances.'

'I hope you find what you're looking for.'

'I hope you do too. Promise me one thing, you won't start drinking again. If you want to keep seeing Liam—'

'I don't need any advice from you.'

Roisin watched him leave. Tears began to fall, and she wondered if she'd done the right thing.

Chapter Seventy

'Glen. Um, now's not the best time—' George had just managed to settle Robbie to sleep.

'Er... You're the one who asked me to come over tonight. I could go home.'

'No, no, it's fine. Come in.'

'Thanks, because if I have to look at one more wedding magazine with Pet, I'll scream.'

'How are the plans coming along?' asked George, distractedly, closing the living room door.

'We ain't set a date yet, but you know what women are like. I was hoping we'd have an engagement party first and wait for a while before planning the wedding, but Pet is all over it. She told me we have to book the place in advance because there's a waiting list. I've left it to her.'

'We're going to have to talk quietly. Robbie's asleep in the bedroom.'

'Wow, she actually allowed him to sleep over?'

'He's staying with me permanently at the moment. Roisin's in hospital.'

'Whoa. What happened?' Glen sat on the sofa.

'I got a couple of text messages from her last night asking me to collect Robbie from school today, and the next thing I heard was she tried to kill herself—that's what the police think, anyway.'

'The police?'

'They were over here earlier, asking questions. It's been a strange day. And, it took me ages to get Robbie into bed because he was upset about Roisin. It was a shock for him to find her unconscious this morning, and for some reason he got it into his head that she was crying because of him last night.'

'Poor kid.'

'He's okay now. I read him a story and he cheered up a bit.'

'Maybe Roisin's fella is one of those domestic abusers.'

'I don't think he is.'

'Could be why his wife left him and took the kid.'

'That was most likely because she found out about his affair.'

'He could have been violent, though. You hear about it all the time. It's always the ones you don't suspect.'

'Maybe. Oh, I don't know, but I met him earlier—he was looking after Robbie—he doesn't seem the type.'

'There isn't a "type", mate. Anyone can be an abuser and it's usually those who are quite charming on the outside.'

'I wouldn't call him charming. He was pretty annoying when I spoke to him earlier.'

'What did he say?'

'He was basically saying Roisin doesn't love me, thinks I'm insane.'

'Huh, why would she have asked you to take Robbie if she thinks you're insane?'

'Exactly. And it sounds like he's to blame for what happened. He walked out on her on Saturday, apparently, and he thinks she was upset; that's why she tried to kill herself. Though, he also tried to blame me.'

'How could he blame you for Roisin trying to kill herself? You're not even with her anymore.'

'He brought up the spider, said he should have called the police about it, he was going on about how it ruined their lives when the baby died.'

'That was nothing to do with you.'

'I put the spider in the house.'

'Rex made you.'

'It always comes back to him. How did we ever get into that situation?'

'This is the part where you blame me.'

'I wish it was that clear cut, but I went along with it, didn't I?'

'It won't do you any good to keep thinking about what went wrong. You've got to start thinking about the future more, leave the past behind.'

'How can I when it's always staring me in the face wherever I go?'

'You should make a fresh start.'

'I've been thinking about that.'

'Good. Pet might have a friend you could date. I'll ask her if she knows any single women.'

'The last thing I need is another relationship.'

'Could be exactly what you need, to take your mind off things.'

'There are more immediate problems to deal with.'

'Rex, right? Can I have a whisky before I listen to this?'

George recalled what Jess had told him. He'd hardly had a moment to think about it with everything that had happened since. He went to the kitchen and poured a glass of whisky for Glen, then returned to the living room and sat next to him on the sofa.

'So,' Glen began as he took a swig of his whisky, 'Rex is back. Tell me more.'

'It's not a joke. He visited me. I'm sure of it. He's in an older man's body, with an American accent, but I know it's him. The eyes, you can't mistake them. They turned black. Remember how Rex's eyes used to turn completely black?'

Glen frowned. 'What did he say?'

'When he visited me, he said he was a detective investigating who was selling those spiders. I gave him Jess's number. He left a message for Jess asking her to give him the details for where he could get a poisonous spider, and telling her to pass on a message to me—saying I'm in his web.'

'Maybe it is a detective. You need a licence to import those kinds of spiders, don't you? Maybe they're looking into it.'

'No. It doesn't add up. Why would a random detective say I'm in his web? That's what Rex used to say: "I've got you in my web".'

'Maybe he meant the Internet. They call it the World Wide Web, don't they? You know what these coppers are like with their jargon.'

'No. He said I'm in his web... Like Rex used to.'

'Let's say it is Rex, what can he do?'

'I'm worried he'll come here to try to find out Jess's address.'

'But you don't know where she lives.'

'She gave me their new address last time I spoke to her.'

'So, pretend you don't know it.'

'I'm worried about what he might do. I have Robbie here.'

'He won't do anything. I think you should forget about it. Don't let him in if he comes here, call the police if you have to. If they catch him impersonating a policeman he'll be in trouble.'

'I was wondering if you could find out how to get one of those spiders for him.'

'Why would you assume I could do that?'

'You're the one who's got the criminal connections.'

'I don't wanna make a habit of contacting criminals. I helped you out with the fake ID because I didn't want you getting locked up for something you didn't do.'

'When will this spider-man leave us alone?'

'Us? He's only after you, as far as I can tell. You're the one who killed him.'

'You're not helping.'

There was a clattering sound from the adjoining room where Robbie was sleeping.

'What was that?' George said loudly as he stood up.

'Maybe Rex is back.'

'This is no time for jokes, Glen.'

Robbie ran into the room holding the gun that George had hidden under the bed. He was pointing it straight at George. 'Daddy! Daddy! Can I play with this?'

'Robbie... put that down. Now!' George's voice came out in a startled scream. He hadn't had an opportunity to think about where to dispose of the gun. What if it was loaded? Robbie was joyfully swinging it around. The colour washed from George's face as he saw Glen stand up and lean towards Robbie, his arm outstretched. 'Glen! It's real! Be careful!' The sound of his own voice reverberated in his head, along with the pulse of a frantic heartbeat, and a terrifying noise joined them as Robbie pulled away from Glen and the gun went off. George's eyes were drawn to the wall and the charred hole left by the bullet. It was shaped like a gaping mouth and, for a moment, in the confusion, the echoes of his own screams seemed to be calling out from within the dense black hole. He collapsed to the floor, sweating profusely.

'What the fuck, George?' Glen was looking from the wall to George and then to Robbie, who appeared stunned and had dropped the gun in all the chaos.

'Don't swear in front of Robbie,' huffed George.

'Sorry.'

There was a knock on the door. A familiar voice sounded. 'George? George? Are you okay in there.' Peter.

George stood up, shakily. He didn't want to pick up the gun, but he couldn't leave it there. With fear, he approached it as one would approach a resting wild animal. Making sure the weapon was facing away from Robbie, he picked it up by the handle, hand shaking.

'Go to bed, Robbie,' he said as gently as he could.

Robbie began to cry.

The knock on the door persisted.

George looked at the gun, no idea what to do with it.

'Do you want me to get rid of that?' asked Glen.

The question gave him hope and he nodded at his friend.

'George? I'm getting worried. I'll call the police,' Peter said, from the other side of the door, his voice grating on George's already shattered nerves.

'We're fine, Peter! Don't call the police! Please go back upstairs.' A heavy sigh followed, as he'd been holding his breath.

'Put it down, George,' Glen urged. 'Take a deep breath. I'll make sure I get rid of it. I'll take it to the local park, dump it in the pond.'

'It's not mine. It was Rex's. You believe me, don't you?'

Robbie continued to cry. 'I want Mummy,' he was saying repeatedly.

George placed the gun back down on the floor, and Glen asked for a plastic bag to put it in. They didn't speak as George found a bag and Glen placed the weapon inside.

'I'll get someone to come round and fix that hole in the wall,' said

Glen.

'Thanks,' said George, still unable to believe what had happened.

After putting Robbie back to bed, he returned to the living room.

Soon George and Glen were seated in the same positions they had been in before Robbie's entrance.

'Bloody hell, George. What were you thinking having a loaded gun like that with Robbie in the house?'

'I'd forgotten it was there.'

'Forgotten? How can you forget you've got a gun?'

'Not forgotten, I had a lot on my mind. Whenever the police came round, it was the first thing I thought about. I was scared they'd get a warrant to search the place, but I didn't know where I could dispose of it, so it stayed there.' He held his head.

'That was close,' said Glen, gazing at the hole in the wall.

George looked at him with wide eyes. 'Robbie could have died.'

'Calm down. It doesn't help to think like that. Be grateful that no one got hurt.'

'This is Rex again. He brought that gun here. He had it when he possessed me, and—'

'I say we forget Rex. If he comes back, call the police. Move away if you have to so he can't find you.'

'It's funny because I was thinking about that before you came. I think it would be best if I was as far away from this place as possible. But what about Robbie?'

'I thought you said you have custody.'

'Not officially, and even if he lives with me he still has to see Roisin.'

'There's FaceTime and Skype, so I'm sure it's fine if you're not living so close to each other; and, in my opinion, it would do you the world of good to move away. You're always wanting to get back with her, it's not healthy.'

'She's the mother of my child.'

'So? She betrayed you.'

'Petula betrayed you, remember?'

'We were kids back then.'

'It could happen again.'

'We're happy. Stop trying to depress me just because you're depressed.' Glen finished his whisky. 'I'm going, but think about what I said. Rex—or who you think is Rex—only has power over you if he knows where you are, right?'

'But what if he just knows where I am, wherever I go?'

'Think about it, if he was that powerful wouldn't he already know where to get those poisonous spiders?'

'I suppose so,' said George, standing up and averting his eyes from the deep recess that remained like a scar after the gunshot. He followed Glen to the front door.

'Me and Pet are thinking of moving away as well, when we get married. Somewhere out in the countryside. Why don't we meet up for lunch tomorrow at the pub and talk about it?'

'I'll see you at lunchtime.'

'And don't worry, I'll get rid of this.' He held up the plastic bag, causing George to instinctively flinch and half close the door.

'Be careful with that thing.' He watched as Glen walked away, sick at the thought of what could have happened when Robbie was holding the gun.

Chapter Seventy-One

I'm home now. I don't know what I was thinking. Robbie should be with me. Thank you for looking after him while I was in hospital.

Roisin sent the text and waited for a response, busying herself with cleaning up the house, trying to forget the past couple of days. Her thoughts kept drifting to George. He'd always been there for her. Reliable. Steady. That was one of the reasons she had strayed. She'd been too comfortable; hadn't appreciated how good her life had been. But was going back the answer? Hadn't her relationship with George caused her to end up in this position? The answer wouldn't come.

George sat opposite Glen in the pub at lunchtime.

'I got a text from Roisin. She wants Robbie back.'

'She's unstable.'

George looked at Glen, narrowing his eyes. 'You've never liked her.'

'For good reason.'

'She's a good mother.'

'Right, a woman who has an affair with the neighbour and then tries to kill herself. Mate, my advice would be to keep Robbie with you. He needs you. That woman'll drive him mad.'

'I'm having trouble finding a nanny, and after Belinda I'm concerned about having anyone new looking after Robbie.'

'You don't have to have a relationship with every nanny you hire, y'know? It's not part of the contract.'

'Ha, ha, very funny. I mean, Robbie will get confused with so many different people looking after him.'

Glen nodded. 'I'm not gonna tell you what to do. I can only give you my opinion. If you think Robbie's better off with Roisin, then give him back.'

'I think he needs his mum. I want to try to give our relationship one more chance. I want to have more children, but I don't want my children to have different mothers.'

'It's the way of the world nowadays, mate. Nothing wrong with it.'

'I'm not saying there is, but it's not for me.'

'There's no ideal world. It is what it is. We've got to make the most

236

of what we've been given. The hand we're dealt.'

'I see you've been reading philosophy again.'

'Ha, ha.'

'Problem is, if I'm being honest, I wish things could go back to how they were before Rex. My life feels like it's in two halves, *before Rex* and *after Rex*. Before Rex was infinitely better.'

'You need a time machine for that. You have to move on. You'll figure it out. Focus on the future, forget the past.'

Chapter Seventy-Two

Hugh had been drinking all day.

Roisin ignored him when she arrived back from hospital late at night. She'd slept in Robbie's bedroom and ignored Hugh in the morning at breakfast. He'd made an effort to start a conversation, but she turned up the volume on the TV.

He'd ended up heading out to work in a low mood and didn't make it to the Tube station, instead deciding to drown his sorrows with a bottle of whisky from the local supermarket.

It was now 3 p.m. and he'd found a temporary home on a bench in the local park, looking worse for wear; his eyes were red, his brain fuzzy. He thought of Abi and that man. It was Liam's birthday today and Victor would be spending time with him. His temperature rose and he sensed injustice all around. With the false confidence he'd gained from the alcohol, he decided to call Abi.

'Abi. We need to talk,' he mumbled, unaware he was slurring the words.

'Hugh? Is that you? You sound... Have you been drinking?'

'I might have had a drink or two. I'm an adult.'

'It's three o'clock. Haven't you been at work today?'

Work? The word fizzed around in Hugh's brain but didn't hold any meaning to him. He distantly recalled that he was due to start a new job this morning, the one he had trained for the week before, but he couldn't remember much about it.

Abi's voice jolted him. 'You told me you'd started a new job recently.'

'I had a day off.'

'You sound drunk.'

'I'm not drunk... I need to see Liam. It's his birthday.'

'Liam's at school. You can call him and talk to him later, if you're not drunk. About six o'clock.'

'Liam wants me to go to his party. Where is the party?'

'The party is for his school friends.'

'Liam wants me there, not your new man. He doesn't like him.'

'That's not true. They haven't even met properly yet. You shouldn't have been talking about Victor with Liam. It's not appropriate.'

'He was the one telling me about him. He said you'll be having a baby with him.'

'You're clearly drunk, I can hear it in your voice. I have to go. I'll tell Liam you said happy birthday. Don't bother calling later. I'll call you to discuss contact later in the week. But if I get any hint of you drinking again, you're not seeing him, is that clear?'

Abigail hung up the phone. She worried that she'd been too harsh on Hugh. Would that lead him back to the drink? It reminded her what life was like when he'd had too much to drink when they were living together. He'd been intolerable then. Her mind was nagging her: she might have made things worse.

She recalled what Victor had said, that he thought Hugh appeared keen to resume their relationship. Is that why he was drinking now, because he'd seen her with Victor and thought she'd left him behind? As much as their reunion had been something she'd hoped for, she knew it could never happen; Hugh was unstable. Her ways in their marriage may have been controlling, but the drink had ultimately driven them apart. It would be unfair to put Liam through that again.

Hugh finished the bottle of whisky and headed home after the phone call with Abigail, darkness infiltrating his mind.

Chapter Seventy-Three

George arrived at Robbie's school just before 3.30 p.m., flustered. His boss had already given him a warning about his timekeeping. He explained that it was exceptional circumstances. 'You're skating on thin ice, George,' his manager had scowled. 'One more incident like this, and you're out.'

It took George a moment to notice Roisin outside the school gates, speaking with one of the other mothers.

He approached her. 'Roisin?'

She appeared pensive, and made her apologies to the woman she had been talking to, before pulling George aside, out of earshot of the other parents. 'You didn't respond to my text.'

'Because I'm concerned about the way you're behaving. You basically dumped Robbie on me and ended up in hospital. I don't think you're in any state to look after my son.'

'Your son? If anyone is unfit to look after him, you are. Or have you forgotten? Do you have amnesia again?' she said, a bit too loudly, attracting the attention of the other parents.

Thankfully, the gates were then opened and the crowd began to disperse.

'You're the one who asked me to take him, said you couldn't cope; then the police came to my flat telling me you tried to kill yourself.'

'I didn't try to kill myself. I accidentally took too many painkillers.'

'Seems coincidental after you sent me a text practically begging me to take Robbie.'

'I was having a bad day. It's not easy looking after a child on your own.'

'I know.' George let out a breath. 'There's something you should know; I've been thinking of moving away with Robbie.'

'You can't do that!'

'No, I didn't mean taking him away from you. I wanted us to talk about it, to see whether you and I could try to give our relationship a chance... for Robbie's sake.'

Roisin's expression changed. The frown was replaced with a look of intrigue. 'You want us to get back together?'

'I'm not saying that we should jump in where we left off, but we could take it slowly. God knows if it'll work, but don't we both deserve a second chance? I'm not perfect, but neither are you. We're both to blame.'

Roisin folded her arms and looked up at him. She appeared to be deep in thought.

'I'm taking Robbie home today,' he said. 'You need time to rest after your hospital stay.'

'But... You said you were going away.'

'Not immediately. I'd like us to talk about it. Come over to mine tomorrow morning, before the school run.'

Chapter Seventy-Four

Roisin walked home in a daze. Letting George take Robbie home with him, was that the right thing to have done? It felt strange returning from school without him, like a part of her was missing. There was no doubt Robbie would be happy to be with George, but that made her yearn for him even more. It was hard to acknowledge that Robbie would probably be equally as contented to live with George as he was with her, if not more so.

She'd surprised herself by giving real thought to the idea of moving away with George and Robbie. Her mind bustled with confusion as she opened the front door. There was unexpected movement in the kitchen; the house should have been empty, Hugh was starting his new job.

Roisin left the front door slightly ajar as she entered. Had she remembered to close the garden door before leaving to collect Robbie from school? She'd left it open earlier, as it was a warm day. To heighten her anxiety, there came the sound of a glass shattering on the kitchen floor. Roisin began to walk backwards.

The kitchen door flew open and Hugh bolted out, nearly bumping into her. He stopped when he saw her, swaying slightly from side to side.

'Hugh? Shouldn't you be at work?'

'I had a day off.'

'You sound drunk.' The sickly sweet and sour smell was now evident.

'I only had a couple of drinks. You're worse than Abi.'

'Abi? Have you seen her again?'

'No, I phoned her earlier and she was being funny about letting me see Liam. It's his birthday today. I wanted to talk to him on the phone, but she won't let me.'

'Why?'

'She wouldn't tell me where his birthday party is; probably doesn't want me going there because her new man is going to be there. Victor. What sort of a name is that? He's taking over. He wants to take my place.'

'Is this because you wanted to try again with Abigail?'

'No. I told you, it's you I love. Why don't you believe me?' He reached out to her.

Roisin pushed him away. 'We talked about this at the hospital. It won't work.'

'You weren't yourself at the hospital. You weren't thinking. You should think about Robbie, too. I'm his dad.'

'George is his dad.'

'It's George. You're back together?'

'Leave him out of this.'

'George and Abi are the past, me and you are the future. We're all we've got, Roisin. I need you.'

'You're drunk. You don't know what you want.'

'No, but you seem to know everything, so does Abi. Everyone else seems to know what I want better than I do!'

'You're irresponsible. You've brought this on yourself.'

'It's Liam's birthday... Abi wouldn't let me speak to him... I was depressed, that's why I was drinking.'

'There's always some excuse, you never take responsibility. Weren't you supposed to be starting your new job today?'

'I'll go tomorrow.'

'You can't afford to lose this job as well.'

He made a gagging sound and then turned around and ran towards the toilet.

Roisin could hear him being sick.

When he came out of the room he looked pale.

'I told you that I wouldn't put up with you drinking. I can't handle this. I thought it would be all right for you to stay here until we decide what to do with the house, but I have to think about Robbie.'

'He's with George. He doesn't live here anymore because you're a lousy mum and you can't look after him.'

'You're pathetic. Look at the state of you. You can't even see straight. Why do you think Abigail doesn't want you near Liam?'

'You're lucky I'm not a drug addict. It's only alcohol, and I have to drink because of Abi... You and Abi. You're not innocent. If you didn't constantly make me feel like you're going to leave me, I wouldn't be so depressed.'

'We're not together anymore, so how could I leave you?'

He pushed past her and walked towards the front door, then turned around. 'Can you lend me ten pounds? I'll pay you back when I get paid.'

'What do you need it for?'

'I'm not a kid. Give me ten pounds.'

'What, so you can go and buy more booze?'

'It's my life.'

'Yes, yes, it's your life. You're on your own, I'm going back to George. We're moving away.'

'I knew it. You've been seeing George behind my back all along.'

'No, I haven't, and I wasn't sure I wanted to take up George's offer to move away with him, but you have made up my mind. I'm going to put the house on the market. You can stay here if you can find the money to pay me back my share.'

'You know I can't afford to do that.'

'That's your problem. If you didn't drink so much maybe you'd be able to hold on to a job for more than five minutes. You've made your own bed.'

'But... You and George? How... Why? Do you not remember what he did?'

'George made a mistake. He didn't know me and Robbie would be in the house when he put the spider in it. You, however, are happy to put my child's life at risk day after day so that you can feed your addiction.'

'That's unfair. I only drink when things go wrong. I'm not addicted. I didn't think you'd leave me when I need you most.'

'You're delusional. How many times do I have to tell you there is no me and you? Anyway, you don't need anyone; you're happy with a bottle of whisky in your hand. You're going to end up as one of those men sleeping on a park bench.'

'You're heartless.'

'Give me the keys. You're not welcome here.'

'It's my home.'

'I'll pay you what you're due from the house sale.'

'You've threatened this before. It's not real. Come on.' He approached her and put a hand on her shoulder. 'Let's be sensible.'

She could smell the alcohol on his breath and it made her nauseous. 'You're a mess.'

'Yes, but you love me. We love each other.'

'No. I don't love you. I'm not sure I ever did. I fell for you because you're a charmer, but you never had love in your heart, did you? You're selfish, and I understand why Abigail didn't want you in her life. I was such a fool. If you don't leave, I'll call the police.'

'My name's on the deeds; I have a right to be here. What can the police do?'

'You're drunk. You're harassing me.'

'Harassing you? I'm your boyfriend, your lover.'

'No, you're not. Not anymore.'

'But we're friends. I thought you were a friend. You're just another selfish woman. Like Abi. I always get it wrong.'

'I want you to walk out of that door, and I want you to stay out.'

'All my belongings are here.'

'You can collect them when you've decided where you're staying.'

'You're going back to George?'

'George is a good man.'

Hugh took his set of keys from his jeans pocket and handed them to Roisin. He hesitated before leaving, looking at her a couple of times as if to confirm that she was being serious. She mused that he would probably be happier now he wasn't accountable to anyone and could drink himself into a stupor whenever he wanted to.

Roisin blinked the tears from her eyes as he closed the door behind him. Her thoughts turned to George, and Hugh's words flashed into her mind: *'You're going back to George?'* She hadn't been sure when she returned from the school run, but she'd had enough of thinking. Her life before she'd left George had been bordering on mundane, but she'd never experienced hollowness like this. She was living in a circus of her own making. Robbie needed stability. It was hard for her to acknowledge that she may have wasted over a year of her life on a wild fancy. It was time to try again. With George. Going back might not be so bad. It could be exactly what she needed.

Chapter Seventy-Five

Three days had passed, and with every hour that went by Rex's frustration escalated. He felt trapped. Huntley Page had asked him to kill a man for him. He had all the details and a gun. If the murder didn't take place by midnight, Huntley's men would be after him.

It wasn't the killing he objected to, he hated being under this man's control. Whatever he asked him to do, he would be expected to do. It reminded him of being inside that prison cell. He wasn't free.

Why hadn't Jess Robson replied to him? If he left her a second message she'd know he was desperate. But what choice did he have? He could practically feel Huntley breathing down his neck.

Time was running out. There must be another way to get a poisonous spider. Jess wasn't an expert in where to find the spiders, after all.

A strange sensation came over him. He stood up and looked in the mirror above the mantelpiece. There were a couple of black spots on his forehead. He moved nearer to the mirror and saw they were bulbous and shiny. He put a hand up and could see his hand through these "eyes". He smiled as he remembered the tricks he'd played on Glen and George back when he'd been in control. This was practically a replay except he was the one turning into a spider. Finally turning into a spider without having to make any effort. A sense of joy overcame him, leaving him breathless. He leaned in closer to the mirror and saw the other eyes appear as the transformation took shape. 'Thank you! Thank you!' he said aloud, not sure who or what had caused this miracle. 'I knew this was my fate, my divine purpose, the reason I was put on this godforsaken planet!'

He fantasised about weaving webs, catching prey, poisoning those he hated.

There were flashes of light before him, making him dizzy. When they dissipated, he started moving involuntarily, crawling on many more than two legs. There were eight.

Mission accomplished. A spider at last. He crawled upwards, upwards, wanting to find a mirror to look into and see what type of spider he had become.

Rex mused that although he'd transformed into an arachnid, he could still think and see and feel like a human. He did not allow this to scupper his mood, however. He soon reached the mirror above the fireplace and crawled along the mantelpiece to get a better look. He was a spider. A glorious black spider. Magnificent. No more would he be accountable to Huntley. A fantasy filled his mind; he could crawl into the den as a spider and poison Huntley. It filled him with pride.

He looked like a poisonous spider, like the spider he had been before Hugh killed him. Hugh. Yes, Hugh must be the next victim.

He began to weave a web as the thoughts cascaded through his mind.

A noise, like a buzzing sound, could be heard: *A fly?* He became excited. He would love to eat a succulent fly right now. But the sound was getting louder, and his surroundings grew darker and darker.

The area around him faded to black. The buzzing continued and began to annoy him. *Where am I?*

'We meet again, Rex Rodenbury.'

No.

'I'm afraid so.'

You said that if I helped George I would be free.

'Unfortunately, you have failed in your mission. You told us that you had learned from your time here, and that you saw the error of your ways. You said you had changed. We didn't believe you, but we gave you the opportunity to return to save George. As we expected, you then reverted to your evil ways. Your soul cannot be saved, Rex Rodenbury. This incarnation will be your last. A spider. A dying man must have his last wish. You will survive for as long as you survive as a spider, and then you will be no more. Your soul will fade to nothing. You have failed; you will return to the darkness from whence you came.'

Wait, what if I do good as a spider? Can I then save my soul?

There was no answer.

Rex found himself in the room once again. He was a spider. A glorious spider. A beautiful, wondrous thing.